The Saucer-Heads

In This Series

That First Heady Burn
True Vermilion
The Dark Shill
A Stack of Sawbucks
The Hillside Roble
The Peroxide Pomp
The Incidental Twin
Brawl in Bardo
The Window-Shade Job
The Convenient Patsy
The Artisanal Grifter
Shrink in the Shadows
Project Chartreuse
From a Desert Playa
The Tired Canary
A Desperate Frame-up
Trail of the Blue Agave
The Saucer-Heads

The Saucer-Heads

The
Saucer-Heads

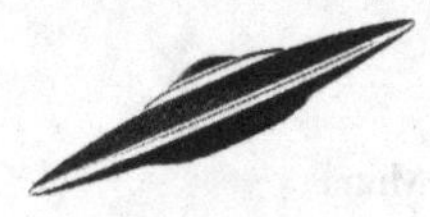

George Bixley

DAGMAR
MIURA
LOS ANGELES

Published by Dagmar Miura
Los Angeles
www.dagmarmiura.com

The Saucer-Heads

Copyright © 2023 Dagmar Miura
All rights reserved. No part of this book may be used or reproduced in any manner whatsoever without prior written permission except in the case of brief quotations embodied in critical articles or reviews. For information, address Dagmar Miura, dagmarmiura@gmail.com, or visit our website at www.dagmarmiura.com.

This is a work of fiction. Names, characters, businesses, places, events, and incidents are either the products of the author's imagination or used in a fictitious manner. Any resemblance to actual persons, living or dead, or actual events is purely coincidental.

First published 2023

ISBN: 979-8-89195-003-0

ONE

S LATER HAD BEEN HERE before, but not in a while. As he reached the top of the stairs, he looked over the low-key bar, the booths lining the back wall, the tables near the windows looking over the street. Outside he could see the array of office towers in downtown LA's Financial District a few blocks away.

The big windows were open for the evening air, but it was still too hot for his faux leather jacket. He loved the way it looked, but he shouldn't have bothered with it. Once he'd got a bottle of Corona at the bar, he found an empty table and folded the jacket over one of the chairs, then sat facing the top of the stairs.

There was some talent here, he saw, surveying the room and sipping his beer. But that couldn't be his focus. He'd been summoned here by text message to meet a client. All he knew about the person was that their name was Truax—he wasn't even sure of the gender.

Slater shifted in the chair to get comfortable and adjusted his glasses. He didn't need glasses, and he wasn't used to these because he didn't wear them very often. They were heavy because of the batteries in the arms. Studding the frames were tiny LEDs that blasted infrared and ultraviolet light, invisible to the human eye but hopefully effective at jamming video cameras and obscuring his identity. His illicit tech supplier, Svetlana, claimed that the colorful pattern on the frames would also mislead facial recognition software into seeing a different face, and wouldn't link it to him.

There wasn't a specific reason for Slater to be in stealth mode, but there were cameras trained on everyone all the time, and the fewer obvious traces he left in the world, the better.

He wasn't sure why Truax wanted to meet here. It would have been easier in Slater's office. This place wasn't a meat market, and there were some women around, but it was mostly gay guys. Even if the idiot stood him up, it was an easy place to hang out.

A guy was approaching him, he noticed, from back by the booths. Lanky and with his top open halfway down his torso, he strode directly toward him. The shirt was some kind of billowy gold fabric, and he was wearing snug white pants, his hair in a pomp. He had some green glitter accenting his cheekbones, and his eyes were hard.

"Truax?" Slater said, subtly shifting his chair back from the table as the guy stepped up.

"You," he said, his gaze intent, and jabbed a finger at him. "You're trash."

"OK," he said evenly, and furrowed his brow.

"You fucked my fiancé."

"Who's your fiancé?"

"Greg," he shouted.

"That doesn't really narrow it down."

"Greg from San Pedro."

He had no idea who the guy was talking about. Slater pointedly looked him up and down. That shirt had to be couture—it had probably cost him a grand.

"I see Greg's tastes run to"—Slater paused for effect—"cheap."

With an audible gasp, his face contorted with anger and he lunged at Slater. Quickly out of his chair, he sidestepped his flailing hands. The guy had no idea how to brawl, and grabbing one of his wrists, Slater twisted his arm behind his back, spinning him around, and pulled him close.

Overpowered, the guy froze. Slater knew other people in the bar would be watching, so he pivoted toward the windows, using his body to block the view of what he was doing. He put his other hand on the guy's throat.

With his free hand the guy clawed at Slater's arm, tugged at it. Why did they always do that? It had to be instinctive, but it was completely ineffectual.

"You feel that?" Slater growled in his ear, shoving his arm farther up his back. "It's one of the bones in your forearm, and it's about to dislocate. Why do you make me do this to you? Why do you make me hurt you?"

He yelped and pawed at Slater's fingers on his throat. "Let go of me, you dick."

"How did you find me?"

"I wasn't looking. Greg showed me your profile on the hookup app. You're hard to miss. A Mexican guy in a very white bar."

"I am not Mexican," Slater said through his teeth. He heard it all the time, as he had his father's dark coloring, but it was still irritating. "Are you going to come at me again?"

"No."

Slater loosened his grip and let him turn around. "What is this fabric?" He brushed a loose fold of the golden shirt with his fingers. "It's so soft."

Scowling, the guy adjusted his collar. "A minute ago you said it looked cheap."

"You know that it takes two to tango, don't you, toots? I didn't cheat on anybody. That was Greg. And next time, choose a better man."

"Scum," he hissed, pushing past him as he walked away.

Lots of eyes were on him, he saw, as he ran a hand

through his dark hair and sat down again, but luckily the bouncer hadn't tuned in.

From the direction of the bar another guy approached his table. Built thick, he was wearing a mauve dress shirt and dark pants, like he'd come from casual Friday at an office job. With blue eyes, his longish dirty-blond hair was carefully coiffed behind his ears. Basically fuckable, Slater decided.

"Truax," Slater said.

"You look busy."

"Not anymore. Sit down."

Truax dropped into the chair across from him. "Those are unusual glasses."

"You said in your text you needed my help."

His expression sobered. "I need to find someone. My boyfriend."

"He's missing?"

"Almost a week now."

"Did you talk to the cops?"

"There's no point." Truax waved a hand. "You know as well as I do they won't do anything. I'm worried something happened to him. That he got into some kind of trouble. If I just knew where he was, that he was safe, I could stop worrying."

Watching him talk, Slater suppressed a sigh. Most of what he'd just said was almost certainly bullshit.

"If you need a hookup, this place is full of guys." Slater waved at the room. "Maybe it's time to move on."

Truax frowned. "I'm not going to do that. I need to talk to him. I need to know what happened."

"What's the guy's name?"

"Finley López."

"Is he Anglo or Latin? His name sounds like both."

"I guess he is both," Truax said. "With me he's Anglo, but he looks kind of Latin. Kind of like you."

"Do you have a photo of him?"

"On my phone." Truax leaned back and pulled it out of his front pocket. "I'll text it."

Slater dug his own phone out of his jeans and studied the image. Looking straight into the camera, Finley was wearing a collared shirt and had a lanyard around his neck. This was an ID photo, from a job or a school. Finley's dark hair was neatly trimmed. He looked to be around thirty, and he was smiling.

"This is from his ID," Slater said. "Not the kind of photo most people would show of their boyfriend."

His brow furrowed. "Well, that's what I've got."

"Did you talk to his family?" Slater said.

"Our relationship wasn't like that." Truax held his gaze, raising his eyebrows, working hard to project sincerity. "We didn't really visit each other's parents."

"I'll need contact info for mom, dad, any relatives. Do you know any of his friends?"

"I've already talked to our mutual friends."

"Where does he live?"

"Finley has an apartment in Chinatown. I'll send you the address." Truax looked down at his phone and tapped at it. "He didn't have a roommate."

"What does he drive?"

"A gray Camry. It's parked at his apartment. It hasn't been driven." He briefly looked up to meet his gaze. "I checked."

"Where did he work?"

"We work at the same place. That's how we met. Magnesia Motors."

Slater knew that name. He'd seen photos of the Magnesia roadster. Magnesia was one of several electric car startups trying to cash in on all the tax breaks and subsidies of the great transition to electric vehicles.

"I've never heard of it," he said.

Truax frowned. "We're an electric vehicle manufacturer."

"Are you actually building them, or is it just another tech-industry hype story? 'We'll have an actual product for you in two or three years; for now, just give us money.'"

"It's for real. I drive one myself. It's actually a great car. I got the first one that the factory did with a red paint job. Before that, they were all gray or white."

"What did Finley do at Magnesia Motors?"

"He was in IT," Truax said, and gestured impatiently. "Don't bother talking to Magnesia. I have a friend in the HR department. In her eyes, Finley abandoned his job. They have no idea where he is."

"What about work friends?"

"I talked to his manager, and people in his department. Nobody knows anything."

"Where's the factory?" Slater said.

"Texas, but we have an office here. In the Arts District."

He gestured expansively. "So why did you call me? And why are we here?"

"My contact said you did this kind of job, and that you were gay, so you'd be familiar with that part of it."

Slater pursed his lips and watched him for a moment, thinking it through. This guy didn't seem gay. He usually had a pretty good sense of that. But maybe it didn't really matter.

"I'll need two grand up front."

"I'll bring a check to your office this week. When can you get started?"

"I can get started when I get the two grand," Slater said. "And it needs to be in cash."

He scowled but pulled out a billfold, holding it down by his thigh to riffle through the cash. Eventually he handed Slater a wad of bills, folded in half.

Not bothering to count them, Slater rose and stuffed them into the hip pocket of his jeans. "I'll let you know what I find out."

TWO

RUAX STOOD UP AS Slater grabbed his jacket, and they walked out together, down the stairs to the street. It was dark out, but still warm, the concrete and asphalt radiating the heat of the day.

"You do this kind of work regularly?" Truax said.

"All the time."

"I'm at the end of the block," he said, waving ahead of them.

"Me too."

"Do you smell that?" Truax said as they walked. "Is it one of those guys upstairs wearing too much perfume?"

"It's night-blooming jasmine."

"I don't see any flowers anywhere."

"It grows like a hedge," Slater said. "The scent is potent. It's probably in a walkway or a courtyard behind one of these buildings."

When they got to the Thunderbird, parked at the curb, gleaming black under the streetlights, Slater stepped into the street behind it.

"Sweet ride," Truax said, pausing on the sidewalk to look it over.

"I know."

Climbing in behind the wheel, Slater pulled off his stealthy glasses, and clicked off the tiny power switch on the arm with his fingernail. Glancing out the windshield, he saw Truax walking farther up the block. On his phone he thumb-typed a text to Max, his business partner:

You around tomorrow?

Twisting the key in the ignition, he fired up the engine, sounding as smooth as it had when it rolled off the assembly line half a century ago. Before he popped it into gear, Max's reply came:

I'm in the office in the morning.

Nosing the big car into the street, Slater headed onto the freeway, just a couple of exits to his hilly neighborhood, north of downtown. He had to smile at the thought that Pike was there, that they were full-on shacked up.

Slater hadn't had this house for long—he'd bought it to make room for the relationship with Pike, thinking that they'd need space to figure it out, room to make it work. It was a boxy new construction, one of just a handful in the neighborhood of century-old bungalows. On the ground floor was the garage and an ADU, with a pair of bedrooms one flight up, and above that, on the top floor, a kitchen and living space.

He pulled into the garage and trudged up the stairs. When he got to the kitchen he could hear house music on the radio, turned down low, and when he walked through toward the deck, he found Pike stretched out on the sofa, eyes closed, slack-jawed, sound asleep. The French doors to the deck were propped open for the night air.

Pausing to admire his sleeping form, Slater felt his heart start to pound, just from the sight of this beautiful man. Arms folded, his black hair was slicked back, and he wore a sheer white T-shirt that revealed the perfect paunch above his belt. Poking out of his drab green cargo shorts, one knee was propped on the back of the sofa.

Pike didn't stir, and Slater went back into the kitchen, where he pulled a fifth of bourbon from the cupboard, and poured the amber liquid into a tumbler. His booze rules said that his ration was half an inch. But it was Friday night, and he'd been working. A little extra wouldn't hurt.

He slurped at the tumbler, closing his eyes to relish the heady burn, then poured a little more and went back to the sofa, kneeling next to Pike on the patch of lawn that surrounded the coffee table. It looked exactly like Bermuda grass, but touching it revealed that it was plastic. Pike had put it here instead of an area rug, and it actually kind of worked.

Waking when Slater touched his leg, Pike flashed a sleepy smile.

"I must have drifted off. There's good music on Friday night."

"You're so fucking beautiful." Slater leaned in, and wrapped his arms around him, and mouthed his neck, eliciting a contented sigh.

Once he'd pulled back, Pike sat up, swinging his bare feet onto the grass.

"How was your meeting?"

"Turns out it's a missing-person type deal."

"Why did he want to meet you in a bar?"

"Good question." Slater massaged Pike's bare calf. "He didn't look like a bar rat."

Pike leaned toward the coffee table and grabbed a book. "So are you going to read to me?"

"Is it my turn?"

"It has to be. I can't keep my eyes open."

Slater sat up on the sofa, leaning back on him, and got comfortable in Pike's big arms before he flipped open the book. They'd been reading *The Odyssey*, not because either of them was especially enamored with it, but it had become a habit, reading mythology. No way could he read a straight translation either—this was an annotated rendition that explained all the characters and the symbolism and the background.

Once he'd found where they'd left off, Slater started to read aloud. "Hermes donned his golden sandals and set off, flying over land and sea as fast as the wind. When he reached the island, he found Calypso, in the wide cave where she lived, singing in a sweet voice as she worked on her loom."

"Where's Odysseus when this is happening?" Pike said.

Slater turned to look at him sidelong, but Pike's eyes were closed, his head resting on the back of the sofa. "He's on the beach, remember? He goes there to cry every day."

"That poor fuck."

"Violet and parsley bloomed in the nearby meadow," Slater went on. "Hermes paused to marvel at the beauty of the place …"

After he'd read a few pages, Pike's breathing had become regular. Sitting up, Slater set the book on the table, then drained his tumbler, coughing at the fumes in his nose.

"Come on," he said. "Let's crash."

"It's not that late," Pike mumbled, but rose and followed him through the kitchen and down the stairs to the bedroom.

Pulling off his shirt, Slater unbuckled his belt, and popped his fly, then stretched his back, rotating left and right.

"Oh, come on," Pike said, from the other side of the bed, his brow furrowed, hands on his hips.

Slater frowned at him. "What?"

"I'm totally wiped out, and then you stand there looking like that." He grabbed the crotch of his fuggly cargo shorts. "It's a turn-on."

"You don't have to do anything about it if you're tired."

"I'm not too tired for that."

Once he'd pulled off his boots and ditched his jeans, Slater climbed on the bed and waited for Pike to get naked. When he lay down, Slater moved close to him, and Pike groped his cock.

"You're hard."

"Of course I am," Slater said, "with you emitting your man-stank. It's like a sexual chemical weapon."

Pike kissed his neck, then met his mouth, and stroked his cock.

"Just lie back," Slater said. "I'll do everything."

Reaching for the back of his neck, Pike pulled him closer, pressing their mouths together.

After a moment Slater pulled away, and shifted down the bed, and took him into his mouth. Pike groaned, and as he worked him, Slater could feel him getting closer, his body vibrating, and eventually he came, grunting as he thrust into him.

Moving up, Slater kissed him, hot and sloppy, and mouthed his jaw.

"That's so damn hot," Pike said.

"Let me fuck you between your thighs."

Slater grabbed the lube from the bedside drawer, and straddled him, then pressed down into him, shoving his arms under Pike's shoulders, focused on his mouth. Pike pulled him closer, a hand on the back of his neck, and squeezed his thighs tight together. Pounding him, Slater climaxed, and strained into him, mouthing his neck and his cheek.

They lay that way for a while, sweaty and content, as his breathing slowed. He stirred awake when Pike spoke.

"I should go shower."

Slater climbed off him, and was vaguely aware of the

sound of the water going on. This was the best time of day, with this feeling, being sated and a little buzzed, and he rapidly sank into oblivion.

THREE

BRIGHT DAYLIGHT WAS STREAMING in the windows when Slater woke. Pike was already gone. He had some gun thing at a shooting range, he remembered. He wasn't sure if it was for work or just him and his work friends messing around and blowing holes in paper targets. Scrabbling for his phone on the nightstand, he checked the time. He needed to go meet Max.

Once he'd washed up and run a hand through his hair, he pulled on a short-sleeved shirt and sniffed yesterday's jeans. They were still clean enough. He tied his boots and hustled up the stairs, where Pike had left the coffeepot on for him. Pouring some into a mug, he dropped in an ice cube and swirled it around until it was cool enough to slam it. Grabbing a bagel, he bit into it on the way down the stairs.

The Fashion District was a quick trip on Saturday morning, and he parked in the surface lot across the street from the century-old building that housed his office, and hustled across in a break in the traffic. The neighborhood was a jumble of fabric suppliers and factories and small retailers. Even though it still looked like an office building, today it was mostly sewing factories, except the suite he shared with his business partner, Max, around behind the elevator shaft on the ninth floor.

Sliding open the steel accordion as he stepped off the elevator, he could hear the sewing machines cycling on and off, even on Saturday. Twisting his key in the deadbolt, he admired the lettering on the office door:

SLATER IBÁÑEZ
MAXIMILLIAN CONROY
INVESTIGATIONS

Inside were three small rooms, one for him and one for Max, and the front office between them, with a desk that no one used, except their operative Etta, who sat there occasionally when she was on a job for one of them. Perched on the front desk next to the computer screen was a white plaster statue of Rey Pascual, a skeleton holding a scythe and wearing a crown. Etta always turned him to face the front door when she left, as if tasking him to monitor the comings and goings.

Etta had changed other things, and he had to admit they were all improvements. She'd had the place painted, and brought in deco-era furniture and light fixtures, elevating the vibe from its prior utilitarian spareness, softening the edges of the seedy work they did.

Stepping into Max's office doorway, he found Max behind his desk, wearing a bright yellow necktie, his gray suit jacket hung on the coatrack in the corner. His tie was several shades lighter than the warm mustard-yellow color Etta had picked for his office walls.

Max leaned back in his chair, his gut bulging over his belt, the holster for his weapon visible under his arm. He had thinning brown hair, but at least he kept it short. Unlike Slater, Max was a licensed PI, and among other things that meant he could carry the sidearm and had access to databases that Slater couldn't get into on his own. Sharing resources worked well, and they'd built a rapport, even though Slater regularly wanted to punch the guy in the face. But then he felt that way about most people.

"Do you have time for me?" he said.

"Always." Max waved at the chairs in front of his desk. "Step into the mustard suite."

"Are you in the field today?"

"I'm meeting a prospective client later. A window-shade job."

"You make it sound like it's a grind. I know you love it."

Max chuckled. "Romantic problems pay the bills."

"I landed a client last night too. A missing person." He explained Truax's ask. "Can you look up my target?"

Max sat up and pulled his keyboard toward him. "What's the name?"

"Finley López, with a z." He looked at his phone, at the details Truax had sent. "Lives on Alpine Street."

Max met his gaze, his eyes narrowing. "That's China-town, Slater."

"I'm aware."

Tapping at the keyboard, Max peered at the screen. "Finley doesn't have a record. He's been at that address for two years. Do you need his vitals?"

"Yeah, send all that."

"Let me see if I can get a photo."

"From a different source?"

"Right." His thick fingers jabbed at the keys, and a moment later he glanced up. "I just sent it to you."

Slater looked at his phone. The image was a head shot with a blue background—a DMV photo. It was definitely the same guy, although he looked darker, more Hispanic than in his employee ID photo.

"He has a four-year degree," Max said, peering at his screen. "He's worked at Magnesia Motors for three years. Based on his date of birth, he's twenty-seven."

"So Magnesia Motors might be his first serious job."

Eventually Max looked up. "That's all I got."

"Can you look up my client?" Slater said, and spelled

his name. "I don't know where he lives, but he works at Magnesia too."

Max worked the keyboard, and a moment later said, "Is he about forty? Blond?"

"That's the guy."

"He's been popped several times. Once they charged him with assault."

"Here?"

"San Diego … He wasn't convicted. There's no other details on that one. There's also a federal charge. Impeding interstate commerce."

"What the hell does that mean?" Slater demanded. "Parking your car on a rail crossing?"

"This says it's a felony. It also says it was resolved, but he wasn't convicted."

"Is it some kind of white-collar thing?"

"Who knows? It's pretty vague. Do you need his photo?"

"Just the vitals."

Max clicked his mouse and rolled it around his blotter. "Nothing here says he works at Magnesia Motors. That doesn't mean he doesn't."

"I thought the EV business was all smoke and mirrors and prototypes, but he claims that he's driving one."

Pushing the keyboard away, Max leaned back and laced his fingers behind his head. "I think they're building them. So far Magnesia just has the one model."

"I've seen pictures. A fuggly little coupe with a bustle back."

"Of all the dead design trends, right?" Max scoffed. "Why would they bring that back?"

"Preach, brother." Slater sighed. "It's probably stupid to be investigating my client. I wish I knew more about him. Something's just off. I can feel it."

"Ask your ex. Maybe he can get details about the

assault charge."

"I appreciate the help," Slater said, and rose.

Max waved a hand. "It goes both ways."

Stepping into his own office, Slater sat behind his desk. The paint color Etta had picked for his walls, a shade of turquoise, made this office feel cooler than Max's. It suited him, he'd decided, and made it easy to work in here.

His ex, Conrad, was a cop, and had access to deeper resources. The guy was also a dick-smack, and usually gave him static when he asked for information. Just the thought of Conrad was infuriating, made him grit his teeth. But he dialed his number anyway.

"What do you need, Slater?" he said when he picked up.

"That's a dick way to answer the phone."

"You're lucky I answer at all. I know you're not calling to ask about the condition of my psyche."

Slater suppressed an acerbic retort and took a breath. "I'm looking for a guy. I figured you'd be able to tell if he's been reported as a missing person."

"What's the name?"

He recited it, and added, "Age twenty-seven. Lives in Chinatown."

Even though he'd called his cell, Conrad was at work, he realized, as he could hear several other voices over the clacking of his rapid keystrokes. While he waited, on his own computer he pulled up the vitals that Max had sent, and scanned through them.

"Nobody with that name has been reported missing," Conrad said finally. "I did find Finley. He gets parking tickets on a regular basis. Mostly downtown. He's paid them all."

"So if Finley's not officially missing, is my client a stalker?"

"I can't open police files for you."

"You can if you think this guy is a knucklehead."

That vague suggestion, that there might be a threat to his safety, was usually enough to get Conrad to come across. It was his ham-fisted attempt to shield Slater from danger.

Conrad huffed and lowered his voice. "What's the name?"

He recited it, and listened to Conrad typing.

"I'll call you later. I need to do this in a smart way."

"Chop-chop," Slater said. "Time waits for no one."

"Fuck you, Slater," he said, and ended the call.

Rising, he called good-bye to Max and went down to the street, and across to the surface lot. He drove the Thunderbird the few blocks to Andy's place, on Broadway, and parked in the lot behind his building. Walking through the lobby, he went up to Andy's floor, and rapped on the door to his loft.

It took Andy a minute to get there, and when he pulled open the door, he was wearing a white tank top and boxers, a few days' stubble on his face, his scruffy brown hair a perfect mess.

"You should text before you ... come over," Andy said, and frowned. "Boundaries, remember?"

Slater threw up his hands. "You're here, aren't you?"

Andy turned and led him inside. His loft was mostly one big room, with a bed and a desk and a little table. The tall multipane windows, original to the building's former incarnation as a textile warehouse, overlooked the square.

His desk had an array of computer screens around it, like he was running a damn TV studio, and Andy ambled over and dropped into his desk chair.

Slater stood facing him. "So how's married life?"

"Pretty sweet. It's mostly ... psychological, but being

married intensifies the … bond. It feels good."

"Just remember that you can get out of it any time you need to. You're not trapped."

"Thanks for that," he said flatly, and frowned.

"If you ever need to give spouse B a tune-up, just say the word. I'll track him down. No questions asked. He'll never know what hit him."

Andy raised his voice. "Slater, focus. Why are you … here?"

"Can you hack my target? I need to know whether he's missing by choice or if someone grabbed him."

"I don't hack."

"Do a deep dive, then, or whatever euphemism you prefer. The cops say no one has reported him missing."

"You checked?"

"Max's databases, and Conrad's sources. He has no criminal record."

"Text me what you … know about him."

Slater put his hands on his hips. "Speaking of spouse B, where is that little weasel?"

"Kyle is with his family today."

"Does he even sleep here?"

"Sometimes."

"So when are you moving to the OC?"

"He's not from the OC." Andy chuckled. "Why do you insist on … saying that? His parents aren't either."

"It sure seems like he is." Slater waved a hand. "That's on you. You married him."

"I did. And it's freaking … great. When are you going to … take the plunge?"

"Why would I do that?" he demanded. "I don't need that kind of entanglement."

"You're fine on your own, are you? No assistance needed from … me or Max or your ex?"

"All that is transactional."

"Well, I can say the sex is … way hotter when there's a ring on it."

"That's not what you said when I was balls deep in you."

"For real, though." He held his gaze. "It's the best."

Watching him, Slater could feel his heart pounding. "Damn it."

Andy frowned. "Don't get steamed."

"I'm not steamed," he said, raising his voice.

"Your hands are balled up in … fists. Do you even know you're doing that? You're not allowed to … take a poke at me."

"Just do the work," he said, and walked out.

Climbing into the Thunderbird, he knew that Andy had a point—punching people in the face was his go-to solution, and it usually made things better. But he could never do that to him, sweet Andy, perfect apart from his deeply flawed taste in men. Tapping at his phone, he sent him what he knew about Finley.

FOUR

B ACK IN HIS NEIGHBORHOOD, Slater pulled into his garage, and as the door rolled down, he got out and walked past the nose of the Thunderbird. Along with the laundry machines and the rack for his gardening tools was his gear cabinet. It was built to look like an innocuous sheet-metal storage cabinet from an office supply store, but in reality it was a well-armored gun safe.

Slater didn't have any weapons, but he kept his surveillance tech inside. It wasn't that he was afraid of it getting jacked—most of it was blatantly illegal. He grabbed the lock-reading probe and the heavy key binder, with sheets of little pouches with numbered ghost keys, and heaved them into his black duffel bag, then lifted it into the trunk of the Thunderbird. Once he'd hit the button to roll the garage door up again, he got behind the wheel, and checked Finley's address on his phone, and copied it to his navigation app.

Alpine was a crowded street, and even though Chinatown wasn't an old neighborhood, it was dense. He found Finley's apartment building on the slope leading down from the freeway, and pulled to the curb farther down the block.

Reaching into the backseat, he grabbed a couple of black latex gloves from the box he kept on the floor, and tucked them into his hip pocket. Switching on the camera-jamming eyeglasses, he put them on, then pulled on his blue ball cap, and climbed out.

It was already stupid hot out, the sun brilliant in the cloudless summer sky. Once he'd heaved the duffel bag out of the trunk, he slammed the lid and walked up to the building's front door, pulling his cap low over his glasses. The security door wasn't locked, opening wide when he tried the handle. That was sloppy, especially these days, considering how many homeless nutjobs were prowling around and doing break-ins.

Three floors of outdoor hallways studded with windows and front doors surrounded a courtyard with some raised beds. The plantings were mostly succulents, some chalky *Dudleyas* and strings of different *Curio* species. He paused to take a closer look. They'd put in some kind of gorse. Who would do that? It was a damn invasive. When Slater had been studying horticulture, he and his whole class had spent hours one day ripping this stuff out where it had spread wild on the college campus.

"Idiots," he muttered, and glanced at his phone to check Finley's apartment number. It was on the second floor, and he climbed the staircase, finding the door marked 204 in the far corner. It was mostly out of view of the courtyard, which gave him some cover. Wriggling his hands into the latex gloves, he squatted to study the lock. As expected, it was a standard setup with a locking handle plus a deadbolt, both with a familiar hardware-store logo. Most landlords went that way, not bothering to shell out for higher security.

When he connected the probe's cable to his phone, Svetlana's lock-reading app popped up, displaying a black screen with the Cyrillic letters "готов." At the end of the cable was a key-shaped probe, and he slid it into the deadbolt cylinder. The phone screen went red and said "ошибка." Slater didn't know the word, but he knew it meant it wasn't working.

Sliding the probe out again, he wiped the sweat off

his brow with the back of his hand, then breathed on both sides of the probe to get some moisture on its surface. This time when he eased it into the lock, the screen turned green, and displayed 147.

Slater glanced over his shoulder to make sure he wasn't being observed, then pulled open the duffel bag and flipped through the heavy pages of the key binder to find the pouch marked 147.

When he tried it in the deadbolt, it twisted freely, withdrawing the bolt with a solid *thunk*. The handle below it wasn't locked, and Slater lifted the duffel as he rose, then stepped into Finley's apartment, pulling the door closed behind him.

It was dark inside, and warm, the air stale and cloying. He called out "Maintenance," then stood listening. There was no sound of movement. He set the duffel bag on the floor. Next to the front door was the kitchen counter, with a window over the sink that looked out on the courtyard. The curtains on it and on the windows across the room were all drawn, and he flipped on the room lights to do a quick survey of the place.

The bathroom was small, with a 1950s tub and shower, and in the lone bedroom the bed was made. Slater opened the closet door, one of the only places in the apartment that someone could be hiding from him. There was nobody here.

Standing in the middle of the main room, he spent a minute assessing the place. All the furniture was still here. It felt like Finley had just stepped out, not that he'd moved out. Slater pulled open the kitchen cupboards and the icebox. There was no food except condiments and spice jars and a lone box of dry cereal. Clearing out anything that would rot showed planning—that meant Finley's absence hadn't been unexpected. Unless someone had come in later and cleaned the place out after he'd disappeared.

Back in the bedroom he pulled open the bureau drawers to find shirts and skivvies and socks, but only a few of each. The closet was less than half full of dress shirts and pants on hangers. There was no luggage either, no suitcase, no backpack. Finley had taken clothes with him. You didn't do that if you were being abducted.

In the main room a TV perched on the table opposite the sofa, and a desk stood under the windows, but there was no computer, just an empty space on the top of the desk where a laptop would sit. The desk drawers contained stationery but no paperwork, no wallet, no passport, no phone. In the top drawer was a paper sleeve the size of a credit card. There was nothing inside it, he found, prodding it with a latex-clad finger. Looking closer, he saw that it was made of thick foil, not paper. The sleeve was printed with a star logo with swirls around it and the words GLOBAL ENTRY.

Digging out his phone, he looked it up. It was a federal program — you could get a card to get through immigration faster when you came back from abroad. Finley had taken the card with him but not the wrapper. Was he headed overseas, or had he just taken anything that might be of value to a burglar?

On the floor next to the desk was a black plastic wastebasket, and Slater picked it up and dumped the contents on the desktop. There were advertising flyers, and two halves of a letter that had been ripped up. When he held them together, it was addressed to "Finley López or current occupant." Junk mail. The only other thing in the trash was a sheet of printer paper, folded in half.

In the corner of the page was a QR code, and in big letters "A Night with Olivia." Below that it said, "Online and in person, talk with lauded contactee and renowned author Olivia Howard." The venue was a ballroom at the

Baltimore Hotel downtown, and the date of the event was last Saturday. Finley had paid sixty bucks for this. Digging out his phone again, Slater photographed the sheet, then put everything back in the trash can.

In the lower desk drawers were pens, and printer paper, and sheets of labels, and some thick padded envelopes. Pulling one out, he read the printing along the flap: "Fold twice to make an RF-proof seal." These were radio-silencing envelopes, and Finley had three of them. Not many people needed those in everyday life.

Putting it back, he pushed the drawer closed and stood erect, looking around the room. No food, no computer, no documents. The cleanup was methodical, deliberate, targeted. It hadn't been anybody else. Finley had cleared out of here himself.

On the wall next to the TV was a shelving unit, and Slater stepped over to it. There were haphazard stacks of paperbacks on the lowest shelf, and he squatted to scan the titles on the spines: *Death Comes to Bakersfield, The Fish Store Murders, Who Slew Auntie Roo.* Murder mysteries. On the shelf above that was a thick English dictionary, and a Spanish one, and then at eye level, two shelves of neatly organized books. He cocked his head to read the titles. *I Rode a Flying Saucer* was a worn hardcover, and *Inside the Space Ships,* and a thick paperback called *UFO Crash at Corona.* They were all UFO books, some of them new, some worn and faded cloth hardbacks, some with dust jackets chipped with age. Pike would love this collection—he was a saucer-head, and the day they'd met, out in New Mexico, he'd taken Slater to a saucer crash site. That had been their first date. Was that weird? But he had no way to know that, no way to be objective about Pike, given the way he felt about him. Everything about the guy distorted reality.

Three of the books were by Olivia Howard, he saw,

the author Finley had shelled out to see at the Balti-more. On the upper shelf was an empty space, where a book was slumped on its neighbor. It was the only gap on the shelf—a book had been pulled out.

Slater pushed the leaning volume upright. The one that had been removed had been thick. Finley clearly valued these books. If he'd pulled one out, he would have neatened the row after he'd taken it. Unless he'd been in a rush.

Repositioning the books the way he'd found them, he photographed the bookshelves, making sure the titles were legible in the images, then tucked his phone away. Stepping to the middle of the room again, he took a last look around. He didn't want to miss anything.

What was this thing? On the coffee table, next to the TV remote, was a little black box. At first glance he'd thought it was another remote, but on closer inspection, it didn't have any buttons on it. He turned it over in his hands. It was heavy, and it had a lone USB port, so it was electronic. But there was nothing else, not even a power switch. A solid-state hard drive, maybe? It seemed odd that Finley would leave something like that behind when he'd taken his laptop.

Striding over to the desk, Slater grabbed one of the radio-proof envelopes, and slid the black box inside, then folded the flap to seal it. Once he'd tucked the envelope into his duffel bag, he killed the lights and let himself out, locking the deadbolt with his ghost key.

He trotted down the stairs to the courtyard, and found the door marked PARKING. Inside was a stairwell, and he hustled down to the garage. The parking stalls were marked with numbers stenciled on the concrete, and they seemed to follow the numbering of the apart-ments. In space 204 was a gray Camry, like Truax had described. Stepping to its front end, he leaned in to examine the windshield. The glass bore a visible layer of dust. It hadn't been driven in a while.

Heaving his duffel onto his shoulder, Slater took the stairs back up to the courtyard two at a time. As he approached the door to the street, a guy stepped in, his brow furrowing at the sight of him. In his twenties, maybe, he had buzzed hair and wore a striped collared shirt and baggy black shorts. His gaze lingered on Slater's heavy bag.

"Can I help you?" he said.

Slater ignored him, striding toward the door.

"What's with the gloves?" he said, and then louder, "Excuse me."

He'd almost made it to the door when the guy grabbed his arm from behind and spun him around. Scowling at him, Slater set down his bag.

"I can't believe you did that. You weigh, what, a buck forty, and you're going to mix it up with me?"

"What were you doing in the garage?" he demanded.

Slater slapped him, right and then left, a firm kovac. The latex gloves made the blow sound loud, with a crisp *smack*.

"Why do you make me do this to you?" Slater growled, and grabbed his shirt collar in his fist, and landed another slap. As the guy tried to push him off, Slater shoved him backward.

His face red now, the guy held a palm to his cheek. He had that look that civilians always got, anger and alarm, not sure whether to be afraid or to escalate. Guys like this weren't used to anybody standing up to them. They usually reacted by fighting back. Slater balled his fists and raised his eyebrows, a tacit challenge.

"I'm calling the cops," the guy spat.

"You came at me, remember? If that's the way you want to play it, you're the one who'll go down for assault."

His eyebrows shot up, and he scoffed, but Slater could see the doubt in his eyes now. He wasn't going to call anybody. Heaving up his duffel, he walked out the front door, and down the block to the Thunderbird. He looked back before he opened the trunk. There was no sign of the guy.

"Idiot," he muttered, and climbed in behind the wheel, and peeled off the gloves, wiping his sweaty palms on his jeans.

FIVE

S LATER GOT ON THE freeway, accelerating on the
short ramp to match the speed of the traffic. The
Thunderbird revved contentedly with the task,
and he quickly merged left to get on the 5. His illicit
tech supplier, Svetlana, worked in a run-down part of
Glendale. The neighborhood she was in hadn't yet seen
the tidal wave of sterilizing urban renewal that turned
everything into a bland copy of everything else.

Her workshop was a low-slung midcentury commercial building with a sagging roofline. As Slater pulled up
in front he saw that the ivy and fast-growing shrubs were
starting to disguise the structure's seediness. He'd helped
her find a landscaper to put in the plantings. They were
a lot cheaper than renovating the place, and it would
keep the city officials at bay for a few more years.

Climbing out, it felt even hotter here. From the Thunderbird's trunk he grabbed the shielded envelope and
walked around the building to the alley, where the lone
functioning entrance was. At the heavy steel-lined back
door, he rang the bell and looked up into the camera.

The door buzzed open, and he stepped into the small
anteroom, and waited to be scanned by the electronics
that studded the walls and the ceiling overhead. Presumably Svetlana was concerned about weapons, but he
knew her tech could also sniff out explosives. Eventually the lock on the inner door snapped open, and he
stepped into the dimly lit interior.

The workbenches lining the room were strewn with plastic and wire and circuit boards. The place always smelled like machine oil, but at least she had air-conditioning, and it wasn't as hot in here as it was outside. Perched on a stool at the workbench, Svetlana was curvy, in her fifties, today wearing a bright red and yellow dress. She always wore bright colors. Slater wasn't sure if it was to perk up this drab cavern, or something else—schizophrenics liked bright colors. But he'd never seen any other sign of that.

Svetlana swiveled to greet him, her Slavic accent flattening the vowels. "Lovely to see your face. Do you need some new equipment?"

"I actually wanted you to identify something for me."

She gestured to the envelope. "I know it's electronic. The scanner shows you have it inside a shielded envelope."

"And you let me in anyway?"

"The other scanner shows it's not dense metal like a weapon. More like foil to stop low-energy radio frequencies."

"That's exactly what it is." Slater folded open the envelope and pulled out the little black box, stepping closer to hand it to her. "What can you tell me about this?"

"No commercial markings." She turned it over in her hands, studying it. "One computer port. Let's connect it to a computer."

"Is that safe?" he said, watching her climb off her stool.

"I have a computer that's air-gapped. That means it's not connected to any network. Like quarantine for people."

Slater followed her deeper into the workroom, where she took a stool in front of another monitor that sat next to a computer on the workbench. Briefly peering at the port on the device, she scrabbled in a plastic tub of cables, pulling one out and connecting it to the device, then to the front of the computer.

Working the mouse, Svetlana pulled up a software interface. It showed several columns of numbers scrolling up the screen. She sat studying it for a moment, then clicked through some other menus and windows.

"The device is outputting a large quantity of information," she said finally, swiveling toward him. "It's not expecting any input through this port."

"What kind of information? Is it like a flash drive?"

"A drive needs input and output. This box is output only." She locked the computer screen and disconnected the device from the cable. "Let's look inside."

Rising, she took it to the workbench at the far end of the room, and Slater watched as she opened and closed several of the little drawers in a tool organizer. The tool she eventually pulled out looked like a drill bit. Stepping closer, he saw that the tip was flat, like a wedge. From the wall rack Svetlana took down a ball peen hammer, and deftly positioned the tool along the seam on the narrow side of the box. Without hesitating she raised the hammer and delivered a single decisive blow. The box cracked loudly as it split into two halves.

There were blue circuit boards inside, he saw, one attached to either half of the housing. Svetlana pulled on the eyeglasses that dangled on a cord around her neck. The lenses had jewelers loupes built into them. She studied the boards, and used the wedge tool to pry one away from the plastic housing so she could study the other side. Eventually she pulled off the glasses and let them drop to her breast.

"No manufacturer's name," she said, meeting his gaze, "so I'm thinking a small operator built this."

"Someone like you?"

"Exactly. Or a hobbyist. The device has many sensors.

Some I don't recognize, but it can receive radio waves in several different frequency bands."

"So it's a radio?" Slater said, folding his arms.

"It's definitely a radio receiver, but I can't see a broadcasting function. The output is only from the port, and it's just numbers, not any standard audio or video signal." She shrugged. "I'm sorry I can't tell you more."

"That's more than I knew a minute ago."

She took a moment to press the circuit boards back into the housing, then snapped the halves together, then handed it to him.

"You don't need to keep it in the radio-shielded envelope. It's not broadcasting anything."

Slater nodded. "What do I owe you?"

"*Nuil*," she said flatly. "Zero. Included in your subscriptions and service for a regular customer."

"I appreciate that." He followed her toward her usual workstation near the door to the alley.

"How are things going with your federal employee boyfriend?" Svetlana said, climbing onto her stool. "Mr. Pike?"

"He moved in with me. His job is here now."

"Do you plan to get married?"

Slater laughed. "No."

"Remember that a married spouse can't be compelled to testify against you in legal matters, and vice versa. Marriage has its benefits."

"I'll keep that in mind."

"Does he work remotely?"

He put his hands on his hips and furrowed his brow. "Sometimes, but mostly he's in the office, or in the field."

"If I could get a few minutes alone with his laptop, I might be able to get access to some valuable federal information. Databases." She waved a hand. "He would never find out. I'm very good at what I do."

"I know you are. He doesn't leave his computer around, though. He takes it when he leaves. Even if I did have access to it, that feels risky."

She raised her eyebrows. "I can make it worth your while. Your subscriptions would cost zero for two years, plus I could give you some devices for free."

Slater nodded. "I'll think about it."

"Just keep an eye open for an opportunity," she said, and waved a hand. "I can be at your house in thirty minutes, and return the device in a few hours."

When he stepped into the alley, he winced at the sudden brightness of the day, and walked around to the Thunderbird. On the way downtown, cruising south on the 5, he thought about his exchange with Svetlana.

When she'd first found out about Pike, Slater had worried she might cut him off because he was getting too close to the long arm of the law. Logically she'd be suspicious that Pike would find out too much about her business. But this was a different reaction, and still far from optimal, asking him to betray the man he was crazy about. At least she was using the carrot with him, not the stick. Either way, it would be a disaster if the outcome was that she stopped working with him.

Traffic was slowing as he came up on Griffith Park, and he rode the brakes in the sea of vehicles stretching out ahead. No way was he going to betray Pike, no matter the incentive, no matter the threat. Svetlana was smart, but the feds were smart too, and they had a lot more resources. The whole scheme would undoubtedly get caught out and blow up in their faces. And Pike would be the one to snap the cuffs on him.

SIX

ONCE HE GOT TO the Fashion District, Slater parked and headed across the street to his building. The lot was mostly empty as the factories cleared out over the course of the afternoon. Upstairs he flicked on the office lights and double-clicked his tongue to greet the statue of Rey Pascual. Briefly sticking his head into Max's office, he made sure he really was alone.

At his own desk he leaned back in the chair and swung his boots up on the desk, pulling his keyboard into his lap. He eyed the office's other plaster tchotchke, a statue of Pollux, naked and standing with a horse, positioned next to his monitor. Rey Pascual had been a gift from the woman who sold him pupusas, but this one had sentimental value—a gift from Pike, it had motivated Slater to get into it with him, get into a relationship, dive deep into their narrative complex.

Shifting his focus to the screen, Slater went through the photos he'd taken in Finley's apartment. He had no idea what the radio receiver was for, but at least he had a better idea now of what the hell it was. Searching Finley's pad hadn't told him much. The only evidence on his movements before he disappeared was the ticket for that event at the Baltimore, a chance to meet the lauded Olivia Howard.

A search for her name brought up her bio. Olivia first found fame for a book she authored in 1966, *My*

Saucer Trip to Venus. Looking at the photos he'd taken of Finley's neatly organized bookshelf, he rotated them to read the spines. *My Saucer Trip to Venus* was there, and it looked like an old copy, with a plastic-wrapped dust jacket.

Olivia had an active website. Her portrait depicted a woman with her hands folded on a desk, a subtle smile on her face, her gray hair in a short natural Afro. Chunky amber and gold jewelry glistened at her neck. In this photo she could be as young as sixty, but doing the calculation in his head, if she was writing books in the mid-1960s, she had to be pushing eighty.

The website explained that Olivia still wrote articles, provided commentary in UFO documentaries, and occasionally presented lectures around the country and abroad. The last line of her bio said that "Olivia lives with her family in Los Angeles, where electro-planetary conditions facilitate easy communication with other parts of the solar system."

He pulled up the photo he'd taken of Finley's ticket for Olivia's lecture at the Baltimore. It didn't say anything about the event's organizers. But maybe he could talk to Olivia Howard herself.

Her website had contact info, including a phone number, and Slater dialed. It rang a couple of times, and then a woman's voice answered.

"This is Olivia."

Slater sat up. "I was expecting a machine."

"What can I do for you, dear?"

"I want to ask you a few questions about a lecture you gave at the Baltimore last weekend."

"I'd be happy to speak with you, but my time is paid. Unless you're writing for an accredited media outlet."

"Accredited?" he said flatly. "You mean by your friends on Venus?"

She laughed. "What do you want to ask me about?"

"I'd rather do it in person. Especially if I have to pay for it. What are your rates for nonaccredited interviews?"

"One fifty per hour," Olivia said, not missing a beat.

Slater scoffed. "I guess I can handle that. When are you available?"

"How about tomorrow morning?"

"Sunday? Don't you have to be in church?"

"If you'd listened more carefully at the lecture," she said, "You'd know I don't do that."

Olivia recited her address, and Slater typed it into his contacts, then ended the call. While he'd been talking a text had come from Conrad:

I have something for you. I'll be at the central market if you're around.

His stomach had been growling, and that was as good a place to eat as any. He texted back:

I'll be there in 15.

Once he'd locked his computer, and flicked off the lights, and twisted his key in the deadbolt, he rode the elevator down to the street. On the way, his phone buzzed in his pants. It was a text from Pike:

Where you at? Dinner?

Slater sent him a reply:

Headed to the central market right now. Lots of food there.

The parking lot had cleared out so late in the day, and the attendant was gone, but he saw a guy standing near the nose of the Thunderbird, wearing a long heavy coat despite the August heat. Slater quickened his pace, and as he approached, saw that the guy was zipping up his pants.

When he caught sight of Slater, he took a few steps backward, away from the car. Scanning the vehicle, Slater saw a wet spot under the front bumper.

"Did you just piss on my car?" he demanded.

"I didn't touch your car." He took another step back, scratching absently at his scruffy beard.

The guy looked lucid, his gaze level, and he was enunciating clearly. He wasn't strung out on dope. Slater looked over the fender. An unmistakable patch of droplets beaded the paint in front of the wheel well.

"It's still wet. What the fuck is wrong with you?"

"Have you ever heard the saying, screw the bourgeoisie?"

"I am not bourgeois."

Slater rapidly strode toward him. The guy's eyes grew wide, and he raised his forearms, but he wasn't quick enough. Suckers always did that, the instinctive defensive move. It was predictable, and that made it easy to work with.

Maneuvering around his wavering upheld arms, Slater punched him in the face, a fast right hook. The guy's head snapped sideways.

"Why do you make me do this to you?" Slater said through his teeth. "Why do you make me hurt you?"

He landed another blow, a left to his jaw, and the guy yelped and stumbled back a few steps.

"Asshole," he shouted. "Violence is the weapon of the weak."

"Pissing on cars is the weapon of the psychotic, you stupid fuck." Fists balled, Slater strode after him, but the guy hustled away, loping toward the gap in the parking lot's fence, the pedestrian exit to the street.

Slater watched him until he was out on the sidewalk. Briefly looking over the wet spot on his car, he wrinkled his nose, then climbed in behind the wheel.

The market was just a few blocks away, and there was lots of traffic on Saturday evening, but nothing like the gridlock that happened on weekdays. He soon pulled into the parking structure next door and walked into the market hall.

The traditional produce stalls and vendors in the sprawling space had gradually been displaced by trendy eateries. These days it felt more like a restaurant hall than a market, but it still had the old neon signs, and they still scattered wood shavings on the floor under the dining tables.

Conrad was sitting at a table near the Hill Street side, gazing at his phone, an iced drink in front of him. He was wearing a tan summer suit without a necktie. The look suited him, and the cut of his jacket flattered his barrel chest. He was letting his thick black hair grow a little longer now that he wasn't a beat cop anymore. Such a beautiful man.

As Slater dropped into the chair across from him, Conrad greeted him and flashed a smile.

"You were working today?" Slater said. "That suit is so PD it makes me nervous."

"I thought I looked pretty natty. You, on the other hand, look stressed out. More than usual."

"I caught some homeless pinko pissing on my car. When I confronted him he started quoting Marx at me. As if I was the one with the problem."

Conrad frowned. "Is he still breathing?"

"I chased him off. I'm not crazy."

"You're getting soft. It must be Pike's influence. I've watched you get into a fistfight because someone over-watered their geraniums."

"Most people deserve a punch in the face most of the time. That's just science." He waved an arm. "It feels like nobody is doing anything wrong, but things keep getting worse. How did we get to this?"

"You got me." Conrad shrugged. "I can tell you it goes way beyond this city. Local government alone can't fix it."

"Can we just do this?" He shifted his chair closer to the table. "Pike is coming for dinner. I don't need him to be eavesdropping on my work."

"Nice." He grinned. "My favorite fed."

Slater jabbed a finger at him. "You keep your grubby paws off that man."

Conrad guffawed, throwing his head back. "I'm not going to hit on him. It wouldn't matter if I did—he only has eyes for Slater. It's actually weird. Like he's got some serious mental block. Did you take him to a hypnotist, or drug his breakfast cereal?" Picking up his phone, he tapped at it. "And why not get him to do your dirty work? Feds have all kinds of juicy data."

"I don't have anything to motivate him with."

"You mean blackmail. You don't have anything to blackmail me with either."

"There are certain photos you wouldn't want spread around," Slater said, "what with your new position. It would be a shame if your colleagues got an email blast with an image of my dick down your throat."

Conrad met his eye. "I help you because you're my friend, Slater. The extortion thing is bullshit."

"Whatever you need to tell yourself to get through the night." He gave him the once-over. "You're allowed to wear better suits than that, you know. Or are you undercover, posing as a homeless accountant?"

Looking at his phone, Conrad ignored that. "This guy Truax. There's no bunco charges on him, but he has been arrested a few times for strong-arming people. He got charged with assault in San Diego. Some white-shoe lawyer got it thrown out."

"What kind of assault?"

"It says he messed with somebody's car."

Slater frowned. "How is that assault?"

"I guess it caused injury, or he tried to cause injury. Maybe he disabled the brakes or something."

"So he's a lowlife."

"I'd say so." He looked to the phone screen again. "There's also a federal arrest, but no conviction. The charge was interfering with interstate commerce. The feds don't share anything unless you need to know, but the file says it involved a big rig. He tampered with the tractor."

"So he's a serial automotive tamperer. Interesting that he works for a car manufacturer."

"Truax also smacks his wife around," Conrad said. "He wasn't charged for it, but the police visited their place and detained him. She wouldn't squawk, so they had to let him go."

"You're sure it's a wife? Not a husband?"

He glanced at the screen. "It doesn't specify gender, but the spouse's name is Melissa. There's not too many men with that name."

"So he's straight."

"Is anyone really?" Conrad's brow furrowed. "Sexuality is a spectrum."

He scoffed. "Tell that to a straight guy."

Looking into the distance, past Slater's shoulder, Conrad broke into a smile and raised his hand in a big wave.

"Pike's here already?" Slater said, and looked across the market hall.

It wasn't Pike—a scrawny guy with frosted hair waved back.

"The fuck is that?" Slater demanded.

"Sullivan. The guy I've been seeing."

"He just happened to wander in here?"

"We had plans to meet before I talked to you."

Turned sideways on his chair, Slater watched him approach. Sullivan was significantly younger than Conrad, and dark, his thick Latin hair cut straight across his forehead in a trendy style. He was wearing a sleeveless T-shirt, even though he wasn't muscular, and tight green short shorts.

"Isn't it a little late in the day for booty shorts?" Slater said quietly.

"It's never a wrong time for booty shorts. He's working a look."

"I get it. The guy is stacked. He's also built like a stick insect."

"He says he has Aztec blood, so he's tougher than he looks."

Slater wanted to point out that Aztec ancestry didn't automatically confer resilience, but the guy was already here.

Sullivan leaned in to kiss Conrad, lingering in it, then set his paper coffee cup on the table, and sat down. Conrad introduced them, and Sullivan dipped his chin, briefly meeting Slater's gaze, and said, "Hello."

Slater folded his arms and looked him over. "I'm thinking you're not on the police force."

Sullivan chuckled. "Can you imagine?" He pointed a finger in the air and mimed a gunshot. "*Blam-blam.* I'd totally get split ends."

"It's not all about gunfire, pumpkin," Conrad said, and squeezed his hand.

"Gentlemen," Pike said, announcing his arrival as he stepped up to the table, a wry smile on his face. He was dressed for the weekend—a short-sleeved shirt with a colorful hibiscus print and tan cargo shorts.

Reaching for his shoulder, Slater pulled him down

and kissed him on the mouth, holding him there for a long moment.

When he stood erect again, Pike was blushing. "Let me find a chair."

"Take mine," Sullivan said, and got up. "I never come in here. I'm going to do a drive-by of all the shops."

Once he'd strolled away, Slater eyed Conrad and raised his eyebrows. "Pumpkin?"

"I love the hot pants," Pike said, watching him leave. "It makes me wonder what's under the gravy."

"More gravy," Slater said. "He's clearly stacked."

"He's a sweet kid," Conrad said, "but I don't think he ever did anything where he scored in the top decile."

Slater jutted his chin. "He seems a little jittery. Is he a duster?"

"He's not on angel dust, but I think he does coke." He gestured helplessly. "I just have to look the other way."

"I was only half serious. Why are you dating a wastoid?"

Conrad groaned. "He's for right now."

"Are you allowed to do that?" Pike said. "Ignore the drug use?"

"He doesn't do it at my place. I figure I'm off-duty. This isn't a long-term arrangement anyway—big picture, he's a wrong guy. If he pisses me off I can always pop him."

"Dope is a one-way ticket to a world of pain," Slater said flatly.

Pike chuckled. "Is that the voice of experience?"

"I've never been a doper."

"He's not anti-drugs for any high-brow reason," Conrad said to Pike. "He's anti-drugs because he knows if he got into it, it would destroy him."

"Spread out," Slater said through his teeth.

Pike raised his eyebrows and eyed Conrad. "That

actually has the ring of truth."

Slater jabbed a finger at Conrad, then at Pike. "I don't need either one of you chuckleheads psychoanalyzing me." He looked to Conrad. "I fucking hate that you know me that well. It's like you can see right through me. Like I'm some demographically predictable chump."

"You're a lot of things, Slater, but I wouldn't call you demographically predictable." He sat up. "I should go track down Mr. Right Now, before he gets lost or locked in somewhere overnight. Pike, always a pleasure."

As he walked away, Slater called after him, "Ditch him." He took a breath. "He called that twink 'pumpkin.'"

"He looks more like a string bean," Pike said. "There's so many dating options in the big city."

"And I had to go way the hell out to the middle of rural New Mexico to find you. Voirrey's fricking Corners."

"So I'm your Mr. Right?" Pike grinned. "An upgrade from Mr. Right Now?"

"You're mister fucking everything," Slater said intently. "The sunrise and the sunset. Every note in every song. Every sweet snack treat in the deli case. Seed plants and ferns and all the bryophytes. The fiery beating heart of our multidimensional narrative complex."

Pike nodded. "I like that better than 'pumpkin.'"

SEVEN

P IKE AND SLATER WALKED around the market, studying the food options, and eventually chose a salad
place, the only vegan option. Parked at a table near
the street entrance, they'd finished eating when Slater's
phone buzzed. It was a text from Andy:

Drop by.

Summoning him without providing any details, the
same way Conrad had, was actually good news. It meant
he'd found something but didn't want to write it down
and potentially incriminate himself.

"Ready to roll?" Pike said, and stood up, stretching
his back.

"I have a work stop to make. I won't be long."

Slater leaned in to kiss him before they parted, and
Pike headed out to Broadway, Slater into the parking
structure. Andy's loft was within a few minutes' walk, but
he didn't know when this structure closed, and he didn't
want his wheels to get stranded.

The lot behind Andy's building was crowded, with
all the clubs and restaurants in the neighborhood, and
he paid the attendant the inflated Saturday evening flat
rate. When he knocked on his door, Andy pulled it open
and greeted him with that smile. Following him inside,
Slater relished the suddenly cool air. He kept the place
cold because his CP made his metabolism run hot.

Andy settled in his desk chair, and Slater pulled a

chair out from the table and sat on it backward, facing his desk.

"I looked into your boy," Andy said, swiveling to face him. "He has a couple of … email addresses, but they're impenetrable. He's got really good … security on them."

"He worked in IT."

"That would make him keenly aware of … the risks of being sloppy."

"You wouldn't have called me over here if you didn't have more dope than that," Slater said.

"Finley hasn't used … any of his cards for a couple weeks, and there's no money going into his … bank account. There were two withdrawals, for utilities and rent."

"So he's still around."

"Those payments are likely automated," Andy said, his head subtly undulating with his rhythmic random muscle movements. "His electric bill was pretty … minimal. It makes me think no one is living at that … address. It's the apartment on Alpine."

"How long can he pay rent from that account before it runs dry?"

"Maybe another six months. Longer if he has … overdraft coverage from another account. I can't tell if he does."

"How did you get into his bank accounts?" Slater said.

"I wasn't in them. I was able to … see data about them."

"Like a credit report?"

"Don't ask. You should maintain your … plausible deniability." He waved a hand. "I wish I could tell you where … he's been lately, but I can't find anything. Do you think someone … nabbed him?"

"My gut says he nabbed himself. He must have some other way to survive without cards. A stack of cash."

"Or a sugar daddy," Andy said.

Slater stood up and shifted the chair back to the table. "Excellent work."

"You have to pay me."

He stifled a sigh. "What's the damage?"

"It was pretty … straightforward. Let's say four dollars."

"If it was straightforward, you could just charge me fifty bucks." Pulling his wad out of his jeans, he peeled off the C-notes.

"It's not just about the … time it takes," he said, and reached for the bills. "It's about my skills."

"Bye, beautiful," Slater said, holding his gaze for a moment, then walked out.

The sun was finally gone when he got down to the street, the sky gray and steadily fading to black, the air already cooler. Back in his own neighborhood, cruising up the block, he saw two people standing in front of his house. He waited to hit the garage button, just in case it was some kind of ambush and he'd have to gun it to get away. But when he got closer he recognized Pike's loud hibiscus-print shirt. He was standing with his hands on his hips, talking to a woman. Slater had seen her around—she lived in one of the houses across the street.

Hitting the button for the garage door, he pulled past them, and rolled inside, and killed the engine. He could see them in the rearview, he realized, and left the door up to watch. Pike had a big smile plastered on his face. He couldn't hear the conversation, but the woman was gesturing to punctuate her words, and he heard Pike guffaw, saw his head tilt back. Eventually she touched his arm and then walked away.

The guy was so amiable, so effortless with people. He'd make a really good con man. Slater climbed out of the Thunderbird as Pike stepped inside the garage.

Embracing him, Slater mouthed his neck, and Pike sighed with pleasure.

"Next you'll be joining the neighborhood watch," Slater said, once he pulled back. "Complaining about suspicious characters on the neighborhood app."

Pike squeezed his shoulder. "In this neighborhood you're the suspicious character. You don't know these people, and none of them know you. Tilly asked me about my 'friend' with the old car." He waggled his fingers to put air quotes around the word. "I told her you weren't really a friend. More like a fuck stick, or a come dump."

"You did not say that." Slater chuckled. "You totally should have, though."

"Tilly is short for Matilde."

"I don't care," Slater said, massaging his biceps.

"You should note that it's not Matilda. Matilde is the Spanish form."

"It's a big responsibility you're taking on, being neighborly. Now you have to remember pointless stuff like that, and be on the lookout for dog dirt, and yell at teenagers to get off the lawn."

"There's no lawn."

"I blame the idiot gentrifiers who built the place," Slater said. "They built right to the street."

Pike leaned in to nuzzle his jaw. "Nothing to do with you, right?" he murmured. "Even though you own the place."

"I feel like you got screwed out of a decent meal," Slater said. "You only got salad for dinner."

"I should probably eat that way more often."

"I know you just ate there with me in solidarity."

Pike pulled back and met his gaze. "I wasn't going to sit and eat carnitas in your face."

"Do you want to walk down to that vegan doughnut joint on Sunset?"

"Great idea." He nodded. "That way I won't get sodium and sugar withdrawal."

Pike hit the button to roll down the garage door, and they went out the front, and walked down the hill. The place was busy, and the clerk promised to bring their doughnuts out to them. They sat on the bench out front, leaning back against the brick facade, with a view of the sluggish traffic on the boulevard.

The clerk who brought out the little pink box had a wild mess of hair, and a great Roman nose, the shop's pink apron tied tight around his waist and accentuating his stocky frame.

"Do you need anything else?" he said, handing the box to Pike.

"I'm fine," Pike said, and lifted the top to look inside.

The clerk raised his eyebrows. "I know."

Pike sat up straighter and met his gaze. "Are you hitting on me?"

"I'm sitting right here," Slater said, scowling at him. "No sampling the merchandise, toots. Hit the bricks."

"I know you're together. You're practically sitting in his lap. It was my lame attempt at a twofer." The clerk waved a hand. "Apologies, fellas."

"Hold up," Pike said. "Nobody said no."

Slater eyed him sidelong. "Are you actually up for that?"

"I need to eat my bear claw first."

"When does your shift end?" Slater said, eyeing the clerk.

"Now."

"Let us eat these, and we'll go to my place. It's just a couple blocks."

He grinned. "I totally didn't think that was going to work."

Pike bit into his bear claw as the guy went back inside.

"These are still warm."

"You're certainly feeling your oats," Slater said, taking the box and fishing out his own doughnut.

"I knew you'd be into it," he said, his mouth half full. "I didn't even have to ask."

"He's definitely a hot tomato."

"His name is Guapo, according to his employee tag. And you're the hot tomato." Pike glanced at him. "I'm just trying to keep up."

After they'd eaten, Pike stepped inside to put the box in the trash, and came out again behind the clerk, minus his work apron. They walked back toward the house, and once they were on a quiet side street, the two of them walking abreast with Slater just behind, Slater spoke.

"Is your name really Guapo?"

"It's a nickname, but yeah, that's me. I know your name, Pike. I saw it on your credit card. I left a sticky note on the transaction printout explaining that I went home with you. So you can't ax-murder me."

"That is such a great idea," Pike said. "A low-cost security measure."

"We can still do that," Slater said. "It's just more likely we'd get caught."

"Nice house," Guapo said, as they approached the front door. Once they were upstairs, and in the bedroom, he started to unbutton his shirt.

Once he'd pulled it off and dropped it on the floor, Pike stepped up behind him, and wrapped his arms around him, caressing his bare chest and his belly. Watching them from the other side of the bed, Slater felt his heart start to pound. He knew he couldn't get upset about this, that he'd signed up for it, but he could still feel a surge of adrenaline.

He crouched to untie his boots, then kicked them off and unbuttoned his shirt. "So what are we doing?"

"You two are going to spit-roast me," Guapo said, stepping out of his pants. He had some muscle tone, Slater saw, along with his curves.

Pike chuckled at that, and draped his hibiscus shirt over the chair, then tossed his shorts toward the closet. He stood there in his bright-red underpants and squeezed his cock, already half chubby.

Slater was out of his jeans now, and Pike stepped closer, nuzzling his ear.

"Are you OK?"

"I'll get there," Slater said.

Guapo approached them, and embraced Slater, and pressed into him, running his hands over his back.

"I like the way you smell."

"Which one of us is going to fuck you?" Slater said.

"Do I have to decide everything?"

"I want to," Pike said, and ditched his underpants, and climbed onto the bed.

"Doesn't Guapo just mean 'hot'?" Slater said, kneeling in front of him.

"Hot, handsome, foxy. Like I said, it's a nickname."

"So it's ironic?"

His eyebrows shot up. "You should do stand-up."

Shifting closer, he pushed Slater back, and took him into his mouth, eliciting a gasp at the intensity of it. Resting a palm on the back of his head, fingers in his unkempt mane, Slater guided him, got him to slow down. Pike was totally hard now, and positioned himself behind Guapo. Steadying himself with a hand on his waist, he gradually penetrated him.

Watching that was a total turn-on, but Guapo didn't seem to notice, actively engrossed in smoking him. Slater watched Pike as he started to pound him, and built up speed, then strained into him, his face contorting. Panting, he pulled away and sat back.

"Now you," Guapo said, sitting up. "Come on—fuck me."

Slater shifted up against the headboard and pulled him close, drawing his knees over his thighs, and pressed up into him. Pike moved behind Guapo, and wrapped his arms around him, and stroked his cock. Over Guapo's shoulder he eyed Slater, and held his gaze.

"Who's the suspicious character?" Slater said through his teeth, glaring at Pike. "Who's trouble?"

"What?" Guapo said, his tone breathy as he bounced on him, his head back, face toward the ceiling.

"Who's your worst fucking nightmare?" Slater growled.

Guapo yelped, his body spasming as he climaxed. Pike held on to him, hands firmly on his torso. His lip curling into a sneer, he jutted his chin at Slater.

That look was enough to push Slater over the edge, and he strained into him, squeezing his eyes shut.

Guapo leaned in to briefly kiss Slater, then turned and did the same with Pike, and extracted himself, rising and padding into the bathroom. A minute later came the sound of the shower. Catching his breath, Slater stretched out, feeling drops of sweat trickle on his torso and in his hair. When Pike lay beside him, he pushed his arm under his neck.

"That was intense."

"It's weird to watch you fuck someone else," Slater said.

"I was only looking at you," Pike said softly.

"That's what made it OK."

"Great shower," Guapo said when he came back. "Do you guys need a roommate?"

"No," Slater said flatly.

He chuckled and snatched up Pike's red underpants from the floor, and pulled them on, and snapped the elastic waistband. "I really like these."

"You can have them, if you want," Pike said.

"Good answer." Guapo got dressed, and buttoned his shirt, then pulled out his phone. "That was fun. Can I get your digits?"

Slater recited his number, and once Guapo had tucked his phone away, he looked up.

"Is the front door locked?"

"Just flip the deadbolt," Pike said.

They heard him trotting down the stairs, then the sound of the front door slam.

"I'm so glad he didn't want to hang out," Slater said.

Pike murmured agreement, not opening his eyes.

Eventually Slater pushed himself off the bed and went to shower, and a minute later Pike stepped in with him. Slater got out first, and toweled his hair, then pulled on a T-shirt and boxers.

Upstairs he took the fifth from the cupboard, not bothering with a glass, and guzzled a few pulls, relishing the burn and coughing a little at the fumes tickling his throat. He bought cheap bourbon, by necessity, because he drank so much of it. Pike's good scotch perched un-molested on the shelf behind it. After one more long pull, he put the bottle back.

Walking into the main room, he opened one of the French doors to let in the night air, then turned on the lamp by the sofa and stretched out. Pike came up a while later and sat with him, and kissed his neck.

"You smell like applejack," Pike said.

"Thank you." He sat up and swung his feet down to the faux grass to make room for him. Even though it was plastic, the blades felt good between his toes. "I can't be-lieve you gave that guy your fire-engine skivvies. I loved those. They made you look like a superhero."

He chuckled. "I guess I'd better buy another pair."

"What's your plan for the morrow?"

"I'm thinking I'll go to the hardware store. Grace needs a shower curtain. I'll put it up for her."

"She's technically my responsibility," Slater said. Grace was the elderly woman who lived downstairs, in the ADU next to the garage.

"I like Grace. She's got great stories. I don't mind pitching in."

"You're into the whole UFO thing, right? Tomorrow I'm going to meet one of the OG contactees from the space brothers era. For my case."

"Which OG?"

"Olivia Howard."

"I know her," Pike said. "*My Saucer Trip to Venus*. It's a good read."

"I can't believe you have the name of her book on the tip of your tongue."

"It's a classic."

"You are such a saucer-head. Do you want to meet her?"

"Oh, hell, yeah. Why is she in LA?"

"She lives here. I hope she's worth her rates."

"She's charging you to talk to you?"

"One fifty an hour."

Pike chuckled. "I guess Olivia needs to get paid. Why are you interviewing her?"

"It's one of the only leads I have on my target. He met with Olivia last weekend."

"Do you want me to read to you?" He reached for the copy of *The Odyssey* on the coffee table.

"It's Saturday night, and we're sitting at home," Slater said. "Is that boring?"

"We ate out, and I got a bear claw, and we just had a three-way with a stranger. Primo sex that almost set my hair on fire. That's the opposite of boring. Plus I'm with you."

"Just checking."

He flipped the book open. "I want to know where Odysseus goes next, now that Calypso helped him build a new boat. He's free at last."

"He might not be going anywhere," Slater said. "She could totally fuck him over and reimprison him. Maybe the whole thing was a fake-out. Or she booby-trapped the boat. That sounds like human nature."

"She's not human, she's a nymph." He shifted to rest his head on Slater's belly, then started to read: "Finally free of the island, Odysseus sailed into the Mediterranean, his spirits lifted by the sight of the endless open horizon, the infinite waves on the sea …"

Slater closed his eyes, his palm on Pike's chest, feeling his breath and his heartbeat, and got lost in the rich sound of his voice. This feeling, the proximity to Pike and the warm glow of the bourbon suffusing from his belly, the gradual descent toward oblivion, made all the rest of it worthwhile.

EIGHT

I N THE MORNING, WHEN he woke, Slater realized he
was in his bed. Pike was here, still out cold. He lay
for a while and watched him sleep. It felt weird to
remember him pounding that guy from the doughnut
joint. It was irrational to be pissed about it, he knew that.
Pike was here, with him, and wanted to be here with
him. Not with that guy.

How had his life gotten this fucking good, that he got
to wake up next to this man, so beautiful in slack-jawed
sleep that he couldn't look away? The very sight of him
made his heart ache.

Eventually Pike stirred, and smiled at him, chipper
and bright even when he was half unconscious. When
they got up, Pike put on a white dress shirt.

"You look like you're headed to work," Slater said,
pulling on his jeans.

"Interviewees tend to be more forthcoming if you
dress up a little. It's something about the formality, or
maybe about subtly projecting authority. I'm not sure if
that's scientific or just what the old-timers say."

"Whatever works." Stepping over to the closet, Slater
found a dark-green collared shirt with long sleeves. It
wasn't exactly formal, especially paired with jeans, but
it was a concession to formality, at least, a nod in that
direction.

Once they'd had coffee and some breakfast carbs,
they trooped down to the garage and climbed in the

Thunderbird. Slater put Olivia's address into his navigation app, and it sent them north on the 101.

As Slater focused on the road, and caught up with the speed of the freeway traffic, Pike was gazing at his phone.

"This is from an interview Olivia did with the newspaper a couple of years ago. She says, 'Since my first contacts in the 1960s, my experiences have continued to expand, and I've continued to gain new insights. The visitors I communicate with come from settlements in the Kuiper Belt, but I have space friends all over the Oort cloud.'"

Slater glanced at his side mirror as he changed lanes. "The fuck is the Oort cloud?"

"Let's find out," Pike said, and tapped at his screen. "Apparently the Kuiper belt is a rocky disk around the sun beyond the orbit of Neptune. It contains all the left-over detritus from the formation of the solar system. The Oort cloud is farther out. It's a sphere surrounding the solar system in interstellar space. It's mostly icy rubble."

"So the space brothers aren't just from Venus."

"It's interesting—sixty years ago, human-like aliens living on Venus was totally plausible. Since then we've sent landers there, and taken photos, so now it looks improbable. Olivia moved the aliens farther out. But not too far—they're not coming from Zeta Reticuli."

"It sounds like you don't believe her."

"Ufology is fun," Pike said, "the same as *The Iliad* and *The Odyssey* are fun. It doesn't mean I think centaurs are real."

"So none of it's true?"

"It's hard to say. I believe the Trojan War really happened, and that was in *The Iliad*. I believe people see unexplained lights in the sky. But so much of the UFO field seems like a grift."

"Like Olivia charging me one fifty an hour," Slater said.

"Exactly." He chuckled. "The older stuff is more entertaining. If you dig too deep in the newer stuff, especially in the nineties, it gets very dark very fast."

"You think everything is a grift," Slater said, "and you're perfectly happy and upbeat about it. I think everything is a grift, and it pisses me off." He slapped the steering wheel. "It makes me want to punch people in the face."

"That's just how I'm wired."

"Can you imagine how frustrating that is?" Slater demanded. "I used to think sunny optimistic people were just delusional. But you're not. You actually have a reasonable grip on how the world works."

"So maybe our narrative complex is expanding your understanding of the world."

"And there it is. The positive spin."

Pike laughed at that, and Slater braked in the long queue to exit the freeway onto Sunset.

"What's with the traffic?" Pike said. "It's Sunday morning."

"It's just ramp congestion. It won't delay us much."

"Man, this town. It's hard to put a positive spin on ramp congestion."

"Max says *you* are the traffic."

Pike looked over at him. "That's actually insightful. It sounds like a Buddhist thing."

"His girlfriend is kind of Buddhist. Maybe he picked it up by osmosis."

Eventually they were on smaller streets, and winding up the hillside.

"Fancy neighborhood," Pike said. "Where are we?"

"I'd call it upper Los Feliz. Griffith Park is just a little farther up the hill."

Pulling up in front of Olivia's address, they found a house with a Tudor facade and a sharp roof, with a lengthy stretch of *benjamina* ficus hedge between it and the next one.

"I'd say the saucer world must be pretty lucrative," Pike said, looking it over.

"Listen," Slater said, and killed the engine. "You can't go all cop on this woman. It's a simple interview. You can ask questions, but I'll take the lead."

Pike popped open his door. "So you want me to leave my handcuffs in the car?"

They walked up the driveway, and Slater pressed the doorbell. Pike stood to the side, next to the wall, well away from the front door. That was such a cop stance.

"Do you even know you're doing that?" Slater said, waving a hand at him. "Nobody's going to bust out shooting at you through the door."

"Force of habit."

Olivia pulled the door open, greeting them with a smile even though she'd never met them before. She was wearing a summery caftan, in a blue and green print, with a chunky glass necklace.

"Mr. Ibáñez," she said.

"It's just Slater. This is Pike."

"Come in," she said, and led them into the front room.

Big windows looked out on the street, and there was a lot of mahogany paneling on the walls, with an ornately carved fireplace at one end of the room. The lounge furniture looked bulky and overstuffed. A man was standing near the sofa, clad in a black polo shirt and jeans, his hands behind his back.

"Gentlemen," he said as they entered. "Coffee?"

"Sure, if you're making it," Pike said.

"That's Arnold," Olivia said, gesturing to him as he walked out. "My masseur."

She carefully lowered herself into the armchair at the end of the coffee table, and Pike sat nearby, on the adjacent sofa. Slater took the lounge chair across from him and pulled out his phone.

"That fireplace is a beauty," Pike said. "I'm from New Mexico, where we build them kiva-style. Simple clay bricks in the corner of the room, plastered into a beehive shape."

"I'm sure this one dates to when the house was built," Olivia said. "Early 1930s."

"The craftsmanship is delightful."

Slater waggled his phone and set it on the coffee table. "I'm going to tape this interview, since I'm paying for it."

"Of course, dear."

"It's such an honor to meet you," Pike said, leaning toward her. "I read your book many years ago."

Olivia preened a little. "Thank you. I've written others, but the first one was the biggest hit."

"I can't believe you're Black."

Slater frowned at him. "Why would you say that?"

Olivia laughed. "He's got a point. Back in those days I didn't advertise. I didn't want those biases to interfere with relating my experiences. Transmitting information from our space friends. Their truths transcend our earthly human pettiness."

"Ufology still has a whiteness problem," Pike said.

"I think it's gradually getting better. Have you heard of Neaploia? It's a saucer research group I'm involved with." She raised her eyebrows. "Ufology also has an old-people problem, but Neaploia has lots of young members too. And it's racially integrated. Having an eclectic mix of people like that means they're dynamic thinkers. They've brought some compelling new ideas to the field."

"I'll look into them," Pike said.

Slater huffed and waved a hand. "Last week you did a seminar in a ballroom at the Baltimore Hotel. I wanted to ask you about a man who attended that event."

"I'm so glad you still meet with people," Pike said. "You're not just resting on your laurels. How was that seminar?"

Slater glared at him, but then it clicked—the flattery, the mindless chitchat. Pike wasn't intentionally trying to be annoying and off-topic. He was priming her to be open with them. Building that kind of rapport, he could question her and she'd be happy to talk.

Striding in from the back of the house, Arnold set a tray on the coffee table. It bore three mugs of steaming java. "That's oat milk," he said, "and that's milk-milk."

"Thank you, Arnold," Olivia said, and he walked out.

Pike sat up to take a mug, and Olivia took one too.

"It was a nice cozy event," she said as she sat back. "Quite a few people attended remotely, but there were only eleven of us in person. It was almost like a round table."

Pike raised his eyebrows as he sipped at the mug. "So you must remember Finley López."

It was instinctive for him, Slater realized, the methodical questions. Like standing to the side of the front door instead of in front of it. Olivia wouldn't even notice she was being interrogated.

"He's such an earnest young man," Olivia said. "He hung on my every word."

"He has a collection of your books," Slater said.

"Is he a friend of yours?"

"He's actually gone missing."

Her brow furrowed. "That sounds ominous. Are the police looking for him?"

"Right now I'm looking for him," Slater said. "What

was your sense of him? Is he a lowlife? Was he running a game?"

"A game?"

"He means did Finley seem unethical to you," Pike said. "Pardon the lingo. Slater keeps rough company because of his job."

"I wouldn't say I got that kind of impression. He seemed quite ordinary."

"In his apartment there's a book missing from his bookshelf." Slater held up his thumb and forefinger, a few inches apart. "About this wide. Does that ring any bells?"

"At the seminar Finley actually talked about a specific book in the ufology field. He said it explained everything."

"What kind of everything?"

Olivia shrugged. "I can't remember what the topic was at the time. But I remember he said, 'It's all in the book.'"

"Do you know what book he was talking about?" Slater said.

"It's called *Saucers over the Southwest,* and it's about that thick." She grinned and held her fingers apart, the way he had.

"Do you have mutual friends in the UFO field?" Slater said. "Other people who might know Finley?"

She pursed her lips for a moment. "He did mention Eustace Burke."

"I remember Eustace," Pike said, and set his mug on the tray. "He started writing around the time you did."

"That's the man," she said. "I've met Eustace, but I don't really know him."

"Did Finley say anything else at the event that stands out in your mind?" Pike said. "Even if it doesn't seem significant."

She shrugged. "Not that I can think of. But Finley has a lot of predecessors."

"Meaning what?" Slater said.

"You know that a lot of contactees have disappeared over the years, don't you?"

"They flew to Venus and stayed there?"

She held his gaze. "They learned things they shouldn't have. They spoke out about topics that those in power wanted kept quiet. Maybe Finley knew too much about flying saucers."

"You think he got abducted because he's a saucer-head?"

She looked away. "It's happened before."

"I think we can wrap this up." Slater sat up and tapped his phone, then dug his wad of cash out of his jeans and peeled off a C-note and a fifty, and set them on the table.

Not glancing at the cash, Olivia rose with them. "You haven't been here the full hour."

"I'm not worried."

"That was good java," Pike said. "Thanks for that."

"It was nice to meet you both," she said, and followed them to the front door. "Keep your eyes on the skies."

They walked down the driveway to the street. It felt warmer out now, the sun hot on his dark shirt.

"You totally went all cop on her," Slater said, climbing into the Thunderbird.

"I thought I was being pretty restrained. I was worried you were going to give her the old paintbrush at one point."

"In Cali it's called a kovac," Slater said, and started the engine.

"You have to admit, I did elicit some actionable information."

"That, you did." He nosed the car into the street. "I'm trying not to be pissed that it's so effortless for you. You're like the perp whisperer."

Pike laughed. "Olivia is a witness, not a perp. I hope you're OK with that crack about you hanging out with rough people. It was a technique to build familiarity."

"I knew what you were doing. Besides, it's the truth. My wheelhouse is the cesspool."

"What's with Arnold the masseur?"

"That was odd, wasn't it?" Slater said. "He could be her grandson. I wondered if he specializes in intravaginal massage. Why else would he be making coffee for her clients?"

"Maybe he's a boy toy," Pike said, "or maybe when you invite strangers into your house it's a good idea to have someone else around."

"What do you think of her theory? That Finley knew too much?"

"That's the traditional men-in-black story. They show up to dissuade people from being too nosy or talking too much about flying saucers."

"Do they disappear people?"

"I'm not sure it's a real thing," Pike said. "There's no agreement on whether they're from some federal agency, or they're aliens, or they're supernatural entities. Abducting people isn't very cost-effective. Logically a much easier way to shut people up is just to discredit them and call them crazy."

Slater braked for a stoplight and eyed him sidelong. "Some federal agency. You tried to sign up for it, didn't you."

He chuckled. "If it's real, it's the Navy."

"I've heard that. Anything hinky that's going on with the federal government is usually the Navy." When he got the green arrow, Slater hit the gas and turned left onto the freeway ramp. "I'm going to get a copy of that book. Did you recognize the title?"

"*Saucers over the Southwest.* I don't actually know it. But it sounds like a barn burner."

"Do you want to hit some bookstores, or should I drop you at the house?"

"I have an idea."

"I remember—hardware store, fix Grace's shower curtain. I could just pay somebody to do it."

"A bigger idea than that," Pike said. "Don't freak out."

"Why would you say that?" Eyeing his side mirror to merge left, Slater raised his voice. "When you say that, it makes me think I need to freak out."

"I thought we could get rings." Pike held up a hand and waggled his ring finger. "It doesn't have to be about licenses and contracts and paperwork. Just a symbol."

Slater took a breath, and reached for his hand, and squeezed it. "That's intense."

"Too much?"

"No. But why do you want rings?"

"To ward off guys. A ring on that finger means I'm exclusive with somebody else."

"Or it does the opposite. Attracts guys because they know you can't get too sticky. It makes you an easy mark. A guaranteed no-strings arrangement."

"I never even thought of that. Of course you did." He chuckled. "So how about it? Will gold bands be the next twist in our narrative complex?"

"It's a bit weird," Slater said, "but it's about you, and about us. Of course I want to."

"Let's go to a jewelry store."

"We'll go to the Jewelry District. It's not far from my office."

"Of course there's a whole neighborhood for that," Pike said. "There's always an angle in this town."

Once they were downtown, Slater nosed into the garage under Pershing Square and parked the Thunderbird. He reached over to take Svetlana's glasses out of the glove box, and clicked the power switch with a fingernail, and pulled them on.

"You're worried about facial recognition?" Pike said.

"There's security cameras everywhere. Especially in jewelry stores."

He popped the door handle and climbed out. "That kind of thinking makes the ufologists sound rational."

Once they'd climbed the stairs into the daylight, they crossed the street and walked into the Jewelry District.

"How about this place?" Pike said, pointing to a shop window that glistened with a display of brightly lit earrings and necklaces and brooches.

"Keep walking," Slater said. "I know a guy who works in there. I don't need to see him."

"How about here?" Pike said at the next storefront. "It's even bigger. Any exes in this one?"

Slater waved him in, and Pike greeted the security guard, a burly guy dressed in black, standing near the entrance.

The long counters around the showroom were lit from above by brilliant blue-white spots, making the diamonds sparkle, the metal gleam. Pike found a case with gold pieces in it, and a woman soon stepped over. She wore dark eye makeup, and a summery polka-dot blouse, and had her hair tied back. She introduced herself as Yaz, then gestured to Slater's stealthy glasses.

"Those are such colorful frames."

"I know."

"What are we looking for today?"

"Two gold rings," Pike said. "The simpler, the better."

Yaz pulled a tray from beneath the counter and handed a couple over. "How about these?"

"This one's too thick," Pike said, setting it on the glass countertop. "But I like this one. Slater?"

"Looks reasonable to me," he said, leaning in.

Yaz found another in the tray to match it, and handed it to Slater. "Try it on."

He pressed it onto his ring finger and rotated it. "It might be a little loose."

"Show me," she said, and waggled her fingers.

When Slater presented his hand, she grasped it and pulled on the ring.

"It's actually about right," she said. "It's not going to fall off, and you don't want it much tighter than that."

"Is there a way to fix it so that he can't take it off?" Pike said.

Yaz chuckled. "That's what weddings are for. Are you two going to jump the broom?"

"No," Slater said flatly.

Pike held up his ring. "Mine won't quite fit. Do you have a bigger size?"

She took Pike's hand and pressed it onto his finger. "It's close. I have a machine to expand it."

Taking both gold bands from them, she set the tray back in the display case, and slid it closed, and locked it.

"Follow me," she said, and they walked after her into a stairwell, descending below street level.

Even though it was farther from the daylight, it was hot down here. The corridors were narrow and ancient and grungy. Yaz stepped into a small office, where a guy was working on a piece of jewelry held in a vise, studying it with loupe glasses, like the ones Svetlana used. His gray hair was unkempt, and he had a pot belly under a thin cotton shirt, unbuttoned to the middle of his chest.

As they stepped in he set down the tool he'd been using, and turned to them, and pulled off his glasses. Yaz spoke to him in another language, and they chatted for a moment.

"Armenian?" Slater said, under his breath, leaning close to Pike.

"I was thinking Farsi. It might even be Greek."

The guy took the ring from Yaz, then gestured to Pike. "Show me your hand."

He pressed the ring onto Pike's finger, then turned to a machine that stood next to his workbench, setting the gold band on a cone-shaped column. When he pulled down on a handle, the top part of the mechanism descended onto the cone. He heaved on it a few times, pushing down on it hard.

Once he'd lifted the handle again, he pulled the ring off the machine with a grubby piece of cloth.

"You have to wait a minute," he said, setting it on the workbench. "Stretching it makes it hot."

Eventually he scooped it up, and flipped it over in his palm, and handed it to Pike.

"I think it fits now," Pike said. "Yaz, what do you think?"

Her brow furrowed, and she took his hand, and prodded the ring.

"It's fine now. Can you pay the man for the adjustment?"

The guy waved a hand. "Just give me twenty."

Slater pulled out his wad of cash and handed the guy a bill. When they got back upstairs, Yaz rang up the sale, and they pooled their cash to pay for the rings.

Once they were out on the sidewalk, they stood to compare their hands in the daylight.

"How swanky are these?" Pike said.

"This is definitely new."

"You're having feelings."

"It's another thread in our narrative complex, right?" Slater said, staring at the gold on his finger as it gleamed in the sunlight.

Pike put an arm around his shoulder and squeezed. "Breathe into it."

"I like that they're simple. We don't need to look like King Tut's tomb or gangster rappers."

"You'd need a lot more bling to get there."

He handed Pike his car keys. "You take the Thunderbird and do your hardware thing. I'm going to bookstores."

"You want me to pick you up later?"

"I'll take the bus." He leaned in and kissed him.

Before he walked away, Pike held up the back of his left hand, fingers spread wide. "I love you, forty-niner. Tangible evidence."

Slater turned and walked toward Seventh Street, feeling a lump in his throat. What the hell was that about? He touched the ring with his thumb and wiggled it. This was going to take some getting used to.

NINE

T HE BOOKSTORE WAS IN a big street-level space, an indie place that mostly sold used books. The shelves stretched past the mezzanine level to the ceiling, with a wheeled stepladder for access to the higher ones. A lot of people lived in this neighborhood, as it gradually shifted from office space to residential, and the café tables along the windows to the street were crowded on Sunday afternoon.

Slater approached the counter and waited for the clerk to step over. The neckline of her thin summery top was wide enough to show her clavicles, and she had her hair up in an untidy bundle, and thick-framed eyeglasses.

"Those are certainly unique glasses," she said, stepping up to the counter.

"Being avant-garde is a grind," Slater said, and waved a hand. "I see you're working a look with the black frames. The harried librarian, or the daytime intellectual?"

She frowned. "I actually need these to see. What can I help you with?"

"I'm looking for a book called *Saucers over the Southwest.*"

Gazing at her computer screen, she tapped at the keyboard. "You're in luck. We have a copy."

She pointed him to the shelf, up the stairs on the mezzanine. When he found the right section, the shelves were crowded with books on the UFO field, like an expanded version of Finley's collection. He spotted *Saucers over the Southwest*. It was a thick hardback with an orangey-red dust jacket with big white lettering on it.

When he took it back to the clerk, she flipped it open to check the price.

"I'll have to charge you thirty," she said, meeting his gaze. "If it didn't have the dust jacket, I'd knock it down to twenty."

"Give me half a minute," he said. "I'll go find one without the dust jacket. I'll need that copy back, though."

She chuckled at that and rang up the sale.

Once he'd paid her, Slater went out into the sunshine, a paper bag with the heavy book in it dangling from his hand, then walked over to the bus stop on Hill Street. Everything around it had changed, but it was in the same place it had always been. He'd stood here waiting for buses before he could drive. Doris would bring him downtown on Saturday mornings to grocery-shop at the central market. She had a car, but they rode the bus anyway, schlepping the shopping bags back to the house. Maybe she hadn't wanted to shell out for parking, or maybe she'd wanted him to get familiar with using transit.

The Sunset Boulevard bus pulled in, and he filed on board with everybody else, and sat at a window near the back, the bag in his lap, gazing out at the city rolling by. When he walked up into his neighborhood from Sunset, he found the garage door up, and the Thunderbird parked inside, looking unscathed. Pike was over at the wall rack of tools and gardening gear.

"Need a hand?" Slater said as he walked inside.

"I just need the drill."

"How's Grace?"

"Thriving, I'd say." Pike embraced him and kissed his

neck. "She has a girlfriend over. They're sitting out in the yard drinking coffee and eating rugelach."

"Nice."

"She offered me some for you, but they're not vegan."

"I don't need pastries."

"I like your ring," Pike said, grasping his hand and lifting it.

"It's weird—it got really heavy on the bus. I could barely hold up my arm. It felt like a ball and chain. Like old photos of Folsom Prison."

Pike chuckled. "I'm not trying to weigh you down. It's just to remind you what we've got."

He grasped Pike's hand and kissed his palm. "I like *your* ring. I do get it. It's kind of hot to wear these. Like handcuffs, or a bondage harness."

"Except with a broader meaning," Pike said. "It goes beyond sex."

PIKE WENT BACK TO Grace's to work on her shower curtain, and Slater went upstairs, and grabbed a Corona from the Frigidaire, and took it and *Saucers over the Southwest* out to the deck, where he got comfortable in a sun lounger.

Even though only one author was named on the cover, Slater soon found the book to be a complicated collection of parts, and not clearly structured. Every story had dense layers of detail, as if more facts made the guy's assertions more credible. What was really going on, according to him, boiled down to three facts: aliens were regularly visiting the earth, they were routinely abducting people, and the government was covering it all up.

Interspersed in the text were sketches, annotated in handwriting, of flying saucers and alien bodies, hand-drawn maps of crash sites around the Southwest, and grainy black-and-white landscape photos.

Flipping to the front of the book, he checked the publication date—1984. Back then the photocopier would have been peak technology, before personal computers were able to do the page design. The author had done all this by hand.

It felt intense, with full-page reproductions of government documents stamped SECRET, many with blacked-out redactions, and photocopied letters and affidavits, newspaper clippings, even death certificates. Several of the stories were about people who had disappeared or died in unusual circumstances, with their last known location or the site of their demise precisely described by latitude and longitude or a street address.

Sometime later Pike brought out a couple of quesadillas, and they ate at the patio table.

"So Grace has a sturdy new shower rod and curtain," Pike said.

"Thanks for doing that."

"How would you feel about me working on that door to the roof?"

Slater swallowed his mouthful before he spoke. "Doors are complicated. Do you know how to hang a door?"

"I've seen it done. I'll watch some videos."

"That doesn't inspire confidence."

"Maybe you can think of it as another part of our narrative complex. Me taking some responsibility for this house." Pike gestured with his half-eaten wedge of quesadilla. "If I screw it up, we'll call a door hanger."

Once Pike had gone, he settled into the lounger again, and got back into the book. Lots of the early ufologists had been Angelenos, it seemed, but he couldn't see an obvious connection to Finley. Why had he said this book contained all the answers?

Slater repositioned the cushion behind his head, and

got into a story about a guy named Dewitt. He'd been writing a book that was going to reveal the Navy's involvement in retrieving a crashed saucer in the desert of northern New Mexico. Somehow Dewitt had obtained internal Navy documents that spelled out details of the retrieval. His book was scheduled to be published in 1963.

Thinking about it, that was decades before Finley had been born. It was hard to believe this was in any way meaningful now. But he kept reading.

Dewitt had been friendly with his landlady, Kathryn. One night, a few months before the manuscript was due to go to the publisher, Kathryn heard a scuffle upstairs in his apartment, along with cries for help. After she called the police, she ventured up to Dewitt's rooms, and found that he'd hung himself. The next day, three guys in dark suits showed up, claiming to be relatives, and said they wanted to pack up Dewitt's things. Kathryn let them in, and when she checked the apartment later, she found that they hadn't taken anything except Dewitt's notebooks and, presumably, the manuscript.

This was one of Pike's men-in-black stories. Like Olivia had said, Dewitt knew too much about flying saucers. Flipping to the next page, he found a photo of Dewitt. It was a candid shot. He looked like an ordinary guy, in his shirtsleeves, his expression serene, his hair in an unctuous mid-century style. The author had also included a photo of the front of the house where he and Kathryn lived, a two-story Craftsman with a porch and clapboard siding.

On his phone, Slater looked up the address. The street view showed that the house was still there. The landscaping was gone, replaced by bare lawn, but the porch pillars and the roofline looked the same as in the book's grainy photo.

The next section was about an event that had gone down in 1974. That was still ancient history in terms of anything that might have impacted Finley. The story was similar in tone, about a UFO researcher named Foster. His neighbor in Burbank, a man named Collier, who owned the duplex they lived in, heard a commotion and found Foster in his unit, unconscious on the floor, bleeding from the head. The room was torn up like there had been a brawl. Foster died a few days later in the hospital, but strangely, his death certificate, reproduced on a full page in the book, listed his cause of death as cancer.

After Foster's funeral, a guy in a dark suit showed up at his place. Collier noticed him on the doorstep and confronted him. The guy said he was collecting personal items and valuables, and showed him that he had a key to Foster's front door. When Collier went in later, the place had been ransacked. He didn't know if anything had been taken, but Foster's wallet was sitting out on the table, with his ID and cash intact.

It got weirder—Foster's phone number had been published in a UFO newsletter. Years after he died, when *Saucers over the Southwest* was being written, the number was still registered to the dead man, listed in the phone book under his name. When the author called it at various times over the course of a couple of years, the response was either silence, or a series of clicks on the line, or a recording of a woman's voice reciting a string of numbers.

The author's theory was that the Navy had kept the line connected as a trap for Foster's associates—they could trace who was calling, then stalk that person at their leisure. Slater frowned, thinking it through. It seemed like an awful lot of effort. But Pike said the Navy was at the root of lots of government chicanery in the UFO field.

A reproduction of the page in the newsletter where Foster had publicized his phone number appeared in the book. It was an advertisement, boxed in by a thick black border:

ATTENTION MILITARY AND G-MEN
Do you work for Uncle Sam?
Do you have inside knowledge about the
saucer phenomenon?
Call us to make a report.
Confidentiality guaranteed.
LOS ANGELES, CALIF. KLAMATH 5-2947

"Klamath" was the name of the telephone exchange, Slater knew, and the *K* and the *L* were capitalized, so those were part of the number. Pulling out his phone, he searched for when telephone exchange names had switched to just the numbers. The process started in 1958 and was completed by 1963. That meant this ad had to date to then, more than a decade before Foster's suspicious death. Staring at the page, he thought about it. No way was the phone number still active.

He and Max used number spoofing when they needed to disguise their identity on outgoing calls. It came up often enough that they'd subscribed to a service. Slater spent a minute configuring it on his phone. When he made a call through the spoofing app, if anyone at the other end paid attention to the caller ID, they would see a fake number, not his real one.

He dialed Foster's ancient phone number and listened. The call connected, and he heard open air, then several heavy clicks, and then it dropped. Pulling the phone away from his ear, Slater stared at the screen. It seemed strange that he'd just had the same response as the author got decades ago when *Saucers over the Southwest* was being written. But that had to be all it was—an oddity. It couldn't mean anything. No way had the Navy set a trap for saucer-heads that lasted fifty years.

He took a breath and flipped to the next section of the book. A name immediately jumped off the page: Eustace Burke. Olivia said Finley knew that guy. Slater read through the story.

At the dawn of ufology, meaning in the 1950s, the author explained that there were regular meetups and lectures for people interested in the strange new phenomenon of flying saucers. Olivia Howard was still doing that today, running seminars for saucer-heads, but it sounded like these had been on a much bigger scale, packing hundreds of mid-century bodies into big auditoriums. The author said that from the very beginning, dark forces were messing with saucer researchers and the organizers of the events, most likely in an attempt to tamp down public interest.

In that era someone had written a book about the systematic harassment of the saucer-heads. It profiled several researchers who had been scared out of the field by shadowy figures uttering threats. Sometimes there was clear evidence that the interference was governmental, as the harassers were identifiable as military, and like Pike said, it was always the Navy. It was easy to scare people back then too—all they had to do was throw out accusations that a person was a commie or a queer. Anyone tarred with that brush could be blacklisted and shut out of academia, and government work, and corporate careers. But sometimes the harassers spoke eerily stilted English and looked and acted strangely, like they weren't quite human. The assumption then, of course, was that they were aliens.

In 1959 a lecture had been planned by Eustace Burke, described as a researcher, at the Baltimore Hotel. It was curious that all these years later Olivia was lecturing at the same damn place, and Finley knew them both. But was that meaningful?

A day before the lecture, the author explained, phone calls were made to strategic people—local UFO group leaders and journalists—telling them that the event had been canceled. Hours later, amid the growing confusion, more disinformation came, explaining that the cancellation was an error, and the event was on again, but the start time was an hour later, and at a different venue, the philharmonic auditorium.

That was a tactic politicians and bureaucrats still used to stifle participation, Slater knew. And he'd never heard of the philharmonic auditorium. It had to be long gone—like so much LA architecture it was just a memory now, ephemeral, temporary, replaced by the next thing. From the description in the book, it hadn't been far from the Baltimore.

So much confusion had been generated that very few people turned up for the lecture at the correct venue. Standing at the back of the ballroom were several stern-looking tight-lipped guys in suits, presumed to be G-men, asking for names and taking notes on everything that was said. Eustace was so freaked out that he didn't say much, visibly nervous and sweating "like a man condemned," one attendee said. He refused to display the photographic evidence he had of saucers over the Mojave Desert, and he left the venue early, slipping out the back way.

Turning the page, Slater found a photo of Eustace from that day, his dark hair nattily coiffed, wearing a light seersucker suit, standing at an old-fashioned mike, a grim expression on his face. He couldn't have been much older than his mid-twenties. Other men stood behind him, some talking to each other, some looking out toward the camera. The whole scene looked chaotic.

Grabbing his phone, he looked up Eustace Burke online. In the biographical data he found, there was no mention of the drama at the Baltimore, but a few years after that, in the 1960s, Eustace had written a book, *Visitors from Planet* W. If he was a grown man in 1959, the guy had to be elderly now, in the same cohort as Olivia. But it was likely he was still alive—Finley had met with him recently.

Slater folded the book closed and sat up to stretch, rotating his back. All this nebulous innuendo. It felt like it was taking him nowhere. He sent a text to Etta:

Can you meet tomorrow? I have a job for you.

With his eyes closed, Slater sat back in the lounger, enjoying the warm sun on his face, and drifted toward sleep. His phone buzzed, and glancing at the screen, he found Etta's reply: "I'm in," with three exclamation marks, plus a heart emoji, then several fireworks emojis.

She must be bored—Etta was apprenticing in the investigation trade with him and Max, but only part-time, a side gig to her main work teaching middle school. On hiatus for the summer, she'd been hanging around the office more, mostly working with Max on his window-shade jobs. Etta wasn't significantly less annoying than most people, but she had a distinct knack for the work, and more important, she had the requisite sangfroid.

TEN

A FTER THEY'D EATEN DINNER, again on the deck, gray twilight started to descend, and it finally started to cool off.

Pike pushed his plate away. "You spent the whole day with *Saucers over the Southwest.*"

"It has a lot of detail. It feels like the author had ADHD but managed to slow down long enough to record his chaotic swirl of thoughts. He gives phone numbers and addresses for ufologists and places where weird things happened. One of them is about four blocks from here. Just up the next hill."

"Seriously? What happened around here that's worthy of a book about flying saucers?"

"A guy named Ray rented an apartment over somebody's garage," Slater said. "He published a UFO newsletter."

"What was it called?"

"*The Saucer Times.* It only ran for a couple of years. Ray's neighbors said they saw unusual visitors sometimes. Guys in dark suits. Then one night Ray just disappeared. No one ever tracked him down."

"That's exactly the kind of story Olivia was talking about. People who knew too much about flying saucers."

"The book is full of those."

"When did this happen to Ray?" Pike said.

"In 1957."

"That's definitely the space brothers era. Is the garage still there?"

"Probably. That neighborhood doesn't have much gentrification churn. Lots of the properties are protected as historically significant."

"Should we take an evening walk?" Pike said. "Just to look the place over."

"I was hoping you'd want to."

After they'd cleaned up, and stowed the dishes in the dishwasher, they went down to the street. The streetlamps had come on as the last of twilight faded. Slater pointed toward their destination, and they set off on foot.

"How is this story about Ray connected to your case?" Pike said.

"I'm not sure it is. My target valued that book for some reason. More than all his other books. He took it with him. And he disappeared just like Ray did. Although Finley took his passport and his valuables. That implies that he left by choice, not in a flying saucer's tractor beam."

They came to a corner, and Slater gestured up the hill.

"What else do we know about Ray?" Pike said.

"Ray's friends said he'd been acting strangely. Paranoid. He told a couple of people that someone was watching his place."

"I like the classic streetlamps here. Our neighborhood has those simple modern ones."

They were antiques, Slater saw, metal stands embossed with ornate designs and elegant fluted glass lampshades on top, glowing warm yellow, unlike the harsh white LEDs on most streets.

"It must be part of the whole historic-district vibe," Slater said. "There's lots of nineteenth-century houses."

They crested a hill, and turned a corner, and soon

Slater pointed to a set of numbers painted on the curb.

"That's the address."

They stood in the street, looking it over. The house was Victorian, with a peaked roof, and gables, and lots of windows. It was hard to tell in the dark but it looked like it had a laurel-green paint job.

"That house was definitely here in 1957," Pike said, his voice low. No one was around to eavesdrop on them, but the street was quiet.

"That'll be Ray's pad." Slater gestured with his chin to the garage across the driveway from the house. Warm light shone in the windows of the upper floor.

"I wonder if Ray had a printing press up there."

"In the book there's a reproduction of the front page of Ray's newsletter," Slater said. "It was totally hand-made. He did it on a typewriter, then had it copied to mail out. I bet he typed it up there."

A shadow appeared in one of the windows, the silhou-ette of a head and shoulders—someone was looking out.

"I think we just got made," Slater said.

"We're not doing anything wrong."

The shadow retreated, and a moment later came the sound of a door opening, then a guy stepped into the driveway. When he walked under the streetlamp, Slater could see he had several days' stubble on his face, and longish shaggy hair. Despite the heat he was wearing a gray hoodie with the hood folded back.

"Can I help you?" he demanded.

"I doubt it," Slater said.

"Why are you looking at my apartment?"

"No reason."

The guy stood staring at them for a moment. "You're not going to intimidate me. I know exactly who you are."

Slater scoffed. "I very much doubt that, toots."

"Saucer-heads come around sometimes, but not at

night." He waved an arm. "Out here skulking around in office clothes on Sunday. You're from the Navy. Don't bother denying it."

"We're not Navy," Pike said.

Slater gestured toward the garage. "Do you give tours of Ray's apartment?"

His eyebrows shot up. "I knew it," he hissed.

"Do you know a guy named Finley?"

"Finley who?"

"Finley López. About your age. He went missing last week. Kind of like Ray did."

"Fuck," he snapped.

Slater could see his chest heaving, his rapid breaths.

"Are you threatening me?"

"Calm down," Pike said. "What's your connection to Ray?"

He took a few steps closer and jabbed a finger at Pike. "You don't get to question me. I moved in here because of Ray. To get insights. To research his disappearance."

"What have you learned?" Slater said.

"None of your damn business. I know you already know more than I do. It's like he evaporated. His sister found his wallet in the dresser, a sandwich on a plate in the icebox, a half-typed page from his newsletter still in his typewriter."

"All that happened a lifetime ago," Slater said. "Do you really think you can learn any more about it now?"

Turning to look at him, his lip curled in disgust. "You'd love that, wouldn't you. For me to just give up and go away. I'd threaten to call the cops right now, but I know you'd just flash them your ID and they'd leave."

"Why would you call the cops?" Pike said. "We're not trespassing. We're not even loitering."

"And nobody's threatening you," Slater added.

He stepped closer to Slater, stopping an arm's length

away. "Are you going to make me disappear too? Just like …" He hesitated and waved his arm. "Farney Sanchez, whatever his name is?"

"It's Finley López," Slater said. "And don't be crowding up my personal space."

"Or else what?" He moved closer and jutted his chin. "I know you guys aren't allowed to escalate."

All the shrinks Doris had sent him to in his youth, and the hemp-wearing hippies who facilitated the anger management classes that the judicial system had forced him to attend, had emphasized the same thing—hold your tongue, don't lash out, just sit with the anger. He knew where the high road was. But Slater wasn't that guy.

"You're woefully misinformed," he said, and threw a fast right.

Standing so close, the guy didn't see it coming. The punch landed squarely on his jaw. His head snapped sideways, and he stumbled back, and held his hand to his face.

"Fuck," he roared.

Slater balled his fists and took a ready stance. "Why do you make me do this to you? Are you hankering to wind up unconscious?"

The guy eyed him and worked his jaw. "That really hurt. Give me your badge number. Your Navy ID. You have to provide that."

"The man already told you we're not from the Navy, you dipshit."

"I don't believe you."

Slater put his hands on his hips. "Tell you what. I'll give you my supervisor's phone number."

"OK," he said evenly, furrowing his brow.

"Are you going to write it down, or do you have a photographic memory?"

He pulled out his phone and tapped at the screen, its

blue glow illuminating his stubbled face and his messy hair.

"You can call anytime, night or day," Slater said. "It's Klamath five, twenty-nine, forty seven."

The guy looked up, eyes wide. "Motherfucker."

Pike put a hand on Slater's shoulder. "Let's go."

Slater walked with him, and after a few paces glanced back. The guy was watching them leave, his phone dangling at his side. Once they were around the corner, Pike spoke.

"You didn't have to punch him."

"He was vibrating. I thought it might chill him out."

Pike chuckled. "When has fisticuffs ever served to calm someone down?"

"It's interesting that he knows all about Ray and *The Saucer Times*."

"He didn't know your target, though. And what was that phone number?"

"It's in the book too. It belonged to a saucer-head back in the day. The author thinks the Navy kept the line connected to trap his associates and other people who know too much about flying saucers."

"So you've given him something to lose sleep over."

"It wouldn't have mattered what I said." Slater waved a hand. "We were Navy guys sent to harass him. Even a knuckle sandwich wasn't going to change his mind."

They turned the corner at the bottom of the hill, and started up the street toward the house.

"What happened to plain old facts, and the truth, and reality?" Pike said. "It feels like it's all getting malleable. Like those quest games. You can just make up new beliefs as you go along, parked on your sofa, pressing buttons on your game controller."

"That's a great question. Why was my target so interested in that book? Finley, and Olivia, and all the space-brother contactees I read about. The hothead in Ray's apartment tonight." Slater waved his hands in a helpless gesture. "These people all seem like deludenoids."

Pike slipped an arm around his waist. "It's always an adventure with you, forty-niner."

ELEVEN

I N THE MORNING SLATER heard Pike leave early. A while later he got up and pulled on his jeans and a clean shirt. Once he was caffeinated, he grabbed *Saucers over the Southwest,* and tucked it into his canvas satchel, and trotted down to the garage. A coherent plan hadn't yet completely gelled in his mind, but he had some ideas.

Opening his secure cabinet in the back of the garage, he disconnected a vehicle tracker from its charging cable. It was about the size of a cell phone, but thicker, with a hard black plastic housing and magnetic metal ribs studding one side. Locking the cabinet again, he dropped the tracker into the satchel with the book.

The mysterious radio receiver he'd taxed from Finley's pad was still in the Thunderbird, and he opened the trunk long enough to retrieve it and put it into his satchel as well.

Climbing in behind the wheel, he backed into the street, and waited for the garage door to roll down, then drove to Chinatown and parked down the block from Finley's building. Grabbing a pair of the black latex gloves from the box in the backseat, he got out and walked back to Finley's building. The front door was still ajar. From the looks of it, it hadn't latched properly in a long while.

In the courtyard he had to scoff at the sight of the gorse in the planted bed. Propagating that stuff was a crime against nature. As he climbed the stairs, he pulled on the gloves, then fished out the ghost key, still in the bottom of his pocket. Glancing around to make sure he was unobserved, he let himself into Finley's apartment.

Just in case, he called out "Maintenance." But there was no sound, and only dim light filtering through the drawn curtains, the air still dank and stale.

Once he'd set the device on the coffee table where he'd found it, next to the remote, he stepped into the bedroom. The bed was still neatly made. Nothing had changed—no one had been here.

On the stairs down to the courtyard he peeled off the gloves, and tucked them into his hip pocket, then drove to his office. Climbing out, he slung the satchel on his shoulder, and waved to the parking attendant over in the little booth. They all knew the Thunderbird, and nobody bugged him unless it was that time of the month, when he had to pay for a new pass.

Upstairs the lights were off, and as he stepped inside he eyed the plaster statue on the front desk. "How you doing, Rey?"

There was no sign of Max, and in his own office he spent a few minutes photocopying the pages of *Saucers over the Southwest* that talked about Eustace Burke. He was shuffling the printouts together when he heard keys in the door.

Etta stepped in and called out a greeting. Curvy, with her dark hair cut short, today she was wearing a white cotton shirt and jeans, a flower tucked above her ear. Stepping into his office, she dropped into the guest chair across his desk. He'd never seen her wear a flower before, but her people were Pacific Islanders, and she could pull it off.

Slater sat back. "I love the plumeria."

"I forgot about that." Etta gingerly tapped at it. "In

Samoa they call it a *sei*. It's just for fun. I was at a thing this morning."

He furrowed his brow. "Did you know you can see your bra through that shirt? You should probably wear white under white, not black."

She scoffed. "It's a look, Slater, not an accident. You think I leave the house without even checking the mirror?"

"I assumed that's how the lesbian ethos works. No makeup, no panty hose, no mirrors required."

"Nobody's worn panty hose since 1980," Etta said. "Except maybe drag queens. And don't be typecasting me."

Slater waved a hand and sat up.

"Whoa," Etta said, her eyes growing wide. She reached for his left hand. "What in god's name is that?"

He let her pull his hand toward her. "The next phase in our narrative complex. No gods involved."

"Did you go to the courthouse?"

"Hell, no. There's no paperwork. It's just a symbol."

"It's so sweet."

"It's also practical," Slater said. "If I put this on, Pike will cut me some slack. It's like greasing the squeaky wheel."

Releasing his hand, she sat back. "I know that's just bluster. You love that guy."

"I can't deny that. Where Pike's concerned, I'm a full-on roundheel. One look at him and I'm staggering around like a stumblebum."

"He's definitely smoothed out some of your rough edges."

Slater frowned. "Thanks for the psych eval."

"See, even that reaction is softer. If I'd said something like that when we first met, you would have threatened to deck me."

"Curious," he said, and thought about it. "I don't

think I've lost my baseline seething rage. But maybe Pike's pheromones have muddled everything. Like when you take a smoke pot around a beehive. The bees get all confused and docile."

"I think it's simpler than that," Etta said. "It's love."

"I'm still not sure why he's with me. He could do so much better."

"That's cause for gratitude right there. So what have you got for me?"

Slater explained Truax's ask, and what he'd found out about Finley. "I want you to find one of the old space-brother contactees. He knows my target. His name is Eustace Burke. The lauded author of *Visitors from Planet W.*"

"Let me make some notes." Etta stepped out to the front desk, returning a moment later with a pen and a steno pad.

"His name and the name of his book are in here." He slid the copied pages across to her. "It's a chapter from this book. It's not very long."

Etta picked up *Saucers over the Southwest* and scanned the back cover, then flipped through it. "This is intense."

"Tell me about it. Reading it feels like walking in quicksand. My target met with Eustace recently, but by my reckoning he has to be in his eighties at least."

"I'm not sure how close I want to get to the paranormal stuff." She folded the book closed and set it on the desk.

"Because you're superstitious. I get it. Maybe the pope will cut you some slack this one time."

Etta met his gaze. "I saw that ape creature out on that desert playa with my own eyes. You did too. It rattled me, Slater. I didn't get into this game to get abducted by aliens."

"Pike says most people who have contact with aliens have positive experiences," he said, raising his eyebrows.

She laughed. "You're not going to tell me Pike is a saucer-head."

"Big time. He's read lots of the books. His assessment is that it's basically a grift. There's no aliens."

"So what was that *meaola* in the desert?"

Slater spread his hands. "Search me."

Etta rose. "I'll do some digging."

Tucking the book into his satchel, he slung the strap onto his shoulder and followed her into the front office. She was settling in at the desk, and Rey Pascual was now facing her, his scythe at the ready.

He called "bye" as he stepped out, then paused to lock the deadbolt. Once he was behind the wheel of the Thunderbird, he pulled out the book to check the address in Hollywood where Dewitt had lived, where his landlady, Kathryn, had found him dead and got played by the guys in dark suits who came to seize his research and his manuscript. He thumb-typed it into his navigation app and pulled into the street.

Cruising off the freeway into the neighborhood, he stopped at a red light on the boulevard. This part of Hollywood had been slower to gentrify than the west side. He turned onto Dewitt's narrow residential street. It was still mostly century-old duplexes and small apartment buildings. There was nowhere to park in front of the house, but he found an open meter at the end of the block, adjacent to the boulevard.

Once he'd plinked some coins into the meter, he walked back toward Dewitt's address. There was only one new structure on this whole block, a three-story full-lot mansion, kind of like his own house. It was still under construction, he saw as he walked past, with a high chain-link fence that surrounded the site. Despite the barrier, the concrete walls of the structure's ground floor had been heavily graffitied with clear expressions of the neighborhood's sensibilities about the wealthy interlopers: GENTRIFICATION IS GENOCIDE said one tag, and GTFO in big letters, and KEEP BEVERLY OUT OF HOLLYWOOD.

No matter how much he wanted to ignore it or deny it, he was part of it too. When he'd bought that bougie house, he hadn't been thinking about income inequality or displacement. But it was undeniable that just a few years ago someone with a lot less resources than him had been living in an older house on that lot. He pushed the thought out of his mind as he walked up on Dewitt's place.

Even though the clapboard was gone, replaced by sandy stucco in some long-ago renovation, the house looked much like it did in the black-and-white photo in *Saucers over the Southwest*. A low chain-link fence encircled the yard now, with a gap in it where a narrow concrete walk led across the mottled turf to the front door. Standing on the sidewalk, he looked over the property. It was hard to tell whether Dewitt's upstairs unit was still a separate apartment.

A woman with dark hair and a red print dress stepped out the front door, and stood on the porch, and called to him in Spanish.

"*No entiendo*, sister," he called back.

"What are you looking for?"

"I'm just looking at the house."

"Why?" she demanded. "It's not for sale."

"A woman named Kathryn owned it in the 1960s."

"Well, I own it now."

"Can I show you a picture?"

She folded her arms as Slater dug out his phone and walked toward the porch. He found a photo of Finley and held it out so that she could see the screen.

"Have you ever seen him around?"

"He's easy on the eyes," she said. "I'd remember him."

"Did you ever hear about Kathryn, or a guy who lived here named Dewitt?"

"I've been here fifteen years, and I never heard of any of them. Do they owe you money or something?"

"Let me show you another." Slater pulled up a photo of Truax and held it out for her.

"I don't know him either."

"Are you sure about that?" he said, watching her face. "I heard maybe he comes around here."

She frowned. "I can't help you."

As she turned to step inside, she pulled the heavy mesh security door closed behind her. Slater took a last look at the porch, and the floor above it. That had to be Dewitt's window.

As he walked back out to the sidewalk, he spotted a guy across the street, standing in the yard that fronted a bungalow, holding a rake. Clad in denim and a broad straw hat, what stood out was that unlike most gardeners in this town, he was Anglo. Slater wasn't sure until he got out to the sidewalk, but the guy was definitely watching him.

He ignored him, but before he had taken more than a few steps, the guy called, "Excuse me."

When he looked back, he furtively waved him over. Slater turned and approached the low steel-picket fence.

"What's up, boss?" Slater said.

"You were asking about Dewitt," the guy said quietly.

"You could hear that from over here?"

"I knew it," he said intently. "What do you know about Dewitt?"

"Only what I've read. He died long before my time." Slater studied his face. "What do you know about Dewitt?"

"Are you a federal agent?"

"Not even close."

"Good." He looked relieved. "Federal agents can't lie about their identity."

That was bullshit, but Slater didn't need to point that out. "Are you a government agent? With the Navy, maybe?"

"Of course not," he snapped.

"So you're just standing here with a rake, in midsummer, when there's nothing to rake up, watching Kathryn's house? It looks to me like you're on a stakeout."

"I live here." The guy gestured to the house behind him.

"Can I have a kumquat?"

He frowned. "What?"

"Your tree still has some fruit on it." Slater gestured to it. "They should have all fallen by now. Maybe it's because you've got lots of shade. They look edible."

"You can eat those?"

Slater stepped through the open gate, and over to the tree, and grabbed a handful of the little fruits. Munching on one, he savored the intense bitter-sour citrus explosion when it popped between his teeth.

"They're still good."

"If you say so. I can't believe you ate the peel and all."

"Tell me about Kathryn and Dewitt," Slater said, and popped another fruit in his mouth.

"I didn't know about the history of the place across the street when I moved in. But I met some of the other people."

"What other people?"

"People who came to look. Like you. People seeking the truth. UFO questers."

Slater ate another kumquat, then pulled out his phone and found the photo of Finley. "Did you ever see this guy?" He held the screen out toward him.

He stepped over to look. "I can't say that I remember seeing him. I know I never spoke to him. Who is he?"

"A quester. Here's another." He showed him the photo of Truax.

"I've never seen him either."

Slater tucked his phone into his jeans and turned to pull another handful of fruit from the tree.

"Are they missing?" the guy said.

"One of them is." He turned and met his gaze. "I think maybe they got him."

The guy's eyebrows shot up. "You mean ..."

He nodded slowly. "He's been missing since last weekend."

"Don't tell me about that," he said quickly. "They're probably watching us right now." His eyes darted furtively around the street. "Go on, now. Get out of my yard." With that, he picked up the rake and turned to walk toward the house.

"You need to harvest the kumquats when they're ripe," Slater called after him. "Even if you don't eat them, you need to take them off the tree."

The guy ignored him, and Slater munched on the little fruits as he walked back toward his car. When his hands were free he checked the map on his phone. There was a coffeehouse a block from here—he didn't even have to drive.

TWELVE

F ROM THE CAR SLATER grabbed his satchel, and dropped more coins into the meter, then walked down to the coffee place. Once he had a soy latte in hand, he sat with his back to the wall and again read through the story about Foster, the guy with the honey-pot phone number.

Foster had seen a saucer landing in a field, and talking about it had got him into trouble. After he'd scanned the details, Slater sipped his latte and flipped to the recommended reading section. There were so many other books on the subject, even back when this one was published.

His phone buzzed in his pants, and he pulled it out. The caller ID said REDDY KILOWATT, and he tapped it to pick up.

"The flying saucers have landed," Slater said flatly.

"That was a fun one," Pike said. "It was really early, like 1952 or 1953."

"Published in 1953. How do you remember that?"

"Listen—some of us are getting drinks later near the Burbank office. I wanted to invite you."

"Invite me?" Slater said. "That sounds so formal. It makes me think it's a trap. Are you working for the Navy?"

Pike chuckled. "If I wanted to bust you, I'd do it in your bedroom."

"You can snap the cuffs on me anytime, son. You

know that. I'm getting chubby just thinking about it."

"Stop," he said, lowering his voice. "I'm at work."

"There's actually a location I could visit in Burbank. I'll come by after."

"You have to promise you won't assault anyone," Pike said.

"That only happened one time. And that guy was pawing you."

"His name is Anton, and he'll be there tonight. These people are my colleagues. Some of them are strapped. You have to behave."

"Sure thing, pop."

Slater ended the call, and folded his arms, gazing out at the cars cruising by on the boulevard. This saucer stuff was starting to feel like a dead end. Maybe the way forward was through Truax. The guy had lied to him. Everyone lied to him, all the time, but usually he could figure out why. Truax told him he was with Finley, but he hadn't mentioned the wife that he smacked around. Why would he lie about all that? He needed to look into Truax.

On his phone he looked up Magnesia Motors. There was only one office in town, in the Arts District. From the overhead image and the street view, it was a low-rise redbrick building with a surface lot next to it. It wasn't a whole lot of office for a flashy tech startup, but maybe this was just an outpost, as the car factory was out of state.

Walking back to the Thunderbird, he phoned Etta, glad that she picked up.

"Are you still at the office?" he said. "I need to use your car for a tail."

"What's wrong with your car?"

"My target already knows the Thunderbird. Plus mine is too beautiful. It stands out. Yours is bland and boring and unnoticeable."

"Not many people would insult me while simultaneously asking for a favor. It's pretty nervy. Unfortunately it's no dice. I need my car."

"We'll swap. You'll still have wheels."

"I'm not driving your old boat."

"It's the same as your car," Slater said, "only better. I just had it tuned up. It runs like it's brand-new."

"Oh, man." She groaned. "It's not for very long, right?"

"I'll text you when I'm pulling up."

Slater got on the 101 and drove to the Fashion District. When he was a few minutes away, he sent Etta a text:

Meet me in the parking lot.

As he pulled into the stall next to her car, a little red Prius, he saw her walking over from the office building. Grabbing his satchel, he climbed out.

"This feels like a trust exercise," she said as she walked up.

He handed her his car keys. "I know you won't harm the Thunderbird."

"I mean me trusting you."

Slater waved at the Prius. "If I total it, there's several million more just like it. You wouldn't even notice if I swapped it out." He put his hands on his hips, looking over the vehicle. "I hope I can fit in there. It's like a doll car."

"Stop trash-talking my ride."

In a false high voice, he said, "Beep-beep."

Etta laughed. "You're such a dick. And you're usually such a control freak. I can't believe you let anyone drive your car."

"Max has his own key, and Pike drove it and didn't crash it. I'm used to the concept."

"So you've tracked down your target?"

"I'm actually tailing my client," Slater said.

"Ouch. That sounds complicated."

"I'll call you when I'm done with it."

He took her key and climbed in behind the wheel. Etta was already headed back across the street, he saw. At least she didn't stay to watch him adjusting the seat and the mirrors and firing it up. That would be understandable, but it would have been annoying.

He pressed the start button, and nothing happened. When he pressed it again all the panel lights went dark. He'd switched it off. The gas motor didn't run unless it needed to, he realized, and pressed the button yet again, then backed out of the stall. It was weird that it was so quiet. It felt like a golf cart.

Rolling out onto the street, he drove to the Arts District. The Magnesia Motors building was on a corner, and the lot had just one driveway. Unfortunately the gate was opaque, and high, so he couldn't see what was inside.

Slater circled the block and parked near the corner, opposite the building, with a view of the driveway. He'd forgotten to grab his binoculars from the backseat of the Thunderbird, but he was close enough here that he could manage without them.

Truax had already told him what his car looked like — it was the first red Magnesia roadster. That didn't mean it was the only red one, but it narrowed it down a lot. On his phone he searched for photos of the roadster model. The front end looked OK, if a little boring, but his teeth gritted reflexively at its profile, with the bustle back. Max was right — it was stupid to revive such a fuggly design.

Keeping an eye on the driveway, he checked the time. It was still an hour or two until the end of the workday for most desk jockeys. Over the next half hour several cars exited through the gate, and only two of them were Magnesia roadsters. Interesting that lots of the company's employees didn't even drive them.

The gate rolled open again, and Slater sat up when he saw a cherry-red vehicle nose out onto the street. The rims were red to match, and it had that obnoxious back end. Both windows were rolled down, and as it turned into the traffic, he got a glimpse of the driver—it was Truax.

Pressing the engine button, Slater pulled into the street. This thing had no acceleration. Would he be able to keep up? He was several cars behind the roadster when he saw Truax brake for a four-way stop. The roadster started rolling again and then honked at a car that had started into the intersection from the left. Truax had barely slowed down, but for some reason he'd decided that he had the right of way.

Slater managed to keep the bustle back in view as Truax went through the intersection, then turned onto the boulevard. Traffic was heavier here—it would be easier to follow him now. He stayed a few cars back, moving to the adjacent lane for a while to be less visible.

The guy was an aggressive driver, changing lanes without using his signal. Or maybe Magnesia had forgotten to put turn-signal technology in their exciting new product. He followed the roadster east across the river, where Truax turned onto the freeway and then got moving fast. Following him down the ramp, Slater pushed the Prius hard, gradually getting up to freeway speed.

For a minute he thought he'd lost him, as he scanned the traffic ahead, but then he saw the distinctive red back end in the left lane. Slater merged left to follow as Truax took the ramp onto the 710.

As the primary road to the port, it was a slow slog south because of all the freight trucks. The roadster drove on it for miles in the left lane, past the dual rows of transmission towers flanking the concrete river channel on one side, and endless warehouses and industrial sites on the other.

Slater almost missed him exiting the freeway, as Truax weaved right in front of a semitruck, not bothering to signal, and didn't even brake to take the ramp. Slater managed to get over in time, slowing the little car as he rolled into the low-rise industrial neighborhood. He didn't have a map out, but this had to be close to Long Beach.

Following the roadster around a corner, Slater braked when he saw the vehicle had stopped at the curb. Truax was striding up a driveway toward a commercial property. Cruising past, he saw the gate was open. It looked like a truck yard. The building fronting the street had no windows, just the street number on a broad white wall.

Farther up the quiet block Slater pulled a U-turn and cruised back, then turned around again and parked close to the corner, facing the roadster's ugly rear end. Taking a breath, he pulled the vehicle tracker out of his satchel, and clicked on the power switch, and palmed it as he climbed out.

The street wasn't busy, and the few vehicles that went by were moving fast. Striding over to the roadster, he glanced around to make sure no one was nearby, then squatted in the street next to the rear tire.

Reaching into the wheel well with the device in hand, he moved it around, trying to find a place where the unit's rib magnets would adhere. But there was no metal here. Still crouching, he stepped along the side of the vehicle, toward the front tire, and moved the tracker along the underside. The surface felt smooth, and just like the wheel well, there was no exposed metal.

"Damn it," he muttered. Was the whole fricking thing made of plastic?

A pickup rolled by, and he turned his head away to conceal his face. This was taking too long. He couldn't risk Truax coming out and spotting him. Rising, he walked back toward his car. If California really was shifting to electric cars, he was going to have to ask Svetlana to build a glue-on version of her vehicle tracker.

Once he was behind the wheel of the Prius, he switched off the tracker and chucked it into his satchel, then pulled up a map. The business was labeled Cali Rock & Mineral, and it was the only structure that used that driveway. That's definitely where Truax had gone. He couldn't find a lot of detail about the company, but it was described as involved in "mineral prospecting and mining supply."

Looking up, he saw Truax stride out of the place with a bundle under his arm. The color and texture of it looked like burlap. When he was working on yards he used burlap as a wind break or a sun shade. It was strong, and biodegradable, a great alternative to plastic. It also made strong sacks for bulbs, or damp soil, or anything that needed to breathe. What was Truax doing picking up burlap from a mineral company?

Truax climbed into the roadster, and a moment later the brake lights flashed, and he pulled into the street, and took the first left. After a minute, Slater followed him. But he'd waited too long, he saw as he rounded the corner. Truax was moving fast, already at the stoplight at the end of the block, making a right turn onto a busy boulevard. He'd just seen it on the map—that was PCH. If there was no traffic, he was going to lose him. Truax had a red light, but he barely even slowed down to make the right. Pushing the Prius hard, Slater tried to catch up.

Even half a block away Slater heard the tires squeal, and then an air horn sounded. Truax must have caused a fender-bender.

"Idiot," he muttered, and made the turn.

But the traffic was moving. A panel truck, rolling slow in the left lane, hit the horn again as the roadster sped past it on the right. Slater hadn't seen what happened, but Truax had clearly pissed off the driver. In the right lane, Slater rolled past the lumbering truck and pushed the little car to accelerate.

Up ahead he saw flickering blue police lights—a motorcycle cop. The bike sped past several vehicles, then pulled in and slowed down close behind the roadster. The cop was after Truax. Most people would pull over right away, but the roadster kept rolling. Was he going to stop? No way could Slater keep up if Truax got into a police chase. Half a block later the cop pulled out and cruised next to the driver's door, and the roadster finally pulled over, in front of a long blue wall painted with big letters that said AUTO PARTS.

Slater pulled the Prius to the curb. There hadn't been a place to stop before this, and now it felt like he was too close, just a few car-lengths behind them. He instinctively shifted lower in the seat. But nobody was looking at him, inconspicuous in the little car.

From here he had an up-close view of the traffic stop, and he watched as the cop, who'd stopped just a few yards behind Truax's vehicle, set the parking stand and stepped off the bike. He strolled toward the roadster's driver's side. That uniform made his butt look great. In those riding boots, even with the helmet, the guy was totally fuckable.

When the cop was almost at the back end of the roadster, Slater saw the right-side door open a few inches, then quickly close again. Had Truax dropped something in the gutter? That was a ballsy move, and hard to pull off. Had the cop noticed?

He approached Truax's window and leaned down,

and they spoke for a minute, then the cop walked back to his bike. Aviator shades and a little mustache, plus that pleasing bulge below the belt. This guy was smoking hot. He climbed on his bike and looked at his clipboard. The roadster was still parked—Truax was about to get a citation for whatever he'd done with the panel truck.

The guy had actually timed it just right, Slater realized. John Law obviously hadn't noticed him open the passenger door. Why hadn't he just stuffed whatever it was under the seat? If the cop had twigged, he definitely would have walked around to see what it was, and things would have escalated. An unregistered handgun or illegal drugs, most likely. Whatever it was, it must be radioactive to make him take that risk.

A minute later the cop walked back to Truax's window, and handed him the clipboard. Truax must have signed it, because the cop took it back, and handed him a copy, and walked back to his motorcycle. Climbing on, he put the stand up and waited.

Truax was still parked, and the cop gestured for him to go, waving his gloved hand forward. The roadster didn't move. As Slater watched, the cop set his parking stand again, and climbed off the bike, and walked back to Truax's window. He couldn't hear the exchange over the road noise of the vehicles streaming by, but the cop was more intent now. Eventually he stood erect and walked back to his ride, and the roadster pulled into the traffic.

Truax had wanted to retrieve whatever he'd dumped, but the cop had other ideas. As the vehicle pulled away, Slater could see now what was in the gutter—the bundle of burlap he'd picked up at the mining supply company.

Back on his motorcycle, the cop sat for a moment, then put up his stand, and killed the flickering blue lights, and pulled into the road. If he'd noticed the bundle in the gutter, he hadn't connected it to Truax.

To him it probably looked like more nondescript street trash.

Slater rolled ahead, past a driveway, and stopped next to the burlap. Popping his seatbelt, he leaned over and opened the passenger door, then reached down to grab it. It was heavy. The burlap was a double-layered sack, and he set it on the passenger seat and pulled open the top. Inside were cylinders of waxy brown paper. His heart started to pound. Not a gun, not drugs. This looked like dynamite.

He gingerly dug around in the bag. It was just the sticks, with no blasting caps. The stuff probably wasn't dangerous without those. Truax would definitely circle back for this. What the hell was he up to? Folding the sack closed, he set it on the floor in front of the passenger seat, then buckled his belt again, and took a deep breath to slow his heart rate, and pulled into the traffic.

With one eye on the road, he checked the map to see which way the freeway was, and headed toward it. As he drove he kept an eye on the rearview, but there was no sign of the red roadster. Once he was up the ramp and on the 710, he phoned Etta, glad that she picked up.

"Where are you at?"

"My place," Etta said. "I was afraid to try to wedge your land boat into my parking stall, so it's on the street out front."

"I'll be there soon."

THIRTEEN

S LATER PUSHED THE LITTLE car to coax some speed out of it, cruising in the left lane past all the slow-moving semitrucks, fully loaded now on their way from the port. On surface streets this car wasn't a bad ride, but on the freeway it felt gutless, like its motor came from a leaf blower or a hedge trimmer.

Eventually he was in Highland Park, and pulled up at Etta's place, and backed into a street space right behind the Thunderbird. Once he'd texted her, he climbed out with his satchel and the burlap bag.

When Etta appeared, she handed him his car key. "How did Ernestine behave for you?"

Slater stepped over to open the Thunderbird's trunk. "Your car has a name?"

"Of course she does. Doesn't yours?" She stood watching as Slater gently tucked the edges of the burlap in next to the spare tire. "What's in the bag?"

"Tampons," he said flatly.

Etta chuckled. "I'm waiting on some calls back, but I'm pretty sure I'll have a report for you by tomorrow about Eustace."

"Excellent," he said, and gently slammed the trunk.

Behind the wheel of the Thunderbird, he spent a minute readjusting the mirrors and the seat. In the rearview he saw Etta pull the Prius around him and into her building's parking garage.

There wasn't time to go back to his house before he

met Pike, but Burbank wasn't far from here. There was time to stop by the duplex where the UFO researcher Foster had lived. Pulling out *Saucers over the Southwest*, he plugged the address into his navigation.

The app directed him north through residential neighborhoods. It wasn't the route he would have taken, but he'd come to accept that the software knew more than he did, specifically about traffic conditions. Eventually it led him onto the freeway, then off again in Burbank.

Pulling up on Foster's address, he realized he should have checked the street view first. The duplex where the guys in dark suits had beat him up was long gone, replaced by four floors of apartments. They hadn't gone up recently either. The style looked like peak 1980s, the garish pink and purple paint job already faded with age.

Slater continued on to the bar where he was supposed to meet Pike and his work friends. It was on a long commercial strip in the middle of the block. It wasn't an upscale place, but not a dive bar either, he saw as he walked in. The vibe was like a sports bar, with a baseball game playing on several TV screens.

Pike was standing with a small group of people at the end of the bar, two of them standing and two on stools. All of them were dressed for the office. That distinct flavor of business-casual was like a uniform, and it marked them as feds. Even the guy at Ray's apartment had pegged them as feds from the way Pike had been dressed.

As Slater approached the group, the one who spotted him first was Anton. Of course it would be him. He was dark, with jet-black hair, and basically fuckable. When Anton recognized him, anger or maybe disgust flashed in his expression, but he quickly masked it.

Stepping up beside Pike, Slater squeezed him around

the waist, and leaned in to give him a pointed kiss. Pike blushed, his eyes bright, a wry grin on his face. Whatever was happening here, it felt like it was important to him.

Pike introduced him to the others. Besides Anton there was a woman named Brewster, her hair pulled back behind her prominent ears, and Hopkins, a chunky guy with his black hair in knobby twists.

"We've actually met," Anton said. "You threatened me one time in a bar downtown. Basically chased me out of the place."

"I remember," Slater said. "Our narrative complex was just starting to unfold. You have to admit you were pawing this guy."

Anton frowned. "No, I wasn't."

"Agree to disagree."

Pike put a hand on his shoulder and squeezed. It wasn't an admonition, exactly, but he was right, they didn't need to get into it.

"Don't get me wrong, Slater," Anton said. "I've been for you since the beginning."

Slater narrowed his eyes. "I guess that's reassuring."

The bartender stepped over and eyed him, and he ordered a small.

"What's a narrative complex?" Brewster said, gesturing with her glass.

"A sprawling multidimensional series of interconnected romantic and erotic events," Slater said. "Squares would call it a 'relationship.'" He waggled his fingers for air quotes. "But that word isn't expansive enough to account for what we've got going on."

"I guess I'm a square, then," Hopkins said, and chuckled. "You're both wearing rings. Are those new?"

Pike held up his left hand and spread his fingers. "It's the next episode in our narrative complex."

The bartender set down a glass, and Slater stepped

over and handed her a sawbuck. Pike and the others tapped their glasses to his.

"We didn't get hitched," Pike said. "It's just so boys and other people don't assume he's single."

"Do you have cute pet names for each other?" Anton said.

"Of course not," Slater said, and at the same time Pike said, "Of course we do."

"He calls me Reddy Kilowatt." Pike eyed him sidelong. "I tased him when we first met."

"Zap," Slater said. "It's not cute. It's just reality. He's the man with a million volts in his pants."

"I have a taser," Brewster said. "If I'd known it was that easy to get dates, I would have tried it a long time ago. What does Pike call you?"

"Forty-niner."

"Slater is threatened by any pants that weren't designed during the gold rush era," Pike said.

"That's hard-core."

"Oh, yeah." Pike nodded. "I wish they all could be California boys."

"So are you two exclusive?" Hopkins said, raising his eyebrows.

Pike scoffed. "That would be like trying to stop a speeding freight train."

"You're all interrogating me like I'm a suspect," Slater said.

"I guess it's a habit." Brewster smiled. "We just want to get to know you."

"You all work together?" Slater said, gesturing with his glass. "Track down rumrunners, smash open barrels of moonshine with fire axes?"

Brewster laughed. "That doesn't come up very often anymore."

He listened and nodded as they talked about their

work. It wasn't uninteresting, and he asked some questions, getting them to elaborate.

When there was a lull in the conversation, Slater said, "So what are the rules about transporting explosives?"

"First, they have to be legal." Hopkins raised his eyebrows. "No do-it-yourself products."

Pike frowned. "What is it with you and explosives?"

"What are you talking about?"

"It's like they're attracted to you. Like stray cats to the milkman. That briefcase from Galliform, then a whole planeload of homemade cartel plastic explosive out in the desert."

"That explains why you're so into him," Hopkins said. "Your worlds intersect."

Slater waved a hand. "It's an innocent question."

"Do you have some explosives you need to transport?" Pike said, holding his gaze.

"If I did, I definitely wouldn't be gossiping about it with this crowd."

"He's taking the Fifth," Hopkins said.

Slater glanced at him. These people were sharp—Slater hadn't denied it, as he didn't want to lie to Pike, since it ticked him off so much. And Hopkins had quickly picked up on the equivocation.

"On public roads or on the rails, explosives have to be transported in a magazine," Anton said. "The size of the magazine corresponds to the weight of the explosives."

"What kind of magazine?"

"It looks like a safe." Anton held up his hands to mime a square. "A big red reinforced-steel box. It has to be secured to the vehicle, not floating around loose."

"You also have to transport blasting caps separately," Brewster said, "unless they're in their own magazine. Then they can go on the same vehicle."

"This is great." Slater hoisted his glass to them. "It's

like having a panel of explosives experts on demand."

"You need to know this for your work?" Brewster said. "Pike says you're a gumshoe."

He waved a hand. "Just curious."

"In private practice you can do things we can't," she said. "We should subcontract with you on the down-low."

"I'd do it," Slater said, "but I doubt you can afford me."

She cackled at that.

"He's serious," Pike said. "Slater makes bank."

"So you're a fancy lad," Hopkins said. "A concierge gumshoe."

"Not even a little. I'm a working stiff."

"Don't listen to him," Pike said. "His house cost three times what mine did. He has a maid who comes in and does his laundry."

"I don't have time to do laundry. I'm too busy hustling to pay for that house."

"It's all about priorities," Anton said.

They drank another round and talked some more, mostly about nothing, before they all left.

As he and Pike walked out to the street, Slater said, "Where's your rig?"

"At the house. I'm riding with you."

"How did you get here?"

"I carpooled with Anton today."

Stepping up to the Thunderbird, Slater unlocked the passenger door for him. "That guy wants into your pants so bad."

"That allegation is so far from reality, I can't even get pissed about it."

They climbed into the vehicle, and Slater headed toward the freeway. The sun was low in the west, painting the city with the golden light of the end of the day.

Pike pulled on his sunglasses and leaned back into the headrest.

"Thank you for being civil," he said, "and keeping your temper."

"You make it sound like I'm a hothead."

Pike laughed. "You're a total hothead. You know you are. You told me that yourself before we even got rolling."

He eyed the side mirror to change lanes. "They're not so bad, your colleagues."

"It's important that you meet them, and get to know them a little."

"Why?"

"It's about having a network."

"I guess I could ask one of them to look stuff up," Slater said, "if you're not around."

Pike squeezed his shoulder. "A social network. Not a business network. Everyone needs that."

"Now you sound like a shrink."

"I know you get what I'm saying."

"Are your friends concerned at all that you're with someone like me?"

"They don't care who I'm with. And there's nothing wrong with you."

"I'm bad news," Slater said. "You know that's true."

"I wouldn't say that. As long as you're not actually transporting explosives in your trunk."

The guy was sharp, Slater thought, if that idea still lingered in his mind. He braked as he exited the freeway into their neighborhood, navigating the narrow ramp.

"How risky is that?" Slater said. "Just talking hypothetically."

Pike pushed his sunglasses up on his head and eyed him. "It depends on what kind of explosives."

"Basic mining industry dynamite."

"Low risk."

As he turned onto their street, Slater said, "What about leaving it in your trunk overnight?"

"Unless you're in Phoenix in the summer, it should be fine."

The garage door rolled up, and he nosed the Thunderbird inside and killed the engine. Pike popped the door handle, and started to climb out, but then paused when Slater didn't move.

"So what do you do with dynamite when you happen to run across it?"

"It's not something I come across incidentally," Pike said, his tone intent. "What the hell is going on?"

"How much trouble is it to get rid of the stuff? I mean, what do you even do with it?"

Pike stared at him for a moment. "Is there dynamite in the trunk of this car right now?"

"I don't want to lie to you."

"What the fuck are you doing with dynamite in your car?" Pike demanded, raising his voice.

"Someone in my case dumped it in the gutter. *Bam*, right there on the side of PCH. I didn't know what it was until I retrieved it and opened the bag. I figured it was better that I took charge of it than some eighth-graders on the way home from school."

"Who throws dynamite in the gutter?"

"I can't really get into it." Slater shrugged. "It's confidential."

"Damn it, Slater, do you know what kind of position that puts me in? If I do what I'm supposed to do, there's a whole investigation, and cops crawling all over this place, and a lot of questions for you."

"Maybe there's another way to just, you know, get rid of it."

"Your target doesn't know you grabbed it?"

Slater shook his head. "No idea."

"Are you sure it's really dynamite?"

"Good question. Do you want to have a look?"

He made a low growling sound in his throat, and reached into the backseat, and snagged a couple of the black latex gloves from the box, then climbed out.

Slater got out too and stepped around to the trunk. As Pike was wriggling his hands into the gloves, he heard him mutter under his breath, "Fuck."

"I feel like I'm stressing you out."

"That's very perceptive," Pike shouted, and smacked the button to roll down the garage door.

"Why the gloves?"

"I don't need to leave my prints and DNA on it."

Slater opened the trunk and pulled open the burlap bag. Reaching in for one of the sticks, Pike looked it over.

"Yup—this is dynamite. At least it's real."

"Meaning what?"

"It's not some homemade version, or the cartel stuff. This is professionally made in a munitions factory. That means it's safe."

"Unfortunately my prints and DNA are probably all over it."

Pike stepped back and folded his arms, his brow furrowed. "Where did this person obtain it? And what were they planning on doing with it?"

"I'm going to find out."

"Technically it's not that big a deal to have this stuff, since it's legit. You're supposed to have a permit, and you're supposed to have it in a magazine if you're going to drive around with it."

Slater nodded, and took a breath, and ran a hand through his hair.

"Here's what I'm going to do," Pike said finally. "I'll call a guy I know who has a permit. He'll be able to sell it to somebody else with a permit. He won't ask any questions."

"That sounds like a great solution. Should I leave it in the trunk?"

Pike scoffed. "I'm not going to invite him here. I'll go to him." He pulled out his phone and tapped at it, then held it to his ear. After a friendly preamble, Pike said, "Can I come see you? I have some paperwork I need to deal with … right … I just need to get it off my desk … text me the address. I'll head over there soon."

Once he'd ended the call, Slater said, "Did he know what you meant?"

"I think so." His phone buzzed, and he glanced at the screen. "Where's Vernon?"

"The other side of downtown. Twenty minutes' drive at this time of day, mostly on the freeway. Do you want me to come with?"

"No," he said flatly. "You know this mishegoss jeopardizes my job, don't you? I could get in serious trouble for this."

Slater stepped closer, and massaged his biceps. "You won't. You're too smart."

"I feel like you're pulling me down into the cesspool you're in."

"I'm trouble, Pike. You know I'm no damn good."

He huffed and stepped over to the trunk of the Thunderbird, and grabbed the burlap sack, then walked to the side door and out to the street.

Once he'd retrieved his satchel, Slater headed upstairs. He felt a twinge of guilt roping Pike into it. He could have dealt with it himself, but he knew Pike would have an easier solution. He also knew he'd be pissed, but it wasn't the kind of trouble that he'd dump him over.

He ordered food from the Thai place he knew Pike liked, and took his boots off, and sprawled on the sofa with *Saucers over the Southwest*, absently squeezing the fake grass between his toes. The delivery driver rang the bell not long before Pike got back.

When he heard Pike coming up the stairs, he met him in the kitchen.

"There's grub," Slater said.

"Good. We can eat outside."

He seemed calmer, Slater decided, and carried the bag of Thai out to the deck. It was dark out, but there was enough light from the French doors to eat by, and the cooler night air felt good.

Slater waited until Pike had some food in his belly, then said, "How did it go?"

He looked tired as he sat back in his chair. "The guy was happy to have it. The stuff was new, so he can sell it for a premium."

"It goes stale?"

"When it gets old, it sweats nitroglycerin," Pike said. "The newer the better."

"He didn't need to know where it came from?"

"This guy deals in it, so selling a little extra on the sly along with a legit order is no big deal."

"It's kind of cool that we can pool resources, you and me. Help each other out."

Pike raised his eyebrows. "So far it's just you doing reckless things, and then me finding a way to weasel you out of it."

"That's true," he said quietly, and looked away. "But you know I'd do the same for you."

"I can't believe you were driving around with that stuff." Pike sat up and dug around with his chopsticks in one of the cartons, then met his gaze. "You're a lot of man, Slater."

"I know."

"Did I tell you I'm out of town tomorrow? Just overnight. We're going out to the Mojave Desert."

"Where in the desert?"

"Near one of the military bases. Twentynine Palms."

"What are you doing out there?"

"Much like your dynamite supplier, that's confidential."

"I bet it's drugs," Slater said. "Twentynine is incorporated, but once you're outside the towns, the Mojave has lots and lots of tweakers."

"Is that so."

"I wonder if they've moved on to fentanyl? That's what's happened in the city. It feels like that came on really fast too. It's why Doris quit riding the metro."

"Meth-heads rage and rampage, throw punches, break windows." Pike folded his arms. "The fetty crowd is actually easier to deal with. They just fall asleep."

After they carried the containers inside and dumped them in the trash, Slater said, "You're hot when you're pissed. It's a side of you I don't see very often."

"It's hot even when I'm pissed at you?"

"It riles me up in the best possible way. Because it's you. Do you want to work some of that out?"

Pike chuckled. It was the first time he'd smiled all evening. "Of course you'd turn it into a sex thing."

"I know you want to throttle me right now. Let's use that."

He waved to the stairs. "So let's go."

Pike followed him down to the bedroom, and stepped around the bed, and pulled open the drawer in the nightstand. He took out a pair of handcuffs while Slater unbuttoned his shirt, and popped the buckle on his belt.

Once Slater had his shirt off, Pike said, "Turn around."

He curled his lip into a sneer. "Make me."

With no hesitation, Pike lunged for his wrist and twisted it to spin him around. Slater didn't resist, and Pike moved fast, snapping on the cuffs with the ease of someone who'd had plenty of practice. Spinning him around to face him, Pike put a hand on his throat, his grip firm but not cutting off his air.

"'I found it in the gutter,' he says. 'Just sitting there on the side of the road.'"

He leaned in, and pressed their mouths together. His mouth was warm and intense, and Slater explored it with his tongue. He felt his dick tightening in his jeans.

Pulling back, Pike unbuttoned his shirt and quickly ditched his clothes.

"You're going to need to get my jeans off," Slater said, reaching around with his bound hands and wriggling his fingers.

"Shut the fuck up."

Pike popped his fly, and pushed his jeans down, and Slater stepped out of them. Leaning in, Pike squeezed his cock, and mouthed his neck.

"I'm going to fuck you senseless," he said, and pulled back.

"Big talk." Slater jutted his chin.

Pike slapped him, hard enough to turn his head.

"What was that?" He met his eye. "I can't hear you."

He slapped him again, then pushed him down onto the bed. Slater shifted so that the cuffs weren't digging into his flesh. In the right position, in the small of his back, they were actually comfortable.

Grabbing a condom and lube, Pike climbed on the bed with him, and shoved his legs apart. With one hand on the back of his neck, he leaned in, probing him with his fingers. Slater gasped at the intensity of it.

"'Clean up my mess,' he says, 'because I don't give a shit about your career.'"

"Spread out," Slater said through his teeth.

Pike shifted closer, his hands pulling on Slater's knees. His cock was rock-hard now, and he pressed into him, and soon worked up to pounding him.

"Psycho," Pike growled.

"Speak up, son. I missed that."

"You're a psycho," Pike shouted, and slapped him again. "A fucking psycho." His face contorted as he climaxed, straining into him, and then he sank on top of him.

The weight of his body and the smell of his sweaty hair was a turn-on, and Slater breathed in his scent, and thrust against him. He only had a small range of movement, but it was enough, and it only took a moment until he came.

Eventually Pike shifted onto his side, one leg folded over Slater's, his breath gradually slowing.

"Why do you do this to me?" Pike said.

"I knew you'd have a solution."

"I don't mean that. I mean this." He caressed his chest. "You get me so amped up. Everything else just fades out."

"It's because I know you. And you know me. You know what I need." Slater took a breath. "I love you so hard."

FOURTEEN

B RIGHT MORNING LIGHT WAS streaming through the sheers when Slater woke. His phone was ringing, he realized. Pike was gone. He scrabbled for the phone on the bedside table. It was Truax.

"I haven't heard from you," Truax said when he picked up. "What's the status?"

"I'm following some leads," Slater said, his tongue thick. "There might be a connection to some UFO groups."

"Don't waste your time. Finley's not off with those nuts."

"How do you know that?"

"Just focus on Finley. Not on that stuff. Quit dicking me around and do the work."

He'd ended the call, Slater saw, looking at the screen. There was a text from Etta from earlier:

Updates. Are you in the office today?

Slater sat up and sent a response:

I'll be there in an hour.

Forcing himself out of bed, he got dressed, in jeans and a dark shirt, then went upstairs. Pike had left coffee for him in the pot. It was tepid now but still tasty, and he slammed a mugful, then drove to the office.

Etta was already here, sitting at the front desk, wearing a blue plaid shirt.

"Are you ready for me," she said, "or do you need a minute?"

"Come on in."

He sat behind his desk and waited for her to take the chair across from him.

"I still can't get over that ring," Etta said. "It creates so much cognitive dissonance. Like a penguin riding a bicycle, or ketchup on ice cream."

"It's just a symbol."

"A symbol that your heart is true," she said, grinning at him, "and that you're a sweet little love bug."

He frowned. "You've been hanging around middle schoolers too long."

"So I was working with Max yesterday. We were on a stakeout. He taught me some of the techniques to use for interviews when you're tracking someone down." She deepened her voice and imitated Max's flat intonation. "First, you look at the drinking glasses, and if there's lipstick on the rim, you know there's a woman involved."

"I know several men who wear lipstick," Slater said, "and lots of women who don't. Then there's everybody who isn't binary."

"I think he just said that to wind me up." Still imitating Max, she said, "First, you talk to the wife, and you don't believe anything she says. Then you find the girlfriend, and you don't believe anything she says."

"He's exactly right about that."

"Everybody is going to lie to you all the time," she said.

"Preach, sister. You have to sift through it to find the places where the stories overlap. That's where you might see a glimmer of truth."

"That's what Max said, and that's what I did."

"So where is Eustace?"

"He actually went to Planet W with the space brothers," Etta said. "He got his green card there, although he still has to file U.S. taxes."

"Bullshit. It sounds like you didn't do enough sifting. Or you believed a wrong guy."

She laughed. "I'm just messing with you. He's in a retirement home. Out in Monrovia. I'll text you the details." Etta shifted in her chair. "I'm not sure how much credence to put in Eustace's book."

"You mean *Visitors from Planet W*?" Slater said. "I assumed it was pure fiction."

"Eustace claims the alien ship from Planet W came when he was stationed at a military base in San Diego in the late 1950s. The thing is, the book wasn't written until 1964. That makes me think he backdated his story."

"To cash in on being an early contactee? I guess you might get more credibility that way."

"Eustace says the crew of the alien ship were all buff white guys," Etta said.

"He said they were white?"

"He compared them to some of the movie actors of the day. They wore tight uniforms, so you could see all their muscles."

Slater chuckled. "They sound like my kind of aliens."

"One of them is the ship's captain, Zanderos. Him and Eustace hang out, and Zanderos tells him all about Planet W."

"As if the captain of an interstellar ship would have nothing better to do than kill time with an enlisted grunt. It doesn't wash."

"I know, right? They go to the beach together, and swim in their underwear, and have a picnic on the sand."

"It sounds like they were sleeping together," Slater said.

"Eventually Zanderos has to leave, and he boards the flying saucer, and it zips away. Then six months later Eustace walks into a diner, out in the desert between here and Vegas. Zanderos is sitting there eating pancakes. He's not in uniform, and he's wearing dark sunglasses, but Eustace recognizes him. Zanderos subtly shakes his head, like, 'Don't acknowledge me.' Eustace realizes, 'Oh, he's undercover.'"

"Or maybe Eustace was really boring to talk to, and Zanderos was trying to ghost him. Nowadays you'd just block him on the hookup app."

"Eustace didn't say they were lovers," Etta said, "but there were definitely homoerotic overtones."

He waved a hand. "I can't believe you read that book."

"I like books. I'm off for the summer, and it was an easy read. My assessment is that it's pretty implausible. In the last chapter one of the other visitors tells him all about Jesus."

Slater scoffed. "Like they'd have the same fictional entity chiseling the populace on another planet."

"Jesus wasn't a chiseler."

"Everyone who uses his brand is. That's why they pass the collection plate. You'd think if their god really was magic, he could manifest some cash for them."

"I don't get how you manage to move through life being so antireligious."

"A shrink once told me the first step to healing is forgiveness." Slater shrugged. "Lo, I've already forgiven myself."

"OK, Slater, I get it." She sat up. "I'd offer to go interview Eustace, but I'm going camping today."

"I should talk to him myself. What's the damage?"

"Two yards?"

"Don't say it like it's a question. That means I have room to push the number down. When somebody talks like that, I automatically offer them sixty percent of the ask. You'd wind up with a buck twenty."

"OK." She nodded. "It's two yards."

"But you read that whole stupid book. Did you have to drive out to Monrovia to do interviews?"

"It was all phone work."

"So maybe you should be billing for what your time is really worth," Slater said.

"All right. Two fifty."

"Don't undervalue yourself," he said, raising his voice, "and don't undervalue your time."

Etta slapped his desk. "Three yards, firm."

"That's more like it." He pulled out his wad, and peeled off three C-notes.

"Sweet old Mr. Franklin," she said, and tucked the bills into her pants pocket. "You're a tough negotiator, ring boy."

The muffled sound of keys came from the front door, then Max called out a greeting, and appeared in the doorway to Slater's office.

"I hear you've been educating our operative about finding people," Slater said.

Max waved a hand. "We had some time yesterday on a stakeout."

"Hours and hours sitting in the Challenger," Etta said. "Without your bird-dog gig I would have died of boredom."

"Stakeouts are definitely my least favorite part of the work," Slater said.

Etta gestured to Max with a thumb. "Did you know this guy eats junk food and then immediately hides the wrappers so his girlfriend won't find out?"

"I'm not hiding anything," Max said. "I'm cleaning up after myself. I put the wrappers in the trash."

"I bet when you were single the wrappers were knee-deep in the backseat," Etta said.

Max eyed Slater. "Five hours of this attitude. It's like

sandpaper on my soul."

"But he loves me anyway," she said, and stood up. "I'm out, fellas."

Max went into his office, and Slater heard the front door close, and the sound of Etta setting the deadbolt. He got up and stood in Max's doorway.

"I should pay you too if you did the work on tracking down my target."

"I didn't do anything." Max sat back in his chair. "I just outlined the tools for her. We were sitting there anyway. With Etta, I only have to explain things once."

"She's a natural, huh."

"It makes me feel dumb sometimes, watching her do the work." He waved a hand. "No debt incurred for training. Showing her the ropes will benefit me on future jobs."

Slater went down to his car, and checked the address Etta had texted him. He put it in his navigation app and got on the 10.

<hr>

PULLING UP ON THE retirement home, not far below the looming San Gabriel Mountains, Slater found a tired low-slung building with a stretch of angle parking in front. As he climbed out of the Thunderbird he looked over the landscaping. A strip of turf fronted the structure. That was just stupid these days, but planted next to the building was coyote brush, well established and trimmed to a few feet high. He stopped to look it over, and saw that it was blooming. He dropped to one knee to inspect it.

A woman in nurse's scrubs, her black hair in myriad little braids, was standing nearby, a cigarette in hand.

"Is something wrong with the hedge?" she said.

Slater briefly glanced at her. "This is actually the

bomb. It's a native species, and its thriving here." He stood up. "These are all male plants. They're flowering right now."

She frowned, and gestured with her cigarette. "Plants have males and females?"

"Some of them." His eyes narrowed. "Your badge says RN. Didn't you have to take any science classes to get that degree?"

"Not the ones about plants." She dropped her cigarette and ground the butt under the sole of her shoe. "Gender is a construct anyway."

Slater followed her into the lobby. There were no interior security doors, but right at the entrance was a front desk, positioned to be unavoidable to anyone walking in. The smoker stepped behind it and gave him the once-over as he stepped up.

"I'm here to see Eustace Burke."

"Are you a relative?" she said.

"His nephew."

"You don't look like him." Her brow furrowed. "Eustace isn't Latin."

"Race is a construct anyway," he said flatly.

"Nephew or grandnephew? He's got a lot of years on you."

"Spare me the chin music, toots. Can I see him or not?"

She frowned and gestured with a nod. "Unit 112. That way."

Slater walked down the hall, following the numbers mounted next to the doors as they gradually counted higher. The door to 112 was ajar, and he walked in. It was like a studio apartment, with a bed at one side, a kitchen counter, and sliding doors onto a sprawling green yard. Sitting in a recliner, his feet up, was a guy with gray hair and glasses, wearing a plaid Western shirt and sweatpants. He was watching TV and had it turned up too loud.

When he caught sight of Slater, he looked up at him with rheumy blue eyes. Slater couldn't see any resemblance to the man in the photo of the derailed saucer event in the 1950s. The intervening years had changed him too much.

Eustace lifted the remote to mute the TV set. "Who are you?"

"I'm a friend of Zanderos," Slater said. "From Planet W."

He cackled at that. "I'm glad people are still reading my books. Pull up a chair."

Slater took one from the little round table by the sliding doors, then sat facing him.

"I'd get up," Eustace said, "but I'm supposed to keep my feet elevated."

"I'm not worried. Do you remember meeting a guy named Finley López?"

"Sure. He's an earnest young fellow. It was a while ago. Maybe in the spring."

"He visited you here?"

"That's right. He had great hair. Like yours. What's your beef with him? And what's your name, anyway?"

"Ibáñez," Slater said, and dug a business card out of his hip pocket, and handed it over. "I'm trying to track him down."

"Insurance," Eustace said, peering at the card. "You don't look like an office type."

"I'm in the field."

"Tracking down deadbeats, I'm thinking. Is Finley in trouble?"

"He abandoned his job, and vacated his apartment. I'm trying to figure out what's going on with him."

"Well, we only talked about ufology. He's not a

researcher, but he's passionate about the field. Lots of questions for me about when I met the men from Planet W. It's so long ago now I didn't have very clear answers for him."

"What about that lecture you gave at the Baltimore back in the day?" Slater said. "Somebody tried to derail it."

His eyebrows shot up. "You've done your reading too. That somebody is your Uncle Sam." His face clouded at the memory. "Or rather a secretive black op funded with your Uncle Sam's money. The cabal that controls access to saucer information. Goddamn spooks. They did derail it. I was so intimidated after that, I didn't talk publicly about the space brothers for years."

"Do you think the feds are still going after people who know too much?"

"My sense of it is that they were trying to suppress anything that might challenge the status quo. In that era there were lots of enemies: communists, and gays, and black people. And then us saucer-heads."

"Did Finley ask you about that event at the Baltimore?"

"He was more interested in the aliens and their ships, not about me. I told him what I remembered." He chuckled. "I was happy to talk to him. I liked the way his pants fit."

"He's stacked?"

Eustace nodded slowly. "Oh, yeah."

"That makes me want to meet him even more."

"You know, you could have been one of the men from Planet W," he said, his eyes flicking over Slater's body. "You're built like they were."

"Weren't they all white guys?"

He chuckled. "It was a long time ago. I had a friend who looked like you once."

"A boyfriend?"

"We didn't call it that, but yes, we were romantically involved. I see you're with someone, judging by that ring."

Slater glanced at it, and touched the inside of it with his thumb. "It's a whole thing. I have sex rules. I'm allowed to do what I want when he's out of town."

"That sounds thoroughly modern. Don't take this the wrong way, Ibáñez, but could I touch your hair?"

"Why not?"

Slater shifted his chair closer, then dropped to one knee at the side of the recliner. Eustace ran his hand into his hair. Leaning in, Slater closed his eyes, enjoying the feeling of his fingers on his scalp. When he met his gaze, he saw the longing in his eyes. Slater shifted position, leaning over him, and met his mouth. With his hand on the back of his head, Eustace pulled him closer.

The guy was good at this, his mouth taut and intent, considering his age. Slater put his palm on Eustace's thigh, and slowly slid it up his sweatpants, into his crotch, and squeezed his cock.

Eustace pulled back and inhaled sharply.

"Too much?" Slater said.

"No—it's just ... it's been a while."

Slater massaged his cock. "You're getting a stiffy."

"Unfortunately that's not going to do anything. But could I touch yours?"

Slater got up, and stepped over to the door, and pushed it closed. Returning, he popped his fly, and sat on the arm of the recliner, and guided Eustace's hand onto his cock. It started to stiffen from the attention.

Eustace stroked him for a minute, taking deep breaths, and Slater massaged his shoulder and the back of his neck. If the guy kept doing that, he could probably climax.

Then came a soft tap-tap-tap at the door. Slater hopped to his feet, and turned his back to the entrance, and tucked his junk away. A woman wearing maroon scrubs stepped in.

"What's going on?" she demanded.

"I'm busy, woman," Eustace said.

"I need to check your blood pressure. Who's this?"

"I'm his nephew," Slater said, glancing over his shoulder as he rapidly buttoned his fly.

"Why does your nephew have his pants undone?"

"I said I'm busy." Eustace raised his voice. "Come back later."

"I have to go anyway," Slater said, turning to him and briefly squeezing his arm.

"I don't understand what you were doing here," she said.

"Don't feel bad," Slater said, briefly holding her gaze. "Lots of people are stupid."

He stepped around her and into the hall.

"Damn it," Eustace said, and called after him, "Come and see me again, will you?"

Walking out to the street, Slater adjusted his crotch, and climbed behind the wheel of the Thunderbird. His phone had buzzed earlier, and when he checked, he saw that Olivia Howard had phoned. As he nosed into the street, he tapped her number.

"I'm glad you called," she said when she picked up.

"You called me."

"I wanted to invite you to a Neaploia event."

"I'm not actually a saucer-head," Slater said. "I'm trying to track down a saucer-head."

"It's a summoning. Where we combine our energy to psychically summon the spacecraft. We're doing it out in the Mojave at Landers."

"I know Landers. Junkyards and beat-up RVs and

meth-heads."

"It's also where Giant Rock is. The event isn't just a summoning. It's like a festival. We had to get a permit to use the land and everything. You'll meet lots of people in the field. I know it's short notice, but it's happening tomorrow, and I thought of you."

"It's also a long drive. I'm going to have to pass."

"You might learn something," Olivia said. "I happened to remember more about Finley."

"Like what?" he demanded. "Can't you just tell me on the phone?"

"If you come to Giant Rock, we can sit down and have a proper chat."

"I'm not paying you again."

She laughed. "It's included in our previous interview."

"What's the name of the event?"

"The Great Mojave Summoning. It's happening all day. Food trucks and speakers and the whole nine yards."

"I'll think about it," he said, and ended the call.

It felt like a trap, Slater thought, accelerating up the ramp onto the freeway. But he couldn't see a motive for Olivia to mess with him, and if it was a public event, it would be safe enough. What he really wanted to do tomorrow was dig deeper into Truax, and find out what he was planning to do with that sack of dynamite. But if Olivia had more dope on Finley, he needed to talk to her.

FIFTEEN

W HEN SLATER GOT UPSTAIRS to his office, Max was gone, and the lights were off. The statue of Rey Pascual was positioned to face the front door, scythe at the ready, watching him with empty eye sockets as he entered.

Slater double-clicked his tongue in greeting. "How you doing, Rey?"

At his computer, he swung his boots up onto the desk and pulled the keyboard into his lap. The Great Mojave Summoning was for real, he found, and it was run by Neaploia. He scrolled through search results about the group. Like Olivia had said, they were an organization of saucer-heads, with "research" as their stated goal. They ran message boards, and put out publications, and held events.

The website for the Great Mojave Summoning had camping advice along with details on nearby hotels, and at the bottom, "Private aircraft can fly in to the Great Mojave Summoning. Look for Giant Rock airstrip. No services."

A search for the airstrip showed that it was technically retired from use, but it was still there, on a sprawling desert playa on federal wilderness land. Even when it had been an official airstrip, it had never been surfaced or even graded. The playa was flat, with no brush, and light planes had always just landed there.

He leaned back and rubbed his eyes. Truax and his

dynamite was a lot more tantalizing than a UFO event, but the job was to find Finley.

Digging out his phone, he dialed Pike, glad that he picked up.

"Am I still in the doghouse?" Slater said.

"I think we worked that out. How could I be upset with you when I can still smell you on my skin?"

"You know I want to be a better person for you."

"Don't do it for me," Pike said. "Do it for you. I'll benefit as a side effect."

"Are you still coming back tomorrow night?"

"Unless Poseidon gets pissed off at me and delays my return. The way he did to Odysseus."

"I don't think that guy has much sway in the Mojave Desert," Slater said. "If you're there until evening, you can drive me back. I have a meeting in Landers. I'll save some time and fly up."

"What's in Landers?"

"The Great Mojave Summoning. At Giant Rock. Olivia wants me to go."

"How cool is that? I've heard of Giant Rock. They used to have UFO events there in the 1950s. Is it near Twentynine?"

"Right up the road," Slater said.

"I'll be done here in the afternoon. I'll drive over."

Next he phoned Max.

"Who's that guy who flew you up to Lone Pine?" Slater said.

"Cappy Dan."

"Is that his actual name?"

"Cappy as in captain," Max said. "I don't know what his real name is. He's not really a captain either. Just a guy with an airplane. He's a little shady. A cash-only type guy."

"That's how we like them. I assume he's licensed?"

"I'm sure. Aviation is pretty tightly regulated. You can't really get away with much."

"Can you text me his info?"

"Let me give him your number first, so he knows why you're calling him. A cold call might freak him out. Where are you headed, anyway?"

"Giant Rock," Slater said. "It's out in the Mojave."

"You want to fly because the T-bird isn't up to crossing the desert in midsummer."

"It might do fine, but it's not worth the risk."

"You can borrow my wheels," Max said.

"I could rent something too. But that would mean I'm admitting that my ride can't do what I need it to do."

"Probably wise to just spend a couple grand, then," Max said, "and avoid the issue altogether."

That was sarcasm, Slater realized as he ended the call, and for a moment the urge flitted through his mind to punch Max in the face. But it was hard to get pissed at the guy when he knew himself that he was being irrational.

Max didn't type very fast with those pudgy fingers, he knew, and it might take him a while to text Cappy Dan. But a minute later his phone buzzed with the guy's details. Slater tapped the phone number and listened to it ring.

When Cappy Dan answered, he said, "Slater."

"You talked to Max."

"He's a good friend," Dan said. "A prince among men."

"He must have paid you well."

He laughed. "What do you need?"

"A ride to Giant Rock," Slater said. "Tomorrow morning."

"Where's that?"

"It's a playa out in the Mojave with no services."

"Let me look it up."

While he waited, Slater heard muffled noises in the background. Eventually Cappy Dan spoke.

"There hasn't been an airstrip there in fifty years."

"But the playa is still there. You can land on it, right? I just need to be dropped off. You don't have to wait around because I don't need a ride back."

"I'll check with some of the desert pilots. If it's doable, I still have to fly back, even if you don't."

"Is that how airplanes work?" Slater said.

"I can do it for eighteen hundred."

"I'll pay you a grand."

"That's not enough. Fuel is way up."

"So make me a counter."

"Fifteen," Dan said.

"Done."

"I'll find out today about landing on the playa. We can leave whenever you want. Only during daylight hours, though. Sunup is at six."

"How long is the trip?"

"About an hour."

"Let's leave at ten," Slater said. "Where's your plane?"

"Upland."

"That's halfway to freaking Giant Rock. I might as well drive. Can you pick me up somewhere closer to civilization? There's an airport in El Monte."

"I can't pick up passengers there."

"What if you say that I'm not a passenger?" Slater said. "Tell them I'm your employee."

"That could work. You could pose as a maintenance guy. If you wear coveralls, nobody will think you're a passenger, just that you're taking a ride to check out the aircraft."

"I can do that."

"Go to a hardware store," Dan said. "You can buy

coveralls there. Get dark ones, not white. I'll put your name on the list. They'll want to see your ID at the airport."

They finalized the details, and Slater ended the call.

Sitting up, he swiveled to the office safe, an ancient hulking black box in the corner behind his desk. He dialed in the combination and heaved open the door. There was some paperwork inside, but most of the space was packed with money. Lots of clients paid in cash, as they wanted the anonymity it provided—if you were checking up on your cheating spouse, you didn't want to pay the private investigator out of the joint account. He and Max had been smurfing the cash into the bank, but it was a slow process, and there were still lots of bundles of greenbacks.

Pulling out a rack, Slater saw that it was already partially depleted, its currency strap hanging slack. He took three grand, then wrote the date and the details on the accounting envelope:

Slater –3G

Thinking about it, he was already close to underwater on this job. He needed to get more dough from Truax. And going to the airport in disguise was shady as fuck.

Closing the safe, he spun the dial to reset the wheels, then rose and tucked the cash into his jeans. Standing in the middle of his office for a moment, he stretched his back and stared absently at his desk and the plaster statue of Pollux with his horse. The corresponding statue of Castor sat on Pike's desk. Sweet beautiful Pike. Their narrative complex had turned his life upside down, changed everything, in the best possible way. They had a groove now, a real bond—to the point that he was comfortable asking Pike to do illicit things like disposing of stray dynamite.

It was too late in the day to track down Truax, as he'd already be gone from his office. He could do one more local UFO visit—*Saucers over the Southwest* described a site that wasn't far away, next to the bridge on Hyperion, where a saucer had come down and parked so that its occupants could talk to a guy. But that would just be a distraction. He should go to his house, and stay there, and get hammered. His deal with Pike, the sex rules, was that he could hook up with other guys when Pike was out of town. But that didn't mean he should.

He tried to picture it the other way around, if Anton or some random guy was pawing Pike and trying to get with him. The thought was infuriating. Rolling open his desk drawer, he pulled out the thin blue book that Pike had made him read. It was a twelve-step book for sex addicts.

Still standing next to his desk, Slater briefly flipped through it, and paused at the heading for "Compulsive Sex." "Compulsive sex is a drug we use to escape from feelings like anger and self-hatred," it said. For Slater it was exactly the opposite—sex made him less angry. And he definitely didn't hate himself. That was about other people.

"Addicts find it difficult to distinguish between love and sex," was another line that caught his eye. He already knew that difference: Pike was love and sex; other guys were just for sex.

"Fuck it," he muttered, and tossed the book in his drawer, and rolled it closed. Maybe he was an addict, and maybe he was compulsive, but nobody was going to get hurt.

The bar where he'd met Truax was just a few blocks away, almost on the way to his house. The clientele were mostly white guys. He knew other places that were more diverse, but they were farther away. In this place, if he stood out a little, it might even give him an advantage.

He found a street space around the corner and backed the Thunderbird in. It was well into the evening, but the sun was still out, low in the west, and it was still hot.

Slater hustled up the stairs and stepped inside. The place was busy, considering it was a weeknight. Most of the talent was in small groups, sitting at tables or at the bar. Why would anyone come to a place like this with other people? It dramatically reduced the likelihood of meeting new guys. If they wanted to hang out with their friends, they should join a damn book club. The booze would be a lot cheaper.

At the service area near the end of the bar, Slater ordered a Corona, and paid for it, and stood surveying the room. A guy came up to the service area and waited for the bartender, bracing himself on the bar with both hands. He looked to be the same bland Anglo type as Truax, with the same long straight hair. His capri pants revealed pleasing musculature.

The guy must have felt his gaze, as he looked up, and tucked his hair behind his ear, and said, "Hello."

"Are you here to chat with your friends," Slater said, raising his voice over the house music, "or are you here to meet people?"

He chuckled. "Both, maybe. Does it matter?"

"I want to meet someone and get out of here before I have to buy another drink."

"You don't mess around. What's your name?"

"Slater," he said, and watched as the guy paid for his beer.

"I'm Otis." He stepped closer and tapped the neck of his bottle on Slater's. "Why don't you just use a hookup app?"

"The problem there is that if you can host, you get a lot of homeless people."

"That's unfortunate."

Slater shrugged. "Homeless people need sex too. I'm just tired of it. It would be nice to fuck someone who's not going to steal from me. You look like you have a job."

"That doesn't mean I won't steal from you."

"It might be worth it." He looked him over. "You're pretty hot."

"What about that ring on your finger?" Otis said, raising his eyebrows.

He rubbed it with the tip of his thumb. "I have a permission slip."

"Where do you live?"

"Not far. The first exit off the 101 once you're past the four-level."

"I haven't been here very long. I'm kind of hanging out with my friends."

"You need to make up your mind, Otis. If you're busy, I need to move on to other options."

"Such a hard-ass." He guzzled from his beer bottle. "It's actually kind of a turn-on. Can I kiss you first? That might be the deciding factor."

Slater leaned in, and grasped his bicep, and met his mouth. Warm and firm, it had the yeasty taste of beer. Otis instinctively worked his tongue, and didn't chomp or prod like a tyro.

Eventually Otis pulled back. "I'm going to tell my friends I'm leaving."

"Chop-chop," Slater called after him.

There were four other guys at the table he went to, and now they were all eyeing Slater. Taking a swig of his beer, he avoided looking back, and instead surveyed the room.

A minute later, Otis returned. "My friends say you look a little dangerous."

"Of course I do. I'm a brown guy in a white place."

He frowned. "This isn't a white place."

"You don't see it because of your privilege."

Otis waved it away. "They don't think I should leave with you."

"I get it. Safety first. I've got two solutions for you." Slater pulled a business card from his hip pocket. "One, give them this. If you disappear they can take it to the cops. Two, let them track you with your phone. Send them all a location share."

"That's actually brilliant." Otis pulled out his phone and tapped at it. "Let me give them your card."

Slater stifled a sigh and watched as he walked over to the table.

When he came back, Otis said, "Let's roll."

"Finally." Guzzling the last of his beer, Slater set the empty on the bar and followed him down to the street.

"I rode with people so that I could drink," Otis said. "You drove?"

"My car's around the corner."

When they got to the Thunderbird, Slater opened the passenger door for him, then went around to climb in behind the wheel.

"This is quite the car."

Slater frowned as he started the engine. "I know."

"My friends thought you were dangerous, but you didn't ask me if I was dangerous," Otis said.

"You're not." He eyed his side mirror as he pulled into the street.

"How do you know that?"

There were so many things that said this guy was a civilian. Anyone running a con would have studied his business card and memorized it. Otis had barely glanced at it, then went to consult with his friends like he was in middle school. And he hadn't asked even one security-conscious question.

"It's because you have such good manners," Slater said.

He chuckled. "So what do you do? I work at USC."

"Oh, god. I'm so sorry."

"What's wrong with USC?"

Slater braked for a red light and glanced at him. "Corruption scandal after corruption scandal after corruption scandal. And then, wait for it, another scandal. It must be embarrassing. Hold up, was that another scandal? I'm sure it's hard to look people in the eye. Plus if you walk two blocks from that manicured campus, outside those gilded gates, you'd see what reality was. It's not all white folks and designer sweatpants and lavender macarons like on the inside."

"I'm not cut off from reality. There's lots of minorities in the student body."

"Rich kids from Red China and black kids for the sports teams. And that thing where you get to slide in because your daddy's an alumnus—you know that's just a way to keep Jewish kids out, right?"

"You're kind of an asshole, you know that?" Otis said.

"I know. I thought you were into that."

"Maybe if we just don't talk."

Exiting the freeway, Slater drove into his neighborhood, and nosed into his garage.

"Nice house for a man without privilege," Otis said. "There's not many like this in the barrio around campus."

"I didn't build it. Some idiot gentrifiers did."

Slater led him up to the bedroom. Otis's pique had faded, he saw, replaced by a glint of anticipation in his eye.

"So what are we doing?" Slater said. "You want the hard-ass treatment?"

He took a breath. "I don't mind it a little rough."

"I've got handcuffs."

His eyebrows shot up. "Not that rough. And no pain. Just, you know, be a man."

Slater nodded. "That, I can do."

He sat on the side of the bed to untie his boots, and Otis quickly got undressed.

"Leave the jeans on for a minute," Otis said, as Slater pulled his shirt off.

The guy was completely naked now, and already getting chubby. Slater pulled his boots off but not his jeans, then reached for Otis's arm and pulled him down beside him.

Caressing his body, he explored Otis's smooth skin, and squeezed his cock, and mouthed his neck. The guy was really into his pants, running his hands over his ass and sliding them into his pockets and under his belt.

Otis sighed and tilted his head back. Running his fingers into his hair, Slater relished the feeling of it between his fingers. He climbed up to straddle him, feeling his woody beneath him through his jeans, and kneaded his pecs. They weren't huge, but they were real.

"You know what comes next, right?" Slater said.

"You're going to fuck me?"

He'd figured that's what the guy wanted, but he didn't want to have to ask.

"I'm going to make you scream."

"Can you leave the jeans on?"

Slater popped his fly and pulled out his cock. Otis took hold of it and stroked him as he leaned over to the bedside table and grabbed lube and a condom.

"A condom?" Otis said. "Is it 2007 again? Why aren't you on PrEP?"

Slater frowned as he rolled it on. "That works for HIV, but not all the other STDs. It's not going to matter to you anyway. You won't be able to tell the difference."

Leaning in to kiss him, Slater slid his hand between his legs, and worked his way into him. Shifting his knee up, he penetrated him, eliciting a gasp. Otis craned to meet his mouth, and reached down to grab Slater's belt, pulling him closer.

As he built up to pounding him, Otis winced and yelped. That reaction was a turn-on, and combined with Eustace having primed the pump earlier in the day, he quickly climaxed, straining into him. Once he was spent, Slater stretched out beside him, and tossed the condom on the floor, and grabbed Otis's cock.

"That was amazing," Otis said.

"I wish I'd been able to go longer. It's because you're so beautiful."

He chuckled. "You've got game."

"What do you want me to do here?"

"Smoke me?"

Slater shifted down the bed.

"Can you lie the other way?" Otis said. "And button your jeans."

Rolling on his back, he took a moment to button his fly and buckle his belt, then moved onto his side and took him into his mouth. Otis wrapped his arms around his butt and kneaded his thighs, pressing his face into his crotch. The guy was really hard, and Slater worked him, feeling Otis's teeth nibbling his now flaccid junk through the denim.

Slater thrust his crotch into his face, and that did it — Otis climaxed, arching his back and yelping.

Slater shifted onto his back, and folded his arm over his eyes, catching his breath, feeling his mind start to sink toward unconsciousness. He could feel Otis's hot breath on his thigh, even through the denim. It was like the guy couldn't get close enough to the fabric. Eventually Otis got up, and the sound of the shower came. He'd have to throw him out, most likely, but he didn't seem like the type to try to steal anything.

That stupid twelve-step book said meaningless sex left you feeling empty. He tried to focus on that. Is that how he felt right now? There was some truth in it, maybe. It didn't feel the same as it did with Pike—it wasn't as intense, or as intoxicating. But Pike wasn't here.

SIXTEEN

WAKING EARLY, SLATER GOT dressed, in a fresh pair of jeans, after that guy had mauled yesterday's. Upstairs he made half a pot of coffee and slurped down a steaming mugful. In the garage he pulled on his gardening coveralls, in a functional flat shade of navy, and his blue ball cap. He wasn't going to be wearing the coveralls all day, but he wanted to bring them back, so he grabbed a small red toolbox and emptied the tools onto the workbench.

El Monte was straight east on the freeway, and he soon pulled up in front of the aviation business that Cappy Dan had told him to use. He took his sunglasses and hung them on his shirt—he knew he'd need them out in the desert.

Inside the business, a guy came out to the counter when he approached.

"I should be on the roster," Slater said, and handed over his driver's license.

The guy briefly put it on the glass bed of a scanner and closed the lid, pulling it out again once bright light had flashed around the edges. He peered at his computer screen.

"I got you," he said finally. "You're good to go." He handed his ID back and eyed him. "Is Tran having trouble with his plane?"

"Who's Tran?" Slater frowned. "I'm here for Cappy Dan."

"People call him Cappy Dan. I call him Tran because that's his name. We have the cultural connection."

"You're both pilots."

"We're both Vietnamese."

Slater nodded. "Got it."

"So what's wrong with the 172? I know he had the carburetor overhauled a month or so ago. The inspector didn't give him any choice. Is it the fuel system?"

"I won't know until I've had a chance to look it over."

His brow furrowed. "I guess it's none of my business."

"Is he here yet?"

"He's due any minute," the guy said, and gestured to the back door.

It led onto the tarmac, and Slater walked out. It was already hot, and the coveralls made it warmer. He set down the empty red toolbox, and pulled off his ball cap, and ran a hand through his sweaty hair.

There was just one runway, stretching toward the horizon. A couple of private jets were parked at the far end of it, in front of a hangar, and closer to this end were several propeller planes arranged in a neat line, their wingtips anchored to the ground with rope. A small aircraft appeared above the far end of the runway, growing larger and losing altitude until it touched down and taxied toward him. Even idling, its engine was loud.

Painted white with a red stripe down the side, it had a single prop, the wings a flat line over the cabin, and tricycle-style landing gear. It pulled up nearby, and the engine died. Slater walked over.

The guy who climbed out was wearing jeans and a blue short-sleeved shirt. In his fifties, maybe, he was rake thin, and basically fuckable. Cappy Dan was wearing the same blue ball cap that Slater was.

Dan pointed to it and beamed. "We're baseball twins."

"I wore it because I'm an aircraft mechanic," Slater said.

He laughed. "You look the part. Come over and stand by the engine. Act like you're talking about it."

With their backs to the aviation business, Slater stood with him next to the propeller. He could feel heat radiating from the engine block, and heard the *tick-tick-tick* of metal parts cooling off.

Dan waved his arm at the engine, then at the wing. "In case anybody's watching," he said in a low voice.

"Do you want to pop the hood? It would be more convincing."

"That's not easily done. I'd have to loosen the bolts. We'd be here for a while. We can just talk."

"Why does your airplane have wheel pants?" Slater said, gesturing to the teardrop-shaped covers on the wheels.

"They're aerodynamic. The landing gear doesn't retract, so the fairing reduces drag. It saves fuel."

"That actually makes sense. On cars they're just for style."

Dan frowned. "I've never seen wheel pants on a car."

"Then you haven't seen any really good cars."

"It's been long enough," he said. "Let's hop in."

Slater waited for him to climb in and open the passenger door for him. He set the toolbox on the floor behind the seats, then pulled on the headphones that hung on the back of the seat. He adjusted the mike so it rested close to his mouth, then pulled on his sunglasses.

Cappy Dan adjusted his headphones too, then fired up the engine, and taxied toward the runway. Slater could hear both sides of his staccato radio conversation with the controller, but it was hard to parse. Dan lined up the aircraft with the long white stripes down the middle of the runway, striated at this end with countless black tire marks, and gunned the engine. It grew even louder, and soon they were in the air.

Once they were away from the airport, Dan said, "We're going north. Around Big Bear. The Gorgonio Pass is just too busy."

"You're the pilot."

"You owe me some money."

Slater unzipped his coveralls, down to his crotch, and dug in the pocket of his jeans for his wad of cash. He counted out the bills and handed them over.

"Sweet, sweet lettuce," Dan said, tucking them away. "I love you all-cash guys. Max is the same way. He's a friend of yours?"

"My business partner."

They chatted some more, with Cappy Dan frequently interrupting to talk on the radio. He stuck close to the mountains, explaining it was so that he could avoid all the air traffic at the airports in the Inland Empire. They flew over the Cajon Pass, with the freeway snaking far below them, then east again, with the San Bernardino Mountains on Slater's side.

From this side of the mountains the Mojave stretched into the distance. The land was mostly dull reddish brown, dotted with brush and scarred by roads. Mountain ranges broke up the landscape, interspersed with playas, the ancient lakebeds still white with alkali residue.

When the nose of the aircraft dipped and they started to descend, Cappy Dan pointed out the window.

"There's your event."

Several long rows of vehicles were lined up at the base of a rocky hill, and a couple of light aircraft were parked nearby. One very large boulder at the center had a chunk broken off. That was Giant Rock. There were a couple of trucks parked near it, and portable toilets on the other side, and lots of people around.

"This isn't really a runway," Dan said, as they passed the gathering and descended toward the playa.

"The planes that are parked down there managed it," Slater said. "You can land anywhere. The playa's flat."

"I know what I'm doing."

He didn't sound very confident about it, Slater thought, but he held his tongue.

Dan flew over the playa, gradually losing altitude, and eventually turned back toward Giant Rock. When he touched down on the sandy alkali, the ground felt a lot rougher under the wheels than it looked. He taxied toward the event and stopped some distance from where the other planes were parked.

"Wait a second, and I'll kill the engine," Dan said.

Once he had, Slater pulled off his headphones. From the ground he could see that two of the vehicles parked near the rock were food trucks. Over by the airplanes, someone in a green spandex body suit with big almond-shaped alien eyes stood facing them. The figure raised its arm and slowly waved.

"It looks like you're in for a good old time," Cappy Dan said.

Slater grabbed his toolbox and climbed out. It was blast-furnace hot, at least a hundred degrees, but it was dry too, so it didn't feel oppressive. Even with his sunglasses on, the brilliant Mojave daylight on the white surface of the playa made him squint. He'd walked most of the way to where the airplanes were parked when Cappy Dan started his engine. Slater looked back to see him accelerating down the playa, the plane soon rising into the air.

As he approached the event, Slater walked around the edge of it, behind the cars, avoiding the crowd of people, in a long arc toward the food trucks. There were a couple of water stations near them and an array of picnic tables. As he approached the trucks, a man's voice called out, "Did someone call a plumber?"

Slater looked over. The guy was sitting at one of the picnic tables. Wearing round sunglasses, he had his natty dreads bundled behind his head. He briefly raised his hand in greeting.

Both food trucks had a few people waiting nearby for their orders, but nobody was behind them, in the space between the trucks and the boulders of the hillside, echoing with the rumble of the trucks' generators. In the temporary privacy of the spot, Slater stripped off his coveralls and stuffed them into the toolbox. When he walked out again, he went over to the picnic table with the guy who had catcalled him.

"Aren't you the plumber?" he said as Slater approached. "Sir, you're out of uniform."

"Funny."

Up close the guy wasn't bad looking, fuckable even, with a few days' stubble on his dark skin.

"I'm looking for Olivia Howard," Slater said. "Have you seen her around?"

"She spoke earlier. Her and the Neaploia board are in that RV over there, but you can't go in. It's a closed-door meeting."

Slater huffed and set the toolbox on the ground, then briefly pulled off his ball cap and mopped his brow.

"They won't be too long," the guy said. "At least there's tacos while you wait. Seriously, why were you dressed like a plumber?"

Slater put his hands on his hips and jutted his chin. "You know why."

He sat up and furrowed his brow. "It's a disguise? They followed you? Fuck me."

A woman stepped up next to him, wearing a straw hat

and a billowy cotton dress with long sleeves. She put a hand on the guy's shoulder. "What's going on?"

"This is the plumber," the guy said. "This is Yu-Lin. I'm Darwin." Turning to look up at her, he added, "Goons from the Navy have been following him."

"Not anymore," Slater said. "I'm pretty sure I lost them before I got to the airport."

"It's good to know the disguise worked," Darwin said.

Slater stooped and lifted his toolbox. "Can I leave this here? I don't really want to carry it around."

"Put it under the table," Darwin said. "Nobody will bother it."

"There's nothing in it worth stealing."

Once he'd set the toolbox down, Slater walked away. It was hard to estimate the size of the gathering, but there were at least a few hundred people, based on the number of bodies and the dozens of cars. In the distance dust billowed on the road leading in as more vehicles came and others left.

The rock was the size of an office building, and he walked around it. On the side facing the playa was a stage for Olivia and the other lecturers—a flatbed truck parked next to the rock, with a mike stand on the back, and big speakers aimed outward.

Not far from the flatbed, a dozen people in lawn chairs sat in a wide circle. There were other people standing outside the group, but not within the circle. Olivia had said Neaploia was multiethnic, and he could see that in this group. They skewed older, but two or three of them might be under thirty. One of the people in the chairs, a guy wearing a floppy canvas hat, pointed to the sky and said, "Right there. Forty degrees."

The others all turned to look, with laughter and oohs and aahs. Slater looked up at the sky. It was cloudless today, the usual rich blue of the high desert, but he couldn't see anything in it. He stepped over to stand next to a woman wearing a wide straw hat and big dark glasses.

"What are they seeing?" Slater said.

"It's the great summoning." Her tone was hushed. "They'll be doing it all day." She glanced at him, then did a double-take. "Are you the guy who got dropped off in an airplane?"

"I drove in." Slater gestured vaguely. "My car's over there. So they're psychically calling the space brothers?"

"They're manifesting UFOs. Not everyone agrees that it's aliens. Some think they're transdimensional beings, or cryptoterrestrials. The feds call it 'nonhuman intelligence' in all their documentation." She gestured toward the circle. "This could also just be a shared archetype experience."

"Is that another word for 'delusion'?"

Someone in the circle pointed at the sky and shouted "There," and all the heads swiveled in that direction.

"There's no delusion," she said. "If you get yourself into the same state of mind, you'll start to see them too. Grab a lawn chair."

Looking toward where the person had pointed, all he could see was a jet vapor trail. "I know what that is, at least. A planeload of earthlings from Boston or New York headed to LAX."

SEVENTEEN

S LATER STRODE TOWARD WHERE all the vehicles were parked. Fronting the first row was a line of vendor booths. One was selling books, and another had cosplay masks and the stretchy green bodysuit he'd seen someone wearing when he landed. Another booth had toy flying saucers and plastic alien figurines and crystals.

The woman staffing the booth wore a broad-brimmed canvas hat, and watched him perusing the wares, a smile on her face.

Slater held up a purple hexagonal crystal. "Do these work against cryptoterrestrials?"

"They actually will," she said, and stepped closer. "That one specifically will keep your energy integrated, so you can resist psychic attacks. It also helps you communicate with the nurturing entities, not just avoid the negative ones."

"Good to know."

The next stand had an array of electronic devices, including one that looked like a voltage meter with an old-school needle gauge. Next to it was a tray of black boxes, similar in shape to the one he'd found in Finley's apartment, but slightly longer. Picking one up he saw that it had no markings, and a lone computer port on one side.

Slater gestured with it to the vendor, a sweaty guy in a white T-shirt. "What's this?"

"That there is a primo UFO detector."

"How does it work?"

"You connect it to a computer," he said, "and download the software that works with it. It scans a whole range of frequencies for anomalies. An alarm sounds on your computer if it senses saucers or aliens."

A woman standing nearby gestured for the clerk, and he stepped over to talk to her. Slater set the box down and walked back toward the picnic tables, over by the boulders and the food trucks.

Yu-Lin, the woman he'd talked to before, was lounging at a table, and waved at him. Darwin wasn't with her now.

As he approached, Yu-Lin said, "Hey, plumber—are you drinking water?"

"Good idea," he said, and changed direction. At the water station he filled a plastic cup, then carried it back to the picnic table, and sat across from her.

"You have to keep hydrated," Yu-Lin said. "It's so dead here. It's the most lifeless place I've ever seen. Like the moon or something."

Slater frowned. "Nothing's growing on the playa, but everywhere else there's creosote bush. As far as the eye can see."

"Those dried out stick things? They seem sad. Like they're barely holding on."

"It depends on your perspective. They're happy here because they're adapted to the climate. Dozens of insects and rodents and lizards make use of them. They're like little desert apartment buildings. The first people used them to treat all sorts of health issues."

"You sound like a scientist," she said. "Compared to the cities, you have to admit this place is pretty dead."

"That seems narrow-minded for someone at a flying saucer convention." Slater sipped his water. "You have to meet the Mojave where it's at, not where you're at.

See it for what it is."

"You're saying I'm biased."

"I'm saying it'll be worth your while. Free your mind."

"I'm not sure I need lifestyle advice from a plumber," Yu-Lin said.

"Do you know Olivia Howard?"

She sat up. "I heard her speak today. She's brilliant. But I never met her."

"What about a guy named Finley López?"

"I don't know that name."

Slater pulled out his phone, and found a photo of Finley, and turned the screen toward her.

"I've never seen him before. Are you a contactee?"

"I'm not." He tucked his phone away. "I'm just doing some research."

"You know what they say about the phenomenon. If you stare at it long enough, don't be surprised if it stares back."

"Has it stared at you?"

Yu-Lin held out her arm and pushed up her sleeve. "Look at these."

He leaned in to peer at where she was pointing. There were a couple of small red marks on the inside of her forearm.

"Mosquito bites?" Slater said. "You must have brought them with you. There's no mosquitoes around here."

"They're scoop marks." She pushed her sleeve down. "When they abduct me, they take samples."

"Ouch."

"I have an implant too."

"Just one?" Slater frowned and studied her chest. "They look pretty symmetrical. In LA they say you don't want a passing grade. It looks like you went with a solid B. You could have gone bigger. I guess there's some value in not overdoing it."

"Not breast implants, you weirdo. An alien implant. In my leg. It's about this big." She held her fingers half an inch apart. "I tried to go after it once, but it sensed the scalpel and burrowed deeper."

"What's the implant for?"

"I assume they're monitoring me." She briefly pulled down her sunglasses to meet his gaze. "If you're here, and you're studying the phenomenon, you probably have one too."

"I've never been abducted," Slater said.

"Not that you remember, anyway. Have you ever found divots in your skin in the morning? Or a lump that you can't explain?" She waved a hand and spoke intently. "They're messing with us."

"I thought there was no agreement about whether it was aliens or some shared psychological thing about archetypes."

Yu-Lin raised her eyebrows. "It's aliens, plumber." She waggled her fingers. "Show me your palm."

Slater held out his hand, and Yu-Lin lifted her handbag onto the table, and dug around for a glasses case, and snapped it open. Both lenses had thick loupes, like the ones Svetlana used to peer at electronics. She traded her sunglasses for them, then took hold of his palm, and studied it, wiping it a couple of times with her thumb. Finally she pulled the glasses off.

"I'm sorry to be the one to tell you, but you've got the fibers."

"What fibers?"

"Plastic fibers growing out of your skin. It's called Morgellons disease."

Slater rubbed his palms together and frowned. "You actually saw that?"

"There's blue and green fibers. They're smaller than hairs, and they grow straight out like bristles. Morgellons is common among people who've been abducted."

Darwin stepped up and greeted Slater, and sat beside Yu-Lin, and set a cardboard tray on the table. It bore half a dozen tacos.

"He's got Morgellons," she said.

"Oh, dude." Darwin's face fell. "How bad is it?"

"Stage one or two," Yu-Lin said, and scooped up a taco.

"We're doing an abductee support circle later today," Darwin said. "You should sit in." He waved at the tacos and picked one up. "Chow down, bud."

Slater absently ran his thumb over his palm. He couldn't feel anything like bristles. "You know, in the early days this was fun. People like Olivia got free rides in flying saucers. She got to visit Venus. Now it's people disappearing and scoop marks and bristle fibers."

"Aliens are different now," Darwin said, through a mouthful of food. "So has the Navy ever interrogated you, or just surveilled you?"

He took a breath. He probably shouldn't have told him that. "I never really talked to any of them."

"They took me in a couple of times," Darwin said, gesturing with his half-eaten taco. "For temporary detention."

"The Navy did that?"

"Well, they said they were police detectives, and they flashed police badges, but I knew who they really were. They used the excuse that my roommate was a fugitive from justice, but I knew what they were doing."

"Was your roommate really on the lam?"

"Sure," Darwin said, "but it was nothing to do with me. It turned out he was in Belize trying to avoid the U.S. cops. They got him anyway." He waved to dismiss it. "So these fake cops had me in this little interview room at the police station."

"Was it a fake police station," Slater said, "or a real one?"

"It's the one the police use. In Hollywood."

"On Wilcox?"

"That's the place. I guess the real police let them use it. So you know how those interview rooms have a one-way mirror so that somebody can watch from outside?"

Slater folded his arms. "Sure."

"Well, I'm answering all their phony questions about my roommate, and then I stood up. But no one was expecting me to do that. Just for a split second, reflected in the glass, I caught a glimpse of one. It was standing in the corner of the room by the door."

"One what?"

Darwin held his gaze. "Aliens. One of them was in the room observing my interrogation. It didn't expect me to stand up, so it wasn't prepared."

"They're invisible?"

"It's some kind of cloaking technology that conceals them," Yu-Lin said. "But obviously not if you move fast and have a big mirror."

Slater watched her for a moment as she bit into a taco. "I'm going to let you two eat."

Rising, he walked away. In *Saucers over the Southwest,* strange things happened to silence people, but these stories were even weirder. Yu-Lin's scoop marks were right on the edge of believable, but it was awfully hard to accept that Darwin was so important that the Navy would impersonate the police just to interview him. The more reasonable explanation was that the pair of them were reality-adjacent but not quite fully immersed in it, not quite clear on what was really happening around them. He absently massaged his palm with his thumb. No way was he going to check himself for plastic fibers.

The door to the RV was still closed, with no one

around it, so he wandered back over to the row of vendors. At the T-shirt stand he dug through the merchandise. Most of the designs were colorful silk-screens of aliens and saucers. The vendor was sitting in the shade, on the rear bumper of a van parked just behind the stand, and he rose and stepped closer. Wearing a Panama hat and cargo shorts, his tight T-shirt bore an image of a speeding flying saucer leaving a trail of smoke. His arms were well muscled, and he had great pecs.

Slater gestured to his chest. "You're your own best advertising, Butch."

"The name is Clyde. You like the design?"

"I like your body. If I had pecs like that I wouldn't even wear a shirt."

His brow furrowed. "Is that all you see? Like I'm a piece of meat?"

"Of course I noticed what a delightful and engaging personality you have," Slater said, "and I can't help but sense the depth of your intelligence, and your boundless compassion. But your taste in recherché fashion outshines them all. I suppose you wear your shirt that tight so that people won't notice your tits."

"That sounds like an insult," Clyde said, "and yet it also sounds like a pickup line."

He raised his eyebrows. "Is it working? I'll smoke you right now."

"Are you one of those sex addicts you hear about?"

Slater put his hands on his hips. "Do you want the blow job or not?"

Clyde scoffed. "Saucer people." He looked around. "It's slow right now. We can do something like that." He called to the woman in the next booth. "Can you watch my stuff?"

Gesturing with his chin for Slater to follow, he stepped back to the side door of the van and climbed in. There was only one row of seats up front, with the cargo space laden with tubs of garments. There was still room in back to stretch out. The only light came from the windshield.

Slater pulled off his sunglasses and knelt on the floor. "It's too damn hot in here."

"Let me get the air blowing."

Moving to the driver's seat, Clyde started the engine, and soon cool air was blowing from the vents. When Clyde came back, he pulled off his hat, revealing his buzz-cut scalp.

"This doesn't happen to me very often," he said.

"I find that hard to believe, Butch. You're a total smoke show."

Kneeling behind him, Slater ran his hands over his chest, and down to his pants, grasping for his junk. Clyde was already getting wood. He turned to him, and unbuckled Slater's belt, and popped his fly, massaging his cock. Slater unzipped Clyde's cargo shorts and pulled out his cock, then went down on him.

Clyde groaned and shifted position, taking hold of Slater's cock and then taking him into his mouth. They brought each other closer, Slater working him intently, and in a moment Clyde came, arching his back. Slater climaxed soon after, then rolled onto his back and folded his arm over his eyes.

Once he'd caught his breath, Clyde said, "I have to get back to work."

Slater reached for his fly, and buttoned it, and sat up. "It's comfortable in here now."

"So are you going to buy a T-shirt?"

He chuckled and stepped out, then walked back toward the flatbed truck with the speakers. A woman with a lanyard around her neck was standing nearby, and Slater approached her.

"Is the board meeting still going on?"

"It must be," she said. "I haven't seen anyone come out."

She walked away, and Slater stood for a minute, looking over the summoning circle. They were still at it, one participant or another intermittently pointing up at the sky.

He could feel eyes on him, and looking around, he spotted a guy standing with his arms folded, a scruffy beard and long hair bundled back, his dark wrap-around sunglasses pushed up on his head. Wearing a coarse linen shirt and grubby jeans, he was glaring at Slater.

"Have you got a looking problem?" Slater demanded.

The guy scoffed. "I thought you weren't supposed to acknowledge your target."

"You're not my target. I don't know you. But you look like you're about to punch me in the face."

"I figured there'd be a few of you here."

"What the fuck are you talking about?" Slater demanded.

"Keep walking," he said, and louder, "Tell your handlers I'm not doing anything."

The guy was tall, and built thick, and if he knew how to fight, he could definitely take Slater. He looked like he might actually have that skill. But it was so hard to resist the urge to mix it up. In his youth the shrinks had spent years trying to talk it out of him, that instinct, the perfectly rational human urge to punch someone in the face. The shrink work hadn't really stuck, but he knew there was a downside if he acted now—he'd get eighty-sixed from the event before he'd even seen Olivia.

One of the things the shrinks said was "Try to feel empathy," but that was impossible with a crazy person. On the other hand, it was obvious this guy was being irrational, and he could use that instead. He forced himself to walk away, and headed toward the taco truck.

Yu-Lin appeared in his path, and beamed at him. "I saw you met Ralph."

"The hippie?" Slater said, glancing back to where he'd been standing. "He seems especially unbalanced. That's saying a lot in this crowd."

"He thinks you're one of his stalkers."

"Who's he that he has more than one?"

"He was in the Navy," Yu-Lin said, "but they kicked him out. Since then they've sent coordinated teams of people to follow him, watch him, break into his apartment when he's not there. It doesn't matter where he goes, there they are. Usually they're in teams."

"Did he take something with him that he shouldn't have?"

"They don't search his apartment or his vehicle. They just move the furniture around."

Slater took a breath. "Have you ever asked yourself why anyone would do that?"

"It's a psychological operation. They're trying to drive him crazy. When he says, 'I saw a saucer that got retrieved from the seafloor,' the Navy can say, 'He's that crazy guy who thinks someone moved his furniture around.'"

"Do they come to your pad when you're not there and move stuff around?" Slater demanded.

She shrugged. "I'm not saying I completely believe him. But I have a policy of not disbelieving anyone in the saucer world."

"If that's the case, I have a bridge to sell you."

"Ralph's life is hard." Yu-Lin waved an arm. "He stopped at a gas station on the way out here, and he said both clerks were in on it. They'd been assigned to watch him, and hassle him in subtle ways when he walked in to pay for his gas and buy snack treats. He says there's at least five people here today on his stalker detail."

"I guess he thinks I'm number six. Have you ever worked with the Navy, or with the feds, or any government agency?"

"Not really."

"In my experience they can barely handle the work they're legally obligated to do. I'm not buying that they're employing hundreds or thousands of people to harass one hippie."

"But they followed you, right?" she said. "Why not him too? It's just a matter of degree. You and Ralph are in the same boat. You should try to have some empathy. Why are they after you, anyway?"

Before he could answer, Yu-Lin looked past his shoulder, and smiled and called a greeting. Briefly touching his arm, she excused herself, and Slater stepped away, and headed toward the taco truck. Over where the cars were parked, he saw a familiar green SUV pulling in, and altered his course toward it. It was less distinctive now since Pike had swapped the New Mexico tags for Cali ones, but it was still idiosyncratic, scratched and dented and very much an A-to-B ride.

Pike climbed out, and beamed at the sight of him, and pushed his ratty old cowboy hat up on his head so they could embrace.

"I haven't managed to pin down Olivia yet," Slater said when he pulled back. "She's in a meeting."

"Excellent. That means I can mingle with the summoners and the contactees."

"I'm kind of burned out on that already. I'm going to sit on a rock over there."

"I see there's tacos," Pike said, gesturing to the food trucks. "Maybe we'll eat later."

As Slater walked toward the hillside, he saw a couple of other people hanging out among the boulders. Before he started to climb, he went to one of the water stations and drank. While he was refilling his glass, he overheard a guy, wearing a Panama hat and standing a few feet away, talking to a woman in a headscarf and sheer green harem pants.

"I think that guy's a fed."

"The one in the white shirt?" she said.

Pike was wearing white. When Slater glanced at them, sipping his water, they were definitely watching Pike as he made his way toward the summoning circle.

"Don't you think?" the guy said. "Look at the way he's dressed. Is he here to spy on us?"

"Of course they're monitoring this event. I'm just surprised they'd send someone so obvious."

"Maybe he's here to keep an eye on Ralph."

Slater walked to the boulders and made his way up, climbing the rocks until he was above the desert floor, almost as high as the top of Giant Rock. He had a decent view from here, he decided, and found a comfortable place to sit. The circle of summoners was in sight, but Giant Rock obscured the flatbed stage and the RV where the meeting was happening.

He could see Pike wandering around, watching the summoners for a while, and talking to people. The guy was enjoying this, interacting with the saucer-heads. At one point he disappeared behind the rock. That guy at the water station had pegged him as a fed—what would Ralph the hippie do when he saw him?

A while later Pike walked to his vehicle, and opened the lift gate, and pulled out a lawn chair. He went back to the summoning circle, where a couple of the participants shifted their chairs to make room for him. Pike sat between them, and folded his hands over his belly, and rested his head on the back of the chair. When someone pointed at the sky, his head swiveled along with everyone else's.

Slater had to smile. The guy was so game, up for anything. It was incomprehensible to Slater, but he loved that about him.

Shifting position on the boulders, he found a comfortable spot to recline, and pulled off his sunglasses, and folded his arm over his eyes. It was too bright to sleep, but he could chill out for a minute. The heat of the sun actually felt good.

EIGHTEEN

H E MIGHT HAVE SLEPT for a while, Slater realized, and when he sat up, he adjusted his cap and surveyed the crowd below. Pike had moved out of the summoning circle now, and he was standing talking to the hippie. Was the guy going to take a swing at Pike? But as he watched, that wasn't the vibe—the hippie was talking intently, and Pike was engaged with him, nodding at his words. Pike briefly put a hand on his bicep, and a minute later the hippie leaned in for a hug. When they separated, Pike clapped him on the back, and the guy walked away.

"Fuck me," Slater muttered.

Pike wandered over to the row of vendors, and spent a minute checking out the crystals, then talked to Clyde, the shirt guy, and bought a black T-shirt, rolling it into a cylinder once he'd paid for it. He felt a pang of guilt about hooking up with that guy. The little blue book for addicts said you have to admit you're powerless in your compulsion. But that didn't really fit—he wasn't compelled to do things like that. He'd just seized an opportunity.

Andy was a twelve-stepper, at one time addicted to painkillers, and he'd managed to drag Slater to an NA meeting once when he'd been at a low point. Someone at the meeting had said, "Check yourself before you wreck yourself." That was probably good advice, considering the guilt he felt. That book said the same thing—you had to take a fearless moral inventory. But that wasn't going to happen today.

Rising, Slater started to climb down the boulders. It took significantly more concentration than the climb up had, but eventually he was on the ground, and he found Pike, over by the flatbed truck.

"You made a new friend," Slater said as he stepped up.

"Quite a few of them."

"That hippie thinks the feds are gang-stalking him."

"I heard," Pike said. "Poor guy."

"Why didn't he think you were one of the stalkers? You look like a fed right now."

Pike chuckled. "Ralph just needs to be heard. Think about it from his perspective—it feels like we're all gaslighting him, telling him his perceptions aren't real."

"It's not gaslighting if it's true. What shirt did you get?"

He unrolled it to show him. It was black with a gray saucer screen-printed on it, with a green beam emanating below it. A silhouette of a human form was caught in the beam, spread-eagled in midair.

"Sweet," Slater said.

"Someone asked me why I was grinding on the plumber." Pike rolled up the shirt. "She said you showed up in a plumber's outfit with a toolbox."

"Was it Yu-Lin? What a gossip. But she's right, I did kind of do that."

"Can I ask why?"

The door of the RV swung open, and a guy stepped out.

"I'll explain later," Slater said. "Right now I think the big meeting is over."

Following a couple of other people, Olivia stepped down out of the RV, blinking at the bright daylight, and pulled on a straw hat and a pair of oversize sunglasses.

"Finally," Slater said, striding over to her.

She chuckled and briefly embraced him, making an air kiss near his cheek. "Have you eaten?"

They walked over to the food trucks, and Pike said, "You two sit. Let me get some tacos."

Olivia sat on a bench at one of the picnic tables, and Slater sat opposite.

"I'm so glad you could make it," she said. "Isn't this an amazing place?"

"I do love the Mojave."

"This site specifically has an intense energy. No wonder the space brothers were attracted to it."

"They used to hang out here too? Pike said the earthlings did."

"In 1952 a saucer landed on the playa, and the space brothers visited the man who leased the land. He started hosting saucer meet-ups here. Thousands of people attended, but by the 1970s it was mostly bikers that showed up, so they quit doing it. Plus the host died."

"Did he die," Slater said, "or did he move to another planet with the space brothers?"

Olivia chuckled. "I didn't personally see the corpse."

Swinging a leg over the bench, Pike sat next to him and set down a paper tray of tacos.

"I don't remember those rings when we met before," Olivia said. "You're both wearing them."

"We just got them," Pike said, and squeezed Slater around the shoulder. "We're together."

"I wondered about that. At my house I could feel the electricity in the air." Eyeing Pike, she added, "I bet this one is a firecracker."

"He's a lot more than that," he said, briefly resting his palm on Slater's back. "I'd say Slater is dynamite."

Slater munched on a taco. "So what am I doing here?"

"I wanted you to get a sense of our people."

"There's definitely some colorful characters here," Pike said. "We manifested several UFOs."

"Good for you, honey, getting into the spirit of it." She scooped up a taco and took a dainty bite.

"You said you remembered something about Finley," Slater said.

"I did." She dabbed at her lips before she continued. "Finley talked about his sister."

"In what context?"

"At the seminar he told a story. His sister remembered a family UFO incident that he was too young to remember himself. She was several years older than him."

"Interesting," Pike said.

She took another bite of her taco. "Contact events tend to run in families, so Finley's parents and his sister were involved."

Pike gestured with his taco. "Do you think the aliens are interested in specific bloodlines?"

"That's a reasonable hypothesis."

"Did he tell you her name?" Slater said.

"He didn't. But you're a detective—it shouldn't be difficult to find out."

"You could have told me that on the phone."

"Then you wouldn't have seen this beautiful place, these delightful people. You wouldn't have been able to luxuriate in the amazing energy here."

"I'm definitely glad we came," Pike said.

Slater grabbed another taco. "I definitely feel immersed. These people don't seem to have very good boundaries."

"When we're with like-minded people, we can forgo formality," Olivia said.

"It's more than that," Slater said. "I can feel the crazy wearing away at me. Grinding me down. In another few hours I'll be one of these people, digging in my leg for implants or pulling plastic fibers out of my palm."

"Not everyone here has those experiences. You should meet some of the more upbeat contactees. The summoners."

"I sat with them for a while in the circle," Pike said. "Upbeat is the right word. It's like a party but everybody's sober."

After they'd eaten, Olivia rose and excused herself.

"Thanks for spending part of your day with us," Pike said. "I know you have a lot of people to talk to today."

"Of course, dear." She beamed and squeezed his shoulder before she walked off.

"That's what I'd call small-town manners," Slater said.

Pike sat beside him again. "She is a titan in her field. And good manners don't cost anything."

"I get it. Butter up the chumps and they'll let their guard down."

He laughed. "That's another spin on it."

Yu-Lin had been sitting nearby, and she moved to sit across from them.

"Everybody thinks you're a fed," she said to Pike. "Why were you interrogating Olivia? She's a well-respected contactee. You should just read her books. And why are you hanging around with the plumber?"

Pike chuckled. "It sounds like everybody's a little paranoid. I'm not working. I'm here because I'm interested in contactees."

"This is Yu-Lin," Slater said. "She's been on plenty of flying saucers."

She frowned at him. "Not willingly."

"She has an implant."

"Seriously?" Pike said. "Can I see it?"

"I tried to dig it out," she said, "but it burrowed deeper. I think it's right next to the bone now."

"Show him the scoop marks," Slater said.

Yu-Lin pushed up her sleeve, and held out her arm, and Pike leaned in to look closer.

"Do you have any memory of the experience?" he said.

"I went to a hypnotherapist once, and we started to pull some stuff out, but it was too intense." She pushed her sleeve down. "I might do it again sometime, but for now I think I have to leave it to my subconscious to sort out. I always know when it's happened, though, because I wake up with oily black residue on my skin. Right around the clavicles. Two patches about this big." She made a circle with her fingers.

"Did you save it and have it analyzed?" Slater said.

"I wanted to, but there was this strong feeling that I was supposed to wipe it off and throw it away and forget about it. Like a suggestion they'd planted deep in my mind."

"Is it possible you were sleepwalking and sleep-polished your shoes?" Slater said. "One of the tranquilizer meds has that effect. People sleepwalk and commit sleep crimes."

"I wasn't sleepwalking." She frowned at him. "What are you even doing here if you're such a skeptic?"

Pike put a hand on Slater's shoulder. "The plumber has a high bar for evidence."

And a low tolerance for bullshit, Slater thought, but he didn't say that.

Yu-Lin rose. "I should find Darwin. It's almost time for the abductee support session." She eyed Slater intently. "I hope to see you there."

As she walked away, Pike leaned in to kiss his neck. "I was told things heat up here significantly after dark. There's another summoning circle."

"I'm ready to hit the road."

"Let's watch the sunset first."

"It is a pretty damn amazing sight in the desert," Slater said. "But let's walk out on the playa. Away from the crowd."

The sun was already low in the northwest, and he retrieved his toolbox from under the picnic table and put it in Pike's car. As they walked away from the vehicles onto the empty playa, Slater explained why he'd worn coveralls and carried the box.

When it felt like they were far enough out to be alone, they sat down on the sandy alkali ground, and soon the blazing orb descended behind the mountains on the horizon, leaving an orange glow in the sky, and dark blue rising in the east.

"Best event of the day," Slater said.

"We have to wait a few minutes. I want to show you something."

There wasn't much more to see out here, Slater thought, but he didn't ask. He leaned back on his hands and watched the light fading from the sky, the colors shifting from orange to pink. As twilight deepened, stars started to appear.

Eventually Pike dug out his phone and tapped at it. "They should be right over there." He pointed to the horizon, not far from where the sun had disappeared, and checked his phone again, and studied the sky. "That's them. See those two? The only stars in that part of the sky. That's Castor and Pollux."

"Who knew there were stars named after those guys," Slater said. "How did you know where they were?"

"The Navy has a website that tells you all about what's in the sky. Traditionally they needed to know that stuff to navigate on the open ocean."

"Don't drop that name back at Giant Rock. You'll cause a stampede."

Pike chuckled and draped his arm on his shoulder. "Pollux is the one on the left. Those two will be there ten thousand years from now, a million years from now, the same as they are today. No matter what happens to us, they'll be out there burning as bright as my love burns for you."

Slater eyed him for a moment, then looked back at the twinkling points in the twilight. He could feel a lump in his throat.

"If they're following the sun," Slater said, "they're going to disappear soon."

"For now. But just like the sun, you know they're still there. Like the way I feel about you even when we're apart."

Sitting up, Slater punched him on the shoulder.

"Ow." Pike laughed and rubbed his arm. "What was that for?"

"Doris said we'd get through the euphoric stage at some point. Then you go and do something intense and over-the-top like this. I can't stand it. I get this rush. Euphoria. It messes up my heart."

Pike shifted to face him, and met his mouth, and leaned into him. As Slater sank back onto the ground, he pulled Pike down with him, until they were lying together.

"I love you, forty-niner."

Wrapping his arms around his shoulders, Slater squeezed him hard, and nuzzled his neck.

"Forever," Slater said. "Like the stars in the sky."

———•———

IT WAS FULLY DARK by the time they got back to Pike's vehicle. Lots of cars were still here, and the food trucks were brightly lit, and someone had built a fire over by the summoning circle.

Pike drove the several bumpy miles back to the pavement. It was extremely dark out here, with only a small patch of the road ahead visible in the headlights. Pulling out his phone, Slater read about the stars.

"Castor isn't actually one thing—it's a complex system of hot bluish-white type A stars. That sounds exactly like you: hot, complex, type A. Pollux is a singular yellow-orange giant." He looked over at him. "Does that sound like anyone you know?"

Pike chuckled. "In the mythology they were brothers, but I like the way we do things better."

Slater tucked his phone away. "I spent the whole day out here just to get one very simple piece of information. Finley has a sister."

"You also got immersed in the vibe of his community. Maybe that counts as useful background information. I think Olivia thought of it that way."

"That's a positive way to look at it. You were totally enjoying those people."

"A lot. They have such wild ideas. It reminds me of a college campus. All the creative energy. I always learn a lot too."

"Like what?" Slater demanded.

"Well, the phenomenon is shifting. Historically it was about benevolent space brothers, then by the nineties it was about the grays and the reptilians. They're sinister at worst and at best indifferent and morally ambiguous. Today I can see a shift from witnesses to experiencers. They're not just seeing saucers—more people are meeting aliens, doing stuff with them. I guess it's a natural progression."

"Did you actually see UFOs in the summoning circle?"

"I think if you look hard enough," Pike said, "you can see anything. There's some element of contagion to it.

Somebody says, 'There's one,' and other people want to see it so bad that they see it too."

"I'm worried now I might have a tracking implant," Slater said. "Or Morgellons disease."

Pike laughed. "I'd bet cash money that you don't have either."

"What about Yu-Lin? Do you believe she gets abducted and they leave black goo on her when they put her back?"

"It's like so much of what's going on in the field. It's an interesting story."

"But is it true?"

"Maybe some version of it is. I want to be open-minded about people's experiences."

Slater thought about that. "As long as you're not so open-minded that your brain falls out."

NINETEEN

I N THE MORNING SLATER woke to find Pike already
gone. The drive home had involved a pit stop at the
airport in El Monte to collect his car, and they'd
crashed as soon as they got in. The desert sun had baked
the energy out of him, desiccated his ambition, but he
knew he needed to shake it off.

Forcing himself to sit up, he texted Andy:

I'm coming over.

Once he'd dressed, and had coffee and some carbs,
he headed down to the garage. Andy's response came as
he was climbing into the Thunderbird:

That's fine. I'm here.

Slater scoffed as he fired up the engine. What a dick
to gatekeep him like that. He parked in the surface lot
behind Andy's building, and when he got upstairs, Andy
pulled open the door and waved him in, and dropped
into his desk chair.

"Whoa." Andy's eyebrows shot up. "What's with the
bling? Show me that."

Slater huffed but stepped closer and extended his
hand. Grasping it in his unsteady wavering grip, Andy
looked over the gold band and cracked a smile.

"It's beautiful."

"I didn't do anything stupid like you did. It's just a
symbol."

"The circle means eternity," Andy said. "The promise that your ... love will last forever."

"Like the stars in the sky. It's a sweet story. In the real world love stories usually end badly. Even when they don't, they always end."

"Such a cynic. I bet it was Pike's idea."

"You'd win that bet." Slater waved a hand. "When you dug into Finley López, was there any indication that he had a sister?"

His brow furrowed. "I remember there was a POD on his ... bank accounts. I'm not sure who it was for. I still ... have that stuff. I can check." He swiveled to his computer screens and pulled on his black plastic gauntlets. They looked unwieldy and confining but they functioned as an input device that compensated for Andy's lack of fine motor control.

"What's a POD?"

"Payable on death," Andy said. "You can do that with your ... accounts—name a beneficiary, so that it's not treated like ... the rest of your estate. It doesn't have to ... go through probate."

He peered at the screen, flicking through a series of what looked like bank statements.

"Finley's beneficiary is Hera López," he said finally. "Same last name, and Hera is ... a woman's name, right? It could be his ... wife, or his mom, but it could be a sister."

"What a stupid fucking name for a kid," Slater said. "Who would do that?"

"Wasn't Hera the ... queen of the gods?"

"She was also a vindictive hard-ass. She hated the Trojans—she basically started the Trojan War. I would not want to run into her in a dark alley."

Andy chuckled. "Hera López's parents probably ... didn't know that."

"I guess they didn't have access to an internet search either, or a library. Or maybe they were just morons."

"How do you know so much about Hera?"

"Pike," Slater said. "When we met he was reading about Greek mythology, so we read *The Iliad* together. Now we're on *The Odyssey*. It's a version with dumbed-down explanations so I can figure out what the hell is going on. But it still covers all the action."

"Sweet." He grinned. "It's like your couple hobby, now that you're … a boring couple, with the rings and all."

"It's more like another curling tendril in our red-hot multidimensional narrative complex. It's so intricate and singular that it can't be expressed with mathematical formulas. I can't even point out certain parts of it because it's in a direction that you can't point."

"Because your emotions are … so much more profound than anyone else's," Andy said.

He threw up his hands. "See? You totally get it."

Andy laughed. "I like you, Slater. Even when you … talk trash. It's part of your unique charm."

"Lo, he likes me. Just not in his bed." He grabbed his crotch. "You used to like this, back in the day. You couldn't keep your paws off it."

"You stood up with me at my wedding," Andy said. "Things are different now. Focus on that ring on your finger."

Slater watched him for a moment. "Bye, beautiful," he said, and walked out.

The drive to his office went fast, as it was still early, and the traffic was moving. The lights were off when he got upstairs. He clicked his tongue to greet Rey, and checked to make sure Max's office was empty, then sat at his desk. A search for Hera López brought up all the usual dross, but sifting through it, she didn't seem to have any social media accounts, at least not using that name.

The name came up in a news article, from over a year ago, about a youth group art exhibition. The list of attendees at the opening included "Hera López and her husband." The source was legit, it seemed—a neighborhood news site that mostly published community notices and updates. The art exhibition had been at the Tweedy Boulevard Temple. Slater knew where that was, and more significantly, he'd heard Doris speak that name— she had a connection to it. Pulling out his phone, he dialed her number.

"My handsome son," she said when she picked up. "Such a rare treat to hear your voice. What do you need?"

"You make it sound like I only call you when I want something."

"So you're calling about coming over to fix my wall sconce?"

He huffed. "What's wrong with your wall sconce?"

"I asked you ages ago to come over and look at it. It doesn't light up."

"You really need me to change a lightbulb?" Slater said. "Ask your deadbeat boyfriend."

"It's one of those new LED ones. You can't take the bulb out. Don't worry about me, though. I'll just sit here alone in the dark, as I descend deeper into my dotage, as the twilight looms. I know I've had a good run."

"You know that's not going to work on me, right? For some reason you didn't manage to instill the guilt response."

"Another of my failings," Doris said. "Pike offered to take a look. He said the whole fixture probably has to be swapped out."

"What are you talking to him for?" Slater demanded. "He's busy."

"Not as busy as my son, the *gantse macher*. Pike

actually takes my calls."

"Do you know how infuriating that is?"

"I know, sweetie. You just have to suck it up. You know, I think he's lost a little weight since he moved out here. You must keep him awfully busy."

Slater growled and forced himself to take a breath. "Listen—Tweedy Boulevard Temple. You know people there."

"I know it's one of the oldest in town. Maybe even prewar. I think your cousin Nurit might be a member there."

"Is she the one who wore a miniskirt to her bat mitzvah?"

"She looked lovely," Doris said. "What do you need to know about Tweedy Boulevard?"

"It's for a case. I need to get into their records, or at least talk to someone in the office."

"I know some of the B'nai B'rith crowd from that congregation. I'm sure I can find out who's working in the office. Let me make some calls."

"Just don't tell anyone about me or my work," Slater said. "That's all confidential."

"Of course, sweetheart. It's exciting to be in on it."

He set the phone on his desk and rubbed his eyes. Why was that woman so infuriating? The phone buzzed, and he picked it up to check the caller ID. Truax. He picked up.

"I haven't heard from you," Truax said. "It's been a whole damn week. What have you come up with for my two grand?"

"We should talk about that. I'll be in my office later today. We can meet there." Slater rattled off the address.

A while later his phone rang, with the most annoying ring tone of all: "*No wire hangers ... What's wire hangers doing in this closet when I told you no wire hangers, ever?*"

"The woman who runs the office at Tweedy Boulevard is named Phyllis," Doris said when he picked up. "I haven't met her, but tell her that you're Dave's nephew. He's done music there, and they love him. That's your way in."

Besides being musical, Doris's brother was the human equivalent of a toothache. He taught music to unsuspecting college students and worked as a cantor on the side.

Once he'd ended the call, Slater checked the temple's website and saw that the office was open today. He locked the front door behind him, and went down to his car, and headed toward South Gate. The navigation app took him on rough and potholed Santa Fe Avenue, through the gritty industrial neighborhood south of downtown. The pavement was always a mess down here because of all the freight trucks.

His phone buzzed in its dash mount. The screen said REDDY KILOWATT. He tapped it to pick up the call.

"Are you at work?" he said.

"I'm in the car," Pike said, over the road noise. "On my way to Fresno. An overnight or maybe two. It wasn't planned."

"Fresno's fun. There's a great bar there. It's downtown somewhere."

"I'll be working."

"I can hear voices. Is that Anton?"

"He's driving. He's on a call right now too."

"You'd better not be sharing a room."

Pike laughed. "You know me better than that. You're the only man for me. The red giant blazing in my night sky. My Pollux."

"I want you to imagine me," Slater said, "red-hot and rock-hard and deep inside you. My hot breath on your neck, our bodies pressed tight together."

"OK," Pike said. "I'm hanging up now."

"I've got a firm grip on your cock, and with my other hand I'm stroking your chest. Just close your eyes and imagine it."

"I love you too," he said, and ended the call.

When Slater pulled into a street space in front of the temple, he saw that Pike had followed up with a text message:

Thanks for giving me a stiffy. I'll have to ride the rest of the way with my jacket in my lap. But when I get back, I'm going to ride you hard.

He replied with a GIF of a dachshund nodding its head, superimposed with the word SOON.

Climbing out of the Thunderbird, he stretched and looked over the building. Concrete planter boxes stood between the sidewalk and the accessibility ramp that led down to the entry door. It was actually a decent design, as it made the place look open and accessible, despite the darker underlying purpose of those boxes — to stop weaponized vehicles and truck bombs.

Doris said the temple had been here for decades, but this had to be a recent renovation. Feathery gray-green grass grew in the boxes, and Slater paused to look it over. It was alkali sacaton, a decent native that didn't need babying. It could handle drought and alkali soil. They'd definitely hired skilled help to implement this.

The front door was locked, and he pressed the button on the video doorbell.

"Can I help you?" a woman's voice said.

"My name is Ibáñez. I'm here to see Phyllis."

The door buzzed open, and Slater stepped inside. The foyer was lit by high windows that faced the street. At the foot of the wide staircase was a sign for YOUTH CHOIR PRACTICE and an arrow pointing up. The sound of a piano and children's voices in song drifted down. On the left was a plaque for SANCTUARY, and on the opposite side was a corridor with the lights on. He walked that way and found the office.

The clerk looked to be in her forties, and had her hair tied back, and wore a green print blouse. From a block away he could have pegged her as one of Doris's peers—competent, smart, no bullshit. He wouldn't be able to run a snow job on this one. As Slater approached the counter, she looked up from her desk and smiled.

"Are you here for the class?"

"Youth choir?" he said.

"You're a little old for that. I meant the introduction to Judaism."

Slater frowned and raised his voice. "I'm already Jewish."

She sat back. "Well, mazel tov. What can I help you with?"

"When was the renovation done? The accessibility ramp and the landscaping."

Her brow furrowed. "Last winter. Why?"

"Are you Phyllis?"

"That's right."

"The name is Slater. My uncle, Dave Moskowitz, works here sometimes as cantor."

She beamed. "We love Cantor Dave. Technically he's a soloist, or a cantorial soloist. Cantor is a full-time job. We can't actually afford one of those."

"That's probably for the best. You wouldn't want that guy hanging around all the time."

"Dave is a delight," she said. "A breath of fresh air."

"That's one way to put it."

"His wife is such a good person too. Always willing to pitch in when there's work to be done. It's a burden, right—the spouses are expected to be part of everything."

"Aunt Abby?" Slater said. "Are they still together?"

Her eyes narrowed. "As far as I know."

"I'm working a missing persons case. There might be a connection to one of your congregants. I need a way to get in contact with her."

"Are you a cop?" Phyllis said.

"Private."

"Who's missing?"

Slater took a breath, willing himself to be calm. "A guy named Finley López. His sister, Hera López, has a connection to this temple."

"You're working for the family?"

"That's confidential."

"If you find him," Phyllis said, "are you going to shake him down, or break his legs, or send him to sleep with the fishes?"

He frowned. "I'm not a gangster. I'm an insurance investigator." From his hip pocket he dug out a business card and handed it over. "My client is concerned that Finley might be in trouble. I want to ask his sister if she knows where he is, whether he's all right. If she's looking for him too, I can get them to pool their resources."

Once she'd scanned his card, she set it aside, then met his gaze. "I know Hera. I don't even have to look it up. They're not members, but her husband used to be. Hera's husband's name is Irwin Ganz." She spelled it. "He's an eye doctor. I'm not surprised someone like you is looking for him."

"Why do you say that?"

"I shouldn't gossip."

"And yet you already started," Slater said, and louder, "Sing, sister."

"Dude—cool it." She frowned, then lowered her voice, even though no one else was around. "His parents are elderly. When they visited from the East, he told them his house was kosher, but it really wasn't."

"I suppose that is a little rude."

"It's deplorable, Slater. They're Holocaust survivors. Lying to them like that. It's total disrespect."

"Do you have a phone number for Irwin or Hera?"

Phyllis eyed him a moment longer, then sat up and tapped her computer keyboard. "That, I'll have to look up. Normally I'd never give out that kind of info. There's so much stalking, and fraud, and identity theft."

"I'm not that guy."

"I have Irwin's cell," she said, and recited it.

Slater tapped the number into his phone. "What about a photo of them?"

"I don't have anything like that. But if you look up *nebbishy* in the dictionary, there's a photo of Irwin."

"Got it."

"That was a joke."

Tucking his phone away, Slater met her gaze. "I figured."

"Do you have a schul? You should drop by tomorrow night."

"I got enough of all that in my youth."

"You became bar mitzvah?"

"I chanted my haftarah, got cake, the whole deal."

"I'm sure you also promised to continue the traditions of the community," Phyllis said, and smiled. "It wouldn't kill you to drop by. What else are you doing on Friday night?"

"What's the thing about improving the world?"

"You mean *tikkun olam*. It actually means repairing the world."

"That's what I'm doing right now," Slater said. "Tracking down a lowlife to make the world better."

"Irwin is pretty self-involved, but I wouldn't call him a lowlife." She sat back in her chair. "You know, there's not a ton of Jewish guys with your kind of swagger."

"I'd say you haven't met enough Israelis."

"Does that ring mean you're off-limits?"

Slater frowned, and absently rubbed it with the tip of his thumb. "I'm on dick, sister."

"I've heard that one before." She waved a hand. "All the good ones are gay or married."

"I'm not a good one," he said, and walked out.

TWENTY

W HEN SLATER GOT BACK to his office, he found
Etta parked behind the front desk.

"How was camping?" he said.

"Uncomfortable."

He beckoned her to follow him into his office, and sat behind his desk, and waited as Etta dropped into the guest chair.

"I got a headache from the elevation," she said. "We were up at Idyllwild. Drinking beer just made it worse."

"That sounds painful. Why do you do it?"

"It's more Safiya's thing."

Slater frowned. "Is she still hanging around? You know she's just holding you back."

"Don't tell me how to run my love life." She shot him a look, then sat up and adjusted the little plaster statue of Pollux.

"Why do you always move him around?"

"He likes to be able to see what's going on. Same with the horse." Etta sat back. "So did you meet Eustace?"

"Eustace was a dead end. The upside is that he's an amazing kisser. Even though the body declines with age, it must not apply to the lip muscles."

She wrinkled her nose. "You made out with him? What is wrong with you?"

"I get asked that a lot."

"Was he even competent to give consent?"

"Eustace still has all his marbles." Slater waved a

hand. "He was pretty tits-out about being into me."

"When I did the research, I got the impression he might have dementia, or some other cognitive issue. If he does, it means you molested him."

"He wanted it."

"That's what rapists always say."

"Woman, *he* hit on *me*."

"Rapists say that too. You assaulted a decorated veteran."

He folded his arms. "I was a little surprised he still got wood."

"I don't need to hear that." Etta scoffed. "When you're that age, you'll be walking around with a woody all the time."

"I doubt I'll live that long." He sat up. "Listen, my client is coming in to talk. His name is Truax. Look him over when he comes in, and tell me what you see under the tailoring and the haircut."

"It's hard to pick up anything if he just walks past me."

A firm knock sounded at the front door.

"Showtime," Slater said, and got up.

"I know I'm late," Truax said when Slater pulled open the door. "There's nowhere to park around here."

Slater frowned. "There's usually meters. And the big-ass block-wide surface lot right across the street."

"I found a meter eventually. Where do you park?"

"In the big-ass block-wide surface lot right across the street." He threw up his hands. "Come in."

They walked past Etta, standing with her hands on the back of the chair at the front desk. As Slater sat down, and Truax sat opposite, Etta wheeled her chair in behind them. She had a steno pad in hand, and a ballpoint pen with a fuchsia-haired doll's head stuck on the end. She sat between them, at the side of the desk.

Truax frowned at her. "Who are you?"

"I'm Etta," she said, and smiled. "Mr. Ibáñez's confidential assistant. I'm just here to take some notes."

"Why?" Truax demanded.

"It's for my files," Slater said. "Anything you say to me you can say in front of her."

"You keep records with a pen and paper?"

Etta chuckled. "It's less intrusive than typing. And I'm sure you don't want your voice to be recorded."

"Whatever." Truax waved a hand. "So where are we at?"

"What do you do, exactly, at Magnesia Motors?" Slater said.

"Why are you researching me? I'm paying you to find Finley."

"Why does Magnesia even have offices here? The factory is in Texas."

"There's a solid labor force there," Truax said, raising his eyebrows, "but to get skilled workers, we have to be in California."

"By 'solid labor force,'" Etta said, "you mean the minimum wage there is half what it is in LA."

Truax laughed. "Exactly. Plus there's comparatively no regulation. We can dump the garbage without the nanny state picking through it." He eyed Slater. "Have you tracked him down?"

"I've made some progress. Did you supervise Finley at Magnesia?"

"No," he said flatly. "The office has nothing to do with him disappearing. Do you have anything you can tell me? Any of your leads?"

"Not yet." Slater held his gaze. "I need a few more days to follow up. I'm also going to need some money."

Truax scoffed. "I'm not paying you any more until you have something tangible. It sounds like what you've got is a big nothing."

"I need to get paid for my work regardless of the out-come."

"Good luck with that," he said, and rose.

Etta followed him out, and bolted the front door once he'd left.

"You want my impressions?" she said, stepping back into Slater's office.

"Fire away."

"The guy is impatient. He just wants results."

"What does that tell you?" Slater said. "The impatient part."

Her brow furrowed as she thought about that. "What-ever he wants with Finley might have a time compo-nent."

"Exactly."

"He sort of flirted with me."

Slater frowned. "Why did I not see that?"

"Because you're not interested in either of us."

"When he hired me he told me that he's a man's man, but he doesn't seem gay to me."

"I'd say he's at least partly straight," Etta said, "based on the way his eyes instantly went to my breasts."

"Classic straight-guy behavior."

"Maybe he's into boys too. Sexuality is a spectrum."

"Not with him," Slater said. "Nothing about him says anything except 'straight.' What I can't figure out is why he'd lie about that."

"To motivate you, maybe?"

"He paid me." Slater shrugged. "I'd still do the work even without the queer bait."

"Well, that's all I got. I have to jet." Etta got up and walked into the front office.

"Hold my calls," Slater called after her.

"Hold them your damn self. I'm not your secretary. The landline is forwarded to Max's cell anyway."

"Type up all your notes, at least, and leave them on my desk."

She laughed. "I just gave you my notes. I didn't even write anything down."

The sound of her key flipping the bolt in the front door came as he pulled his keyboard closer. Land ownership was public record, and if Irwin was a doctor, he was well-paid enough to have some. He searched for the guy's name in the county database and soon found that Irwin owned a residential lot in Palos Verdes as well as a condo in Pico Union.

Palos Verdes was tony and home to plenty of doctors, but Pico Union was gritty, and crowded, and full of newcomers. A lone condo wasn't a rental property investment either—people who wanted to play that game bought whole apartment buildings. A doctor with the resources to own in the hills wouldn't have a pied-à-terre in Pico Union either. It would be in one of those sterile new residential towers around the stadium, built by rich Red Chinese trying to protect their money by investing it outside the motherland.

Irwin had a website for his medical practice, and it showed the physical address was downtown in the Financial District. The text implied that he specialized in cataract surgeries. His portrait showed a round-faced guy with thick lips and a fake smile. Not exactly nebbishy, Slater thought. More like oily. His thinning dark hair was slicked back with some kind of pomade.

Sitting back, Slater thought it through. He could probably pull off a walk-in, especially this late in the day. But if Irwin knew where Finley was, Slater's visit might tip him off, and drive him farther away. He'd try something else first.

Once he'd thumb-typed the address of the condo into his navigation app, Slater went down to his car. The shadows were growing long in the golden light of the end of the day. Driving west, he went under the freeway, into Pico Union. An old residential neighborhood, the streets were narrow, and parking was tight.

As he drove by the condo building, he looked it over. New construction, small units on three floors, with half a dozen identical windows facing the street. Even though it was new, no way would a wealthy medical doctor live here, even if he needed to crash close to his office, or needed a place to warehouse his mistress.

Slater found a parking spot at the end of the block and walked back to the building. The gate in the fence along the sidewalk wasn't locked. Up front the first door was marked UNIT A. Walking along the side of the building, he found unit C at the end, and knocked on the door.

A moment later a muffled voice came from inside: "Who is it?"

"I've got your delivery," Slater said.

He hadn't expected to find the guy right away, but here he was, pulling open the door. Finley looked younger than in his ID photo. His lush black hair was longer now. He wore a stretchy green athletic top, highlighting his lithe musculature. Fuckable, Slater decided.

"You look young for your age, Irwin," Slater said.

Finley's face hardened, and he moved to close the door. But Slater already had his boot inside the frame, and all Finley could do was slam against it.

"Piss off, *ese*, or I'm calling the cops."

"I know you're not going to do that, Finley. You don't want that kind of attention. That's why you're using your brother-in-law's place."

Finley glared at him through the gap. "The fuck are you?"

"I'm the guy who tracked you down." Slater pushed the door open wider.

He kept a firm grip on it and didn't step back. "Did Truax send you?"

"Is there anybody else you're hiding from?"

"Is he here?" Finley said, and craned to look behind him.

"I can get him here, if you want."

"You're no cop. You can't detain me. I'll be gone by the time he pulls up."

"Why is he so intent on finding you?" Slater said. "It can't just be the sex."

Finley scowled. "What sex?"

"He's your boyfriend, isn't he?"

"Did he tell you that?"

"So he's not your boyfriend."

"Are you kidding me?" Finley demanded. "Would you sleep with that guy?"

Slater pursed his lips. "If it was really, really dark. And I'd have to be a little crunk."

"He paid you to track me down?"

"Might be."

"There's more going on than you think."

"Like what?"

Finley glared at him for a moment. "If I let you in, are you going to slap me around?"

"Only if you provoke me. Tell me the truth, and I won't get riled."

He sighed but pulled open the door. "You have me at a disadvantage."

"I didn't touch you."

"I mean your name. You know my name. I don't know yours."

"Slater," he said, as he looked the place over.

It was a one-bedroom, with a kitchen separated by a counter fronted with a couple of barstools. A TV and lounge furniture were in the main room, and on the coffee table sat a copy of *Saucers over the Southwest.*

"So tell me your side of it," Slater said, meeting his gaze.

"Do you want a drink? There's scotch."

"It's a little early for me, but what the hell. Set me up."

It wasn't too early, not even a little, but this guy didn't need to know that. His booze rules said he was allowed one if he was working, or drinking with other people.

Slater watched as he went behind the kitchen counter and produced a bottle, then poured a healthy half-inch into a couple of tumblers. Handing one to him, he tapped it with his own.

"Your brother-in-law buys good stuff," Slater said, inhaling the heady scent and taking a sip.

Finley stepped over to the sofa, and sat with one leg folded under him, his arm draped on the back. Even in baggy shorts his junk looked massive.

"You're not who I expected," he said, giving Slater the once-over.

"Who did you expect?"

"Two burly thugs who'd kick down the door and tear the place apart."

He waved an arm. "What's going on?"

"How much do you know?"

"That's not how this works. I'm asking the questions." Slater raised his voice. "Sing, brother."

Finley scowled. "I worked for Truax. At Magnesia. The guy was abusive."

"What did you do there?"

"Are you going to sit down? You're making me nervous."

Slater scoffed but dropped into the lounge chair across from him, slurping at the scotch before he set the tumbler on the coffee table.

"I was basically doing IT and audiovisual equipment,"

Finley said. "Anything with buttons and flashing LEDs that people can't easily figure out. My job was to set things up and train people on how to use the equipment and the software."

"But Truax wasn't your boss."

"Not directly." Finley was watching him closely. "I can't believe he told you we were in a romantic relationship. It makes me nauseous just thinking about it."

"He didn't seem like a man's man. I thought maybe my gaydar was busted."

"Truax is married to a woman. They have a couple of mouthy kids running around."

"That doesn't mean he wouldn't get dick on the down-low," Slater said. "With lots of straight guys, you get a couple of tequila shots in them, and they're on their knees in the back alley."

"Well, Truax wasn't getting it from me."

"So he's a damn poseur. That rings true." Slater raised his eyebrows. "But it doesn't explain why you're hiding from him."

He gestured languorously. "I'm running out the clock. If I lie low a little longer, my contract will expire, and he can't make me come back to work."

"Truax isn't pursuing you like it's a contract dispute. It feels more like you've got something he wants. Usually that means money, or something worth money."

Finley scowled. "I didn't steal from him. I cannot take that toxic work environment anymore."

"So you're just sitting around here reading about flying saucers?"

"I have to eat, right? I've been remote consulting for IT stuff. Small companies. Just gig work."

"Using Irwin's identity."

"I didn't steal it. He loaned it to me. Along with this place and his Volvo."

"What year is it?" Slater reached for his tumbler and took a satisfying slurp.

"The Volvo? Why does that matter?"

"I'm a car whack."

"It's old. Maybe early nineties. It's a station wagon."

"That's a 940 or a 960."

Finley huffed, and stood up, and set his tumbler on the kitchen counter to pour more scotch.

Rising, Slater drained his own glass and set it beside Finley's.

"In your apartment there's a dark-blue box with a single port in it."

He scowled. "What were you doing in my apartment?"

"You weren't using it. Olivia Howard thought maybe the Navy got to you."

"You talked to Olivia?" Finley demanded. "Why?"

"I thought she might know what happened to you. Quit dodging the question. What's the device for?"

Setting down the bottle, a smirk played on his lips. "I'm not going to tell you that."

"Wrong answer," Slater said, and stepped close to deliver a firm kovac, slapping his face left and then right. He grabbed the collar of his shirt in his fist. At this range he could smell Finley's sweat.

"Let go of me."

"You'll take it, and you'll like it." Slater slapped him again, then released his grip and shoved him back. "Spill it."

Red-faced now, Finley scowled at him. "It's nothing to do with Magnesia." He took a breath. "It's a flying saucer detector."

"How does it work?"

"Did anyone ever tell you that you're a little tightly wound?"

"I hear that a lot."

"Paranormal activity is accompanied by spikes across the electromagnetic spectrum," Finley said. "It's not just in one frequency band—it's all over the place at the same time. No human technology does that. It's weird. Like someone striking all the keys on a piano at the same time. When it happens, that box sends an alarm to my computer." He pushed the tumbler toward Slater. "Am I allowed to sit down again?"

TWENTY-ONE

SLATER MOVED OUT OF Finley's way, and watched as he went back to the sofa, then sat across from him again.

"There's so much going on right now in the field. People who are in contact with the aliens say they think something is going down."

"What kind of something?"

"No idea." Finley shrugged. "But it's something big. People are getting messages to get ready. One woman was told by her alien contact 'Keep your camera with you.' It's weird, right? Nowadays everyone has a camera in their hand all the time."

This story was new, Slater realized, watching him talk. It's what Pike had said about the saucer field, that the paradigm was evolving. It was decades removed from the contents of *Saucers over the Southwest*. The book was sitting right in front of him, but Finley didn't even glance at it.

"I'm not sure what it means, but her alien contacts told her they were doing stuff at this airport in Utah. Then someone over there got a saucer photo." Finley pulled out his phone and tapped at it. "Check this out."

Watching him, Slater realized this guy was a total ci-vilian—he didn't even try to conceal his unlock code when he thumb-typed it. He'd seen it clearly, and he worked to commit the four digits to memory.

Finley held out his phone, turning the screen toward

"

him. It showed a blurry photo of a smudge of light on a black background.

"That's a flying saucer?" Slater said.

He pulled the phone back and frowned. "Of course it's a flying saucer."

"Are you an abductee?"

"I don't think so. At least not that I know of."

"No unusual scoop marks," Slater said, "or lumps under the skin, or plastic fibers growing out of your palms?"

"It sounds like you know the field."

"I've met some saucer-heads."

"People who get abducted share genetic lineage, so it runs in families. I'm not sure why. My parents had unexplained incidents. Missing time." He raised his eyebrows and spoke intently, immersed in his topic now. "Once they were driving at night, and they suddenly got all exhausted and felt compelled to stop. They pulled over to take a nap. When they woke up later in the car, my mom was wearing my dad's shirt, and vice versa. Both their shirts were on inside out."

"What about Hera?" Slater said.

"She's seen things in the sky. Especially when my mother was around. She claims she's never been abducted. But I'm not so sure." His eyes narrowed. "Did you talk to her? Is that how you found me?"

"Would she rat you out?"

"I doubt it," Finley said. "Unless you worked her over."

"Good to know."

"So what's next? What are you going to do?"

"Savor the rest of this bougie scotch," Slater said, "and admire your body."

He chuckled. "You are such a weirdo."

"I hear that a lot too."

"You really think I'm hot?"

"Who wouldn't?" Slater said. "It's objectively true. You're a total snack."

"Flirt much?" he said, and held Slater's gaze as he sipped his drink.

"I'll stop, if that's what you want."

"It's been a while for me. I'm afraid to put my photo on a hookup app in case Truax finds it."

"I can solve that problem for you," he said.

Finley raised his eyebrows. "So what are you waiting for?"

Draining his glass, Slater coughed at the intensity of the fumes, then set it down and rose. Stepping around the coffee table, he knelt in front of Finley and pushed his knees apart.

His eyes bright, Finley inhaled sharply. "We're really doing this."

"I'm not playing, son."

Leaning in, Slater met his mouth. It tasted like the scotch, nutty and warm. Finley was a little methodical, but it was still hot, and he felt his dick tightening in his jeans. Shifting position, Finley stretched out on the sofa, and Slater lowered his weight onto him, and mouthed his neck.

Finley shoved his hand under his belt, squeezing his butt. "Let's go in the bedroom."

Rising, Slater followed him through the doorway, then grabbed him from behind, hands on his waist. Finley gasped as Slater wrapped his arms around his torso, running his hands over his stretchy shirt, then under it, finally peeling it off over his head. Still standing behind him, Slater reached around and popped his fly, and shoved his shorts down.

Finley turned to him, kissing him again, then dropped to his knees and unbuckled Slater's belt, and pulled his pants open. As Slater pulled his shirt off, Finley took him into his mouth and started to work him.

Closing his eyes to relish the intensity, Slater eventually put a hand on his chin to pull him up.

"Slow down, Seabiscuit. I want to enjoy this."

He sat on the edge of the bed to untie his boots and push his jeans off, then pulled Finley down with him. Exploring his body with his hands, Slater squeezed his cock.

"You're a big boy."

Finley chuckled. "People always say that."

"What do you want to do with it?"

"I want you to fuck me."

"Do you have a condom?"

"No—why are you not on PrEP?"

"Why do people keep asking me that?" Slater said. "Condoms are kind of fun, aren't they?"

"I've only tried it once. I couldn't feel anything."

"You sound like a straight guy. Are you on PrEP?"

"All day every day."

Slater kissed him, then reached between his legs, pressing into him. He manipulated Finley onto his side, and penetrated him, and stroked his massive cock, one arm around his chest.

As he worked up to pounding him, Finley moaned, reacting to his thrusts, and eventually grunted and climaxed. The involuntary electric shudder through his body was a turn-on, and Slater came, drawing him closer, straining into him.

Spent, he rolled onto his back and folded his arm over his eyes, lifting his head when Finley shifted next to him and slid his arm under his neck. He was starting to drift off, but he forced himself to sit up.

"Are you leaving?" Finley mumbled.

"I need to piss."

Finley had set his phone on the kitchen counter before

they'd moved into the bedroom, and Slater grabbed it on the way by, and found the bathroom, and sat down. He tapped in the unlock code, then spent a minute installing Svetlana's tracking software. The interface was a mishmash of Cyrillic and broken English, likely because she outsourced the coding to the old country. But it seemed to be working, and the last setup screen asked, "To close and secret running?" Slater tapped on the only button, labeled "начинать," and it disappeared.

Back at the kitchen counter, he gingerly set the phone down, positioning it the way he'd found it. In the bedroom he snatched up his shirt from the floor and pulled it on.

"Now you're leaving," Finley said, propping his head on his hand.

"It's late."

"It's like, ten o'clock." He sat up. "So are you going to rat me out to Truax?"

"He's my client. It's where my loyalty has to be."

"He's lying to you," Finley said. "You know that. The lie is bigger than you think. He wants to hurt me."

Slater stepped into his jeans, watching him. "I actually believe you. I can tell you're really afraid. But it doesn't wash with the story about the contract dispute."

He looked away. "So says the man with the *putaso*."

"Doesn't that mean a punch?" Slater said. "I gave you a kovac. Open-handed."

"Does it matter?"

"If you went after me with John Law for assault, it would definitely matter."

"I'd never do that." Finley dropped his chin. "We have a connection, Slater. I can feel it. I know you can too. I just put out for you."

He scoffed and studied his face. "You're good, son, but I'm not buying it. The sex wasn't about me. You're a level-one dick hound." He sat on the side of the bed to tie his boots. "I shouldn't have fallen for it. I need to keep my dick out of my cases."

"You make it sound like I should apologize for enjoying sex."

"I didn't say that." Slater raised his voice. "I'm saying I'm not going to let you use it to manipulate me."

Finley huffed. "Just wait until tomorrow before you tell Truax. Can you do that? Give me time to get a head start."

Turning, he leaned in and gently ran a hand into Finley's luxy dark hair. "You don't have to run. I'll keep your secrets."

His eyebrows shot up. "You're not going to tell him where I am? Isn't that what he hired you to do?"

Slater squeezed his shoulder, and ran a hand down his arm. "I know now that Truax is lying to me. I need to do some more digging before I come across. What's your number? The one for that phone, not from your old life."

As he recited it, Slater tapped it into his contacts, then texted him a single word:

Slater.

He could hear it buzz softly in the next room.

"I sent you my number. Call me if anything changes." Slater met his eye. "I won't tell Truax anything until I talk to you again."

"I wish I could believe that."

"I get it. You don't know me."

Rising, Slater walked out, and went out to the street. Finley was lying, of course, about some of it. But not about being afraid. Truax was lying too. He needed to sort through all the bullshit. Maybe he could find a kernel of truth in it somewhere.

As he walked up the street, at this hour chockablock with parked cars, he noticed a dark-blue Volvo. It was a 960, and it dated to the mid-nineties—that had to be Irwin's. Those were fun to drive. As he passed it, he looked back at the grill. It was in good shape.

Finley might bolt anyway, no matter what promises Slater had made. He wouldn't have taken his own thin word either. He probably shouldn't have gone soft for the guy, and he definitely shouldn't have slept with him.

———•———

DRIVING BACK TO ECHO Park, Slater's phone buzzed— REDDY KILOWATT.

"Are you in a sleazy motel room?" Slater said when he picked up.

Pike laughed. "It's not too sleazy."

"Is Anton there?"

"He has his own room."

"If he comes knocking in the middle of the night, don't open the door. I know he wants you."

"And I know he doesn't," Pike said. "Nobody's going to be knocking."

"Except skulls, maybe? Did you knock some heads together today?"

"Nothing that exciting. It was lots of interviews."

"I went to a synagogue," Slater said.

"Well, shabbat shalom. You're finally seeking out god's *rachmones*?"

"It's for my case. I miss you. I miss the smell of your hair. The way your skin feels."

"Me too, forty-niner. It won't be long."

They talked some more, and after they'd ended the call, Slater pulled into his garage, and killed the engine, and watched the door roll down in the rearview.

Why was he compelled to fuck other people? Pike

was so good to him, so honest, so real. He'd found stars out in the desert sky to profess his feelings with. Pike wasn't fucking around on him. If he did, it would drive Slater insane. Just the thought of Pike up there with Anton—it was irrational, he knew that, but it made his blood boil. Pike could do so much better than Slater. It was probably only a matter of time until he pushed him too far, one too many reckless things to weasel out of, and Pike would ditch him for some drip like Anton.

Pulling the rearview toward him, he looked into his own eyes. They were bloodshot after the scotch and the hookup.

"You are a piece of trash," he said.

He took his phone out of its dash mount and checked the tracking software for Finley. It was up and running— the green dot on the map was right where he'd left him. He hadn't gone on the lam yet—or if he had, he'd left his phone behind.

Upstairs in the bedroom he peeled off his clothes. He should just go to bed, he knew that, but he climbed the stairs to the kitchen and poured his ration of bourbon into a tumbler, then stood at the French doors and stared out at the glittering towers of the Financial District in the distance. Taking a sip, he relished the sharp burn.

He should quit after his ration; that's what the booze rules said. But Pike wasn't around to behave for. Maybe that's what the blue book meant when it talked about admitting that your life was unmanageable. He couldn't even keep it in his pants for the man he loved.

Back in the kitchen, he poured another inch into the tumbler, already feeling the warm glow in his belly. What else was he supposed to do at this hour? Without the buffer of the golden elixir, it was just too much to ask, that he stare into the void of the long empty night.

TWENTY-TWO

MUTED SUNLIGHT WAS FILTERING through the sheers when he woke and slowly started to come to consciousness. His head hurt. He'd overdone it. Deep breaths before he sat up. That helped sometimes.

Finley, he remembered. And Truax. They were lying to him about what was going on between them. It wasn't personal—everybody lied to him all the time. Except Pike.

The thought of lying to Pike made him wince. It wasn't really lying—he just wasn't telling him everything. He knew that Pike was well aware that he did that, fucked other people, and he knew that Pike didn't want the details. He pushed the thought away.

A heavier memory landed in his mind. That book, *Saucers over the Southwest*. It was half a century old, and none of the UFO stories Finley had related had come from it—Finley's interests were the contemporary stuff, the imminent alien monkeyshines in Utah. And yet he'd taken that book, and only that one, when he'd fled his regular life. *Saucers over the Southwest* had sat there all evening on the coffee table, ignored and unacknowledged.

Slater grabbed his phone and swiped away the texts from Doris, not bothering to read them. Svetlana's tracking software showed the green dot for Finley's phone crawling along the freeway, southbound on the 110.

As he forced himself to get out of bed, his head

throbbed with the exertion. At least the room wasn't spinning. In the bathroom he studied his face. Dark circles underlined his bloodshot eyes.

"Booze hag," he said through gritted teeth.

Upstairs he made coffee, and slurped down half a mugful, and looked in the Frigidaire. The sight of food made him nauseous, and he swung the door closed.

Checking the tracker again, he saw that Finley was off the freeway, headed west on PCH. The guy wasn't running away—he was headed to his sister's place. He probably had to pay regular homage to Irwin for letting him use his pad and his identity.

In the garage Slater unlocked his armored gear cabinet and loaded the key binder and the lock probe into the trunk of the Thunderbird. He drove to Finley's condo and found a street space in front. Before he got out, he checked the tracker. Finley's phone was stationary now, on a winding street in the middle of Palos Verdes.

He didn't need to bother with the latex gloves, he decided, as he'd already been invited in to Finley's place, and leaving more of his prints and DNA around wouldn't matter. There were people plying the sidewalk, and a gardener with a buzzing string trimmer in a nearby front yard, but no one was in the walkway along the side of the condo building. Dropping to one knee at the door to unit C, Slater connected the probe to his phone and eased it into the lock. The software spit out a number on the first try.

Walking back out to his car, he opened the trunk and flipped through the heavy pages of the binder to find the key, then took it back to the condo. When he tried it in the lock, it twisted freely, retracting the deadbolt with a muted *thunk.*

He already knew there were no cameras, no alarm, and he stepped inside and closed the door. The place seemed bigger with daylight streaming in the windows.

The only book in the place was *Saucers over the Southwest.* Slater sat on the sofa and thumbed through it. It bore a few sticky notes, some with annotations, and it was a lot more worn than the copy Slater had bought. The dark-red cloth boards were in rough shape too, he saw, when he pulled off the dust jacket. The little divots in the fabric looked like the scoop marks Yu-Lin had shown him at Giant Rock.

He studied the insides of the hard covers, front and then back, and ran his fingers over the smooth papered surface. There was nothing hidden here, no implanted trackers, no mysterious plastic bristles. It was interesting that it still had its dust jacket. The bookstore clerk had implied that old books tended to lose them. The cloth over the spine pulled away from the binding when he folded the book open. Opening it wider, he peered into the gap, and held it up to the light from the windows. There was something in there. Just visible near the bottom was the folded-over end of a strip of clear plastic tape.

Prodding with his index finger, he could feel a hard spot under the tape. It felt smooth compared to the surrounding ancient dried glue on the binding. He pulled on the end of the tape with his fingernails, and it popped out.

Stuck to the tape was a tiny memory card, he saw, and he peered at it. Smaller than a thumbnail, this size was used for cell phones. It had been well hidden. Is this what Truax was really after?

Once he'd replaced the book in the same position on the coffee table, Slater locked the front door and walked out to his car. He started the engine, and got the air conditioner blowing, then phoned Andy.

"It's better when you text me," Andy said when he picked up.

"Why—have you got cupcake Kyle's dick in your mouth?"

"There's no need to be … crass. What do you need?"

"Can you tell me what's on an SD card, and whether it will take down the power grid, or blow up my computer?"

"It's not going to do that. But sure, I can … check it for malware."

"Can you do it now?" Slater said.

"If I must. You have to pay me."

"I always fricking pay you," he snapped, and hung up before Andy could respond. "Dick," he muttered to himself.

———·———

Upstairs at Andy's loft, Slater rapped on the door, and waited for him to pull it open.

"You look like hell," Andy said, walking to his desk. "Did somebody work you over?"

"It's just a katzenjammer."

He dropped into his gaming chair. "We've talked about this. About laying off … the sauce."

"You really think I should?" Slater put his hands on his hips. "No one ever mentioned that before. This is the first I've heard of it."

He chuckled. "What do you need?"

"It belongs to my target," Slater said, and handed him the little memory card. "I don't know anything about it."

"I'll use my laptop." Andy swiveled in his chair and pulled it open with an unsteady hand.

"Is it air-gapped?"

"Where did you learn … that word?"

"You, probably. Or my Russian supplier."

"No surprise she'd need … equipment like that," he said, peering at the side of the laptop.

Slater watched him manipulate the little card, eventually getting it into the slot. He wanted to offer to help, but he knew better—Andy's intentions usually prevailed through the chaos of his movements. Once he'd pulled on his gauntlets, he studied the screen.

"There's only one file," Andy said. "A video. It's big."

"Will playing it transfer the deed to my house to a Nigerian prince?"

"I doubt it. Want to … watch it now?"

"As long as you remember you're sworn to secrecy."

Andy scoffed, and a video window came up on the laptop screen. The image was a wide-angle view of a conference table, with five people sitting around it. They were talking but not looking at the camera. Above them on the wall was a stylized chrome logo shaped like an M.

The video paused, and Andy turned to him. "The camera is stationary. It's one of those … teleconferencing systems. For video meetings."

"Do you recognize the logo?"

"I don't."

"I'd bet money it's for Magnesia Motors."

Andy hit Play, and they both watched for a minute, then he paused it again.

"Do you get the feeling they don't … know they're being recorded?" Andy said. "None of them have looked at the camera."

"That fits what I'm seeing too."

"Who are these chuckleheads?"

"I know that one on the left," Slater said. "She's on the county board. I think I live in her district, or maybe Doris does."

"You probably both do. Those districts are … huge. There's only five supervisors for ten million people. Do you think it's a … board meeting?"

"The board is mostly women, and this is mostly stupid-looking white guys."

"Do you want me to … find out who the others are?"

"How will you do that?" Slater said.

"Facial recognition. It'll compare them to … the entire internet."

"How long will that take?"

"A while," Andy said. "Take the memory card with you and watch the … video yourself. It looks pretty dry."

"You were hoping for a raunchy sex video."

Andy chuckled. "You know what I like. Let me do … some image grabs first."

He clicked through the video, and eventually pulled out the card and handed it over.

"Facial recognition sites charge … fees for these searches."

"I'll pay your damn fees," Slater said. "When have I ever stiffed you?"

"As I remember it, you subjected me to … your stiffy many times."

"Not anymore, now that you're exclusive with that icy twink. It's depressing. Like someone telling you 'You can only eat vanilla cupcakes for the rest of your life.' Plus I know you're not really exclusive—it's just no sex with me. Like I'm a bad penny, or a drug-resistant tropical disease, or some volatile toxic chemical."

"You should focus on that slab of cream cheese at the nexus of … your narrative complex. If Pike gets boring, there's millions of other … guys in this town."

Slater jabbed a finger at him and raised his voice. "And none of them are you."

He walked out, and when he got to the elevator and hit the button, he realized he was breathing hard.

"Prick," he muttered.

TWENTY-THREE

BACK AT SLATER'S OFFICE, he plugged the little memory card into his computer and copied the video file. When he clicked on it, the counter said it was thirty-two minutes long. He was about to start watching it when his phone buzzed. It was a text from Andy:

Three down. I didn't have to look too hard. The other woman at the meeting is also a county supervisor, name is Alekseyev, and so is the guy on the right with gray hair. That's Knudson. I'll do the facial recognition on the other two.

Slater sent him a thumbs-up emoji and then hit Play. One of the women from the county board was talking, her voice tinny through his computer speakers: "It's a fine line. The law says the bidding process has to be open. There are all sorts of other complicating factors, like the buy-California rule."

One of the men that Andy hadn't identified, the youngest in the group, looked to be in his forties. "If you can't make the call for bids fit only us," he said, "you have to obfuscate the bidding. You people do that all the time. Just don't send the call out to our competitors."

"That's easy enough," the supervisor said, spreading her palms. "We'll distribute it to food suppliers and land-scapers. They'll just delete it."

The other guy who hadn't been identified yet was

in his fifties, his dark hair slicked back, and he sat up to speak. "That will help, but we have to narrow the language so that no one else can take the contract. Of course we'll offer you personal fees for working with us."

"What kind of fees did you agree on?" the gray-haired man said. That was Knudson, one of the county supes.

"There's twenty for each of you," the slick-haired guy said.

"I guess that'll do," Knudson said. "Although it's a lot of work, and there is risk involved."

One of the women spoke, the supe named Alekseyev. "We also can't narrow the language enough to change the fact that your plant is out of state."

Slater paused the video. Texas was where Magnesia built their stupid cars. In a browser window he did a search for the company—the logo was the same as the chrome M hovering over the meeting in the video. He sent Andy a text:

The M in the video is Magnesia Motors. That boardroom must be in their LA office.

Sitting back, he hit Play again. These idiots definitely didn't know they were being recorded. Slater had no connection to bureaucracy and its intricacies, but even he could tell that what they were talking about was blatantly illegal.

The conversation veered off topic as they gossiped about other local politicians, and one of the federal senators, and other names that he didn't recognize. He was almost through to the end of the video when his phone rang—Andy.

"It's better when you text me," Slater said when he picked up.

"Shut up," Andy said. "The other two guys in the … video both work for Magnesia. One is in charge of sales.

The younger one is a … low-level toady. I'll send you their names and details. Have you watched enough to … know what the meeting is about?"

"It seems like they're trying to fix a contract bid with the county so that only Magnesia can win it. They talked about paying kickbacks to the politicians."

"I bet the county buys a lot of cars," Andy said. "You should get … Doris to look at the video. She'll have insights."

"I don't need my mother to help me with my homework."

"She follows local politics. Doris will know how … serious it is, whether it's scandal material or just a mundane business meeting."

"You need to stop hanging out with her," Slater said.

"She's my friend—she danced at my … wedding. And don't tell me what to do. You owe me … six dollars."

"You'll get your money," he said, and through his teeth added, "chiseler."

"You keep calling me that, but then you keep … paying me. And you keep coming back. It makes me think you … like my chisel."

"I'm not allowed to touch it anymore, remember?" Slater said, and ended the call.

He sat for a minute thinking about it all, staring absently at the faded thrift-store painting of a bowl of artichokes that hung on the turquoise of his office wall. Etta's paint job and furniture upgrades made that painting look ratty and cheap. He really should get rid of it.

First he needed to get more money from Truax. He was already underwater on this job. And Finley—keeping that copy of *Saucers over the Southwest* close by was about hiding this video. That meant he was just another nickel rat, blackmailing Magnesia in exchange for not releasing it.

If it was damaging enough, it might even be worth more than a penny-ante grift. Andy was right—Doris would have insight into how explosive it was. He dialed her number and listened to it ring before she picked up.

"Are you at home?" Slater said.

"I am. You saw my text about dinner?"

"I need to show you something. I'll be there soon."

Slater ended the call, then checked the tracking app for Finley. His phone was still in Palos Verdes.

Rising, he locked up the office and went down to his car, and drove to Pico Union. It was early enough that he found a street space on the block where Finley's condo was. He let himself in with the ghost key, then put the little memory card back where he'd found it, pressing the strip of tape with his finger until it had firmly adhered to the spine. Once he'd replaced the dust jacket, he repositioned the book on the coffee table.

Back outside, he climbed into the Thunderbird and fired up the engine to get the air blowing. He dialed Finley's number, and when he didn't pick up, left him a voice mail: "You need to call me."

A minute later, as he was accelerating up the ramp onto the 110, his phone buzzed. It was Finley.

"You never told me what Truax does for Magnesia," Slater said.

"His title is security consultant. Technically he's an outside contractor. Why does that matter?"

"I'm trying to figure out what he's up to."

"Have you talked to him?" Finley said.

"Don't worry about Truax."

"Did you tell him that you found me?"

"I already told you I'm not going to do that," Slater said, and ended the call.

Security—he knew what that meant. Truax was the button man, the fixer, the guy they sent to do the shady stuff. He was officially a contractor so that the company couldn't be blamed directly if he got caught. "We didn't do this; it was our vendor." Slater had the same relationship with the insurance company that hired him to investigate fraud. The desk jockeys brought him in when they didn't want to get their own hands dirty.

Slater exited the freeway in hilly Mount Washington, driving up the winding streets to Doris's house. Pulling into her driveway, he saw that her stupid boyfriend's stupid midlife-crisis convertible wasn't here. That meant he wouldn't have to swallow the urge to punch the guy in the face. But Doris's car wasn't here either; instead there was a strange mud-gray Malibu.

Pausing in the front yard, Slater looked over the ironwood, and stepped closer to inspect the bark and the scaly leaves. The inflorescences were almost gone now, and it was producing lots of seed. It was in good shape. Thriving, even.

When he rang the doorbell, Doris greeted him with an embrace. She was petite, and had some gray in her dark hair. Today she was wearing linen capris and a loose white blouse. Slater leaned in to kiss her, then pulled the door closed.

"You look rough," Doris said, her brow furrowing as she grasped his forearms and looked him over. "Are you hung over?"

"I might have a stomach bug."

"I've heard of that one," she said, turning to walk into the kitchen. "The hundred-proof barrel-aged bug. Do you want a coffee?"

"I drink to make all this tolerable," he said, and waved an arm. Lowering his voice, he added, "Affirmative on the joe."

Doris poured a mug for him and slid it across the counter. As he reached for it, her eyes grew wide.

"What's that?" She leaned in and grabbed his left hand.

"We didn't do anything crazy. It doesn't mean anything."

"It means everything." Doris studied the gold band and rubbed it with her thumb. "Oh, it's so sweet. Simple and elegant. Pike said he was thinking about getting them."

He pulled his hand back and picked up the coffee mug. "You shouldn't be bugging him. He's busy."

"That's not your call," Doris said, raising her eyebrows. "So how's your narrative complex unfolding?"

He sipped at the java. "I guess it's more routine. That electric intensity of the new situation is slowly starting to fade. But it's still good. Really, really good. He found the stars Castor and Pollux in the evening sky, and pointed them out to me, and said his love burns as brightly as they do."

She pressed her hand to her mouth and squeezed her eyes shut for a moment. "I wasn't even there, but it's so romantic."

"It's hard for me to see things like that objectively," he said. "I'm so consumed with him. It's like being inside a whirlwind."

"I think Pike likes it here. He's adapting to the big city. He actually said to me, 'Love you, mean it.'"

Slater chuckled. "That's extremely LA. What's with the Malibu parked out front? Did that old man who's been hanging around finally total his doll car?"

"That's a loaner. The Buick is in the shop. And Albert is not that old."

"He's not even Jewish."

"You don't act especially Jewish either," Doris said, "even though it's your birthright."

"I was in a synagogue just this week."

"To strong-arm the office staff and bad-mouth my brother."

"Phyllis told you that?" he demanded.

"Nobody told me that. But I know you better than anyone."

Slater huffed and folded his arms. "They seem to love Uncle Dave over there."

"Of course they do. He has the voice of an angel."

"Now you're making me nauseous, woman. Listen, can you watch something for me, and tell me what it means?"

Doris's eyebrows shot up. "What is it?"

"Local politics," he said flatly.

In the living room he took a minute to connect his phone to her TV, then grabbed his coffee, and sat in an armchair, and handed Doris his phone.

Perched on the sofa, she peered at the device's screen to start the video, then sat back to watch. After a moment she paused it.

"I know three of them," she said, and rattled off their names. "They're on the county board. The other two I've never seen before."

"The other two work for Magnesia Motors," Slater said. "It's an EV manufacturer. That's their logo on the wall. And before we get into it, you need to remember that this is business. It's totally confidential."

Her brow furrowed. "It makes me sad that you think you have to say that."

She hit Play, and they watched it together. At one point Doris leaned forward, listening intently. After the video ended, Slater eyed her. She looked thoughtful, her lips pursed. He knew she was digesting it.

"I've actually voted for a couple of those crooks over the years," she said finally. "They all play musical chairs when they get termed out."

"I probably did too."

"Fixing contracts isn't really that surprising. It could get them in legal trouble, although that kind of corruption usually gets a pass."

"Even when they're surreptitiously collaborating with the vendor like this?"

"It's pretty good evidence, especially when the company guy spelled out the dollar amount of the kickbacks. 'Twenty each.' That has to mean twenty thousand. I'm surprised a company would be willing to drop sixty grand just to get a contract."

"The county is a big organization, right? It must be worth a lot more than that."

"I suppose this might get some traction if it hit the media," Doris said. "Legally I don't think it would matter locally, but the feds might step in and investigate, maybe even prosecute somebody. They've done that before. What would really be damaging is the subtext. The revelation of things they wouldn't say in public."

Slater waved a hand. "Like what?"

"Well, Knudson called somebody a 'wetback.' That slur is a direct insult to half the people in the county. He called another supervisor a 'chunt.' That has to be a portmanteau of 'Chinese' and a vulgar anatomical word."

"What word is that?" Slater said, and raised his eyebrows.

Her eyes narrowed. "I know you know what I'm talking about."

"Seriously, I have no idea what you mean. You'll have to say it."

"The woman he's talking about is Vietnamese," Doris said, "so it doesn't even make sense."

"I don't think you can expect much rational thought when it comes to racism."

"Alekseyev called the DA a 'retard.' Even back when

I was in the classroom, if a kid used that word, it would trigger a serious discussion."

"None of that even registered for me. I hear that stuff all the time. All that bias becomes part of the background noise."

"Knudson would probably get away with it."

"That's the gray-haired guy?"

"His district is the white-flight exurban part of the county. Lots of his constituents have the same sentiments. The other two might not get a pass. A big chunk of the voters in their districts are covered by some of those slurs. I think it would be damaging."

"Here I thought I was sitting on dynamite," Slater said, "and it might not even matter."

"I think it will matter. Just not in a way that'll change things. And maybe not in the way you expect."

"So they won't lose their jobs?"

"Even if they do," Doris said, "they'll just be replaced by the next piggies at the trough. Their adjutants are always raring to jump in when the boss gets termed out."

"It's a dark thought. Exposing this won't really matter."

"I have a lot less faith in our elected officials since I found out one of my oldest friends was on the take. That was your doing."

"Would you rather not have found out?"

"Of course not." She waved it away. "Can you tell me how you got this video, or is that top-secret too?"

"One of the saps in my case is a damn gonif. I think he's trying to extort the car company by threatening to release this."

"Well, it sounds like you have yourself a murky conundrum." She sat up. "So what did you think of my dinner idea?"

He furrowed his brow. "You texted earlier."

She raised her eyebrows but didn't respond.

"Tonight, right? It would just be me. Pike is out of town."

"I know he is, because he actually reads my texts, and answers them."

"Refresh my memory on the dinner thing."

Doris rose. "There's a brewpub on San Fernando Road that I want to try. Burgers and tacos. They have some of your vegan food. I've heard it's good."

"I'm up for that," he said, and rose. "But first I want to edge that buckwheat."

"Is that the one with the salmon-pink flowers? It's been blooming for months and months. The bugs are at it all the time."

"Pollinators love it," Slater said. "It benefits everybody. You're doing your part for the greater good."

Stepping out the back door into the yard, he looked over the row of buckwheat. It was happy here, exuberant even, to the point that it was encroaching on the pathway and needed to be cut back. In the little garden shed he pulled on a pair of work gloves, and strapped on the gardening kneepads, and grabbed the pruning shears, then set to work, kneeling in front of the plant. It was slow going, as he cut the stems deep into the foliage, varying the depth so that it wouldn't look manicured.

This kind of work was meditative, and gave him time to think, far from his quotidian slog in the human cesspool. Literally getting his hands dirty in the earth for a change instead of figuratively with all the lowlifes and fraudsters.

He couldn't do much about that video. It wasn't his to do anything with anyway. If Finley was chiseling Magnesia, that was their problem. But now he knew what Truax really wanted with the guy.

Doris came outside a while later. "There's little

insects flying all around you in the sunbeams. It's like you have a very active aura."

"They're not bothering me. They're after the blooms."

"Wouldn't it be easier just to use a hedge trimmer?"

"If you do that, it looks great for three days," Slater said. "Then you'll get a growth spurt on that side and it'll double down on covering your path."

"You're pulling out a lot, but it doesn't look like you disturbed it at all."

He stood up, the kneepads puckering his jeans. "I'm almost done. Let me rake up and I'll come inside." Glancing at her, he saw that she had tears in her eyes. "What's wrong?"

"Your father would have been so proud of you."

"I doubt that." He stepped closer, and squeezed her around the shoulders with his free arm, holding her for a moment.

Once he'd raked the trimmings into the green bin, he went inside to wash up.

"Do you want some lemonade?" Doris called from the kitchen.

"I can wait until we get to the brewpub."

"You're buying," she said, and scooped up her handbag as she shooed him out the front door. "Dinner is my compensation for sitting through that odious video."

At the pub, they sat outside, and Doris ordered a small of some exotically named IPA. She was right—the pub fare was actually decent.

After he dropped her at home, Slater drove to his house, and went upstairs to the sofa, and sat to pull off his boots. Rising again, he went to the cupboard and poured from the bourbon bottle. His booze rules said his ration was half an inch, but he poured a little more, even though he hadn't completely recovered from last night's excessive snort. It had been a long day.

He needed to talk to Pike before he got too tight. Slurping at the tumbler, he stretched out on the sofa and dialed his number. When Pike picked up, he sounded sleepy.

"Did I wake you?" Slater said.

"I'm just reading."

"In bed? Are you alone? Where's Anton?"

Pike chuckled. "It's patently ridiculous that you're jealous of him."

"I'm not jealous. If he lays a finger on you, I'm coming for him. That's just cold hard facts."

"Do you remember when Hermes comes to the island to tell Calypso that she has to let Odysseus leave? She gets pissed because the male gods get to do whatever they want with the mortals, but when a goddess starts sleeping around, the rules are different."

"I get it. It's totally a double standard."

"Can you see how absurd it is that you're concerned about Anton," Pike said, "and yet you sleep with plenty of other people?"

"None of that means anything," he said quietly. "You know I'm crazy. An emotional wreck. I've shown you my true colors many times."

"I can handle your crazy. I'm just making a point. In case you hadn't thought it through."

"When are you coming back?"

"Tomorrow, if nothing changes," Pike said. "How's your case going?"

"I have something of a dilemma. The number-one rule in my business is that you dance with the one that brung you."

"You're questioning your loyalty to your client?"

"He lied to me," Slater said, "and he's up to something knuckleheaded."

"Everybody lies to you."

"Yeah, there's that."

"Is your client the dynamite guy?"

"No comment."

"But he's using you as a bird dog."

"That's not really problematic. But I don't want to help him mess with someone else. Although his target is lying to me too, and also doing something stupid."

"I know you'll figure it out," Pike said. "You don't need my input. But I would advise you to do the least illegal thing possible."

"Always, petal."

TWENTY-FOUR

N THE MORNING SLATER'S head didn't hurt. That was a good sign—he must have fallen asleep before he'd been able to get too lit.

He was alone, he realized. Where was Pike? Then he remembered, and the whole weight of the last week crashed into his mind. He groaned and reached for his phone, and peered at it, and found Truax's number, and dialed.

"Can we meet?" Slater said when he picked up.

"What have you got for me?"

"I'll tell you in person."

"Sure, I can meet with you. I'm at my office today. It's in the Arts District."

"I'll find it."

He got up, and drank some java, and drove to the Magnesia office. There was an open space on the street out front, and he nosed the Thunderbird in, and dropped some coins into the meter. The gate to the yard was open now, and the lot inside was mostly abandoned, he saw as he walked by. Lots of small businesses worked Saturdays but obviously these turkeys didn't. Truax's plastic car was here, parked over at the side of the structure.

The door to the building was locked, and he hit the little button marked BELL. A minute later Truax appeared and pressed the crash bar to let him inside. Truax's office was just off the lobby, and it was roomy, considering he was an outside contractor, with a trendy glass-and-steel desk, and shiny white cabinets, and a concrete-gray carpet. Truax stepped behind his desk, and Slater sat across from him.

"Why are you here?" Truax said, reclining in his chair and spreading his hands.

Something had changed. Slater could see it right away. It wasn't just because the guy was in his own element—the impatience he'd shown a few days ago had evaporated.

"Well, I know you're not Finley's boyfriend," Slater said. "Why are you after him, and why are you threatening him?"

"Did he tell you I did that?"

"How do you expect me to work for you when you're not giving me the whole story?"

"You never heard me threaten him," Truax said. "He's the one threatening me."

"So you say. It sounds like another layer of bullshit."

Truax scowled, his face reddening, and studied Slater. After a moment he sat up and rolled open a drawer in his desk.

"Here's the real bullshit." Half rising, he handed a sheet of paper across to him.

It was a printout of an email, Slater saw, scanning the page. The message was brief:

> Transfer ten bitcoins to the wallet listed below, and I'll delete the video.

"Finally," Slater said. "A shard of the truth." He set the paper on the desk. "The sender doesn't have a name. You're sure this is Finley?"

"I know it is."

"So he's running a squeeze play on you. I wish you'd told me that a week ago."

"Would you have taken the job?"

"Hard to say." Slater waved a hand. "It must be a pretty damning video."

"The thing is, he's not going to delete it," Truax said. "Not really. If I pay him, he'll just keep asking for more."

"So why are you looking for him? The logical route is not to give him anything, and let him distribute it. Then get him charged with grand theft and extortion."

His eyes narrowed. "That's not the only solution."

"You'd grease the guy for your corporate masters? That kind of loyalty is medieval."

"Where's your loyalty?" Truax demanded. "I'm the one who paid you."

"About that. I've been on this for a week now. I need more cash."

His head tilted back as he guffawed. "Why would I pay you when you haven't brought me anything?"

"I've been busting my ass on this case." Slater watched him for a moment. "It's interesting that you haven't asked me yet where Finley is, or what leads I've run down, or what progress I've made."

Truax raised his eyebrows. "Where's Finley?"

Slater stood up and walked out.

He'd really fucked things up—Truax already knew where Finley was. That's why he hadn't asked.

Climbing into the Thunderbird, he pulled into the street and headed toward the boulevard. He needed to think. Electric vehicles were a high-tech business. Lots of sensors and processors. A thought struck him.

"No," he said softly.

He turned onto a side street and stopped at a curb cut in front of somebody's gate. From the glove box he grabbed a flashlight, then climbed out, and crouched to look under the car, shining the light at the grubby ancient metal. Nothing here looked out of place. He stepped around to the passenger's side, and dropped to his hands and knees, his head near the grimy concrete gutter, craning to see underneath. When he shone the light into the rear wheel well, he spotted a little gray box.

He pulled on it, and it popped off in his hand. Standing erect, he studied it. Unmarked hard plastic housing, magnetic ribs along one side. It was a lot like the ones Svetlana sold him.

Back behind the wheel, he tossed the device on the passenger seat.

"Fucking royal fuck," he shouted.

Truax must have put it there a couple of days ago. When he'd come to his office. The guy had asked him where he parked. A direct question. Why hadn't Slater picked up on that?

He started the engine, then looked at his phone. The tracking app showed that Finley was back at the condo in Pico Union. He dialed his number, relieved that he answered.

"You need to get out of that condo," Slater said.

"What's going on?"

"Truax knows where you are, or close to it."

His voice rose. "You said you wouldn't tell him."

"He followed me the other night, or one of his thugs did. I just figured that out. I found a tracker on my car."

"Damn it."

"Take whatever you can't live without," Slater said. "You can't take the Volvo."

"Why not? It's registered to Irwin."

"Truax might have identified it too. Just grab your stuff and start walking. Now."

"You're sure he's coming for me?"

"No—but do you want to take that chance? Go," he said intently. "Call me when you're away from there."

He popped the gearshift into Drive and turned onto Alameda. Truax had blatantly implied that he was going to try to croak the guy, and Slater had led him right to him.

A box truck parked in front of a convenience store caught his eye, and he pulled in beside it. Grabbing the little gray box, he climbed out. The shop windows faced the parking stalls, but no one inside was paying any attention to him.

There was a lot of steel on these trucks, and as he walked along next to it, Slater surreptitiously attached the device to the end of the fuel tank, right behind the cab. It wasn't obvious, but it wasn't hidden either. It didn't have to be. It just needed to be somewhere other than on his car. Doing this was likely pointless—he'd already revealed Finley's whereabouts. But it might serve to sow some confusion.

As he climbed back into the Thunderbird, a guy walked out of the convenience store, and got into the box truck, and pulled onto Alameda. Once the truck was out of the way, Slater backed into the street and got on the freeway.

His phone buzzed, and he glanced at it—Finley.

"Where are you?" Slater said as he picked up.

"At a friend's place in Koreatown. I walked and then hopped on the bus. I don't think anyone followed me."

"Does Truax have any firearms?"

"I've never seen him with one," Finley said. "You've met him. Does he seem like a gun nut?"

"He's never been strapped when I talked to him. That doesn't mean he won't be. Do you know where he lives?"

"Way out in the sticks. One of those towns along the Ventura Freeway."

"Does his wife work?"

"The gossip in the office was that she was a sizzler," Finley said. "I doubt she does that anymore. They have a couple of brats, right—you can't be working the pole and pulling singles out of your G-string when you have to cut up orange wedges for soccer practice."

"So she's probably at the house most of the time," Slater said.

"Why do you care about their house? What are you planning to do?"

"Truax got the drop on me. It's my turn to try to outsmart him."

"You know he's dangerous, right? Is that why you asked about guns?"

"He doesn't know what I know."

"If you're looking for where he sleeps," Finley said, "he doesn't commute from the sticks every day. For weeknights, Magnesia rents a townhouse for him closer to the office. I think it's in Silver Lake."

"Do you know the address?"

"I can find out. I copied all of Magnesia's HR files, in case I ever needed leverage."

"Aren't you a sneaky little fuck."

"I prefer the term 'resourceful.'"

"Can you get into those files?" Slater said.

"Easy. They're in a cloud drive. Let me do it now."

Keeping his eyes on the sea of brake lights in the stop-and-go freeway traffic, he left the line open, and heard the intermittent sound of fingers on a keyboard.

"Got it," Finley said finally. "I'll text you the address of his corporate crash pad. So what am I supposed to do now?"

"Whatever you want. Just keep your head down. Don't go back to Irwin's condo, or anywhere near it."

"Well, that sucks. I feel like I'm homeless."

Slater wanted to say *You got your damn self into this,* but he didn't. One of the many shrinks Doris had sent him to in his youth called that "the hot potato"—illustrating the idea that throwing blame at someone served no purpose. That didn't mean Finley wasn't a fucking idiot, but he didn't need to get into it with him either.

"We'll talk later," Slater said, and ended the call.

When he pulled into his garage, he checked the tracking app. Finley really was in Koreatown. On the map it looked like the dot was in an apartment building. Climbing out from behind the wheel, he briefly stepped into the stairwell and called up the stairs, but there was no answer. Pike wasn't back yet.

From his gear cabinet he loaded the key binder and the lock-reading probe into the black duffel bag, and heaved it into the trunk of the Thunderbird. Checking Finley's text, he put Truax's weeknight address into the navigation app, then backed into the street.

It wasn't far, and the software sent him on Alvarado, then into the hills above the reservoir. He pulled up to a row of townhouses on a quiet hillside street. Once he'd scoped out the right house number, he parked a few doors down.

Reaching into the backseat, he pulled on his blue ball cap, and fished a pair of the black latex gloves out of the box, and wriggled his hands into them. He grabbed Svetlana's stealthy glasses, and clicked on the power switch, then put them on.

When he climbed out he pulled the cap low over his brow. There were no security cameras visible out front, but doorbell cameras were pretty ubiquitous these days. As he walked toward Truax's front door, he connected the lock probe's cable to his phone. Svetlana's app popped up and displayed "готов" on a black screen. He glanced around to make sure he was alone before he crouched to study the door hardware.

It was a basic mass-market deadbolt, and he gently eased the probe into the keyhole. The screen instantly flashed green and displayed 215. Tucking his phone away, he strode back toward the street.

A woman stepped out the front door of a townhouse farther down the row, eyeing him as she pulled it closed. Dressed in stretchy black and pink, she had her dark hair tied back, and a rolled-up foam yoga mat under one arm. The timing was precisely wrong—Slater couldn't avoid her without it being obvious. She stepped out to the sidewalk, intersecting his path.

"Hey," he said, and nodded as he walked past.

"What's with the gloves?" she called after him.

"Food delivery." Slater paused and turned back, affecting an East LA intonation. It fit with the way he looked. Confirming people's stereotypes was a quick way to get them to dismiss you and move on. He waggled his fingers in the air. "I don't think you want these grubby paws all over your hamburger sandwiches without protection."

She frowned. "Aren't they in bags? I don't eat burgers anyway."

"Well, your neighbors do." Turning, he walked away.

"I like your glasses," she called after him.

Slater strode past the Thunderbird toward the end of the block, then stepped into the street behind a ratty twenty-year-old Civic. This was the kind of car a delivery guy would drive. With any luck it wasn't hers. Pausing at the vehicle's rear end, he pulled out his phone and studied the blank screen, scanning for the woman in his peripheral vision. She was ignoring him now, and climbed into an SUV, and fired up the engine, a moment later pulling into the street. Once she was out of view, he pocketed his phone and walked back to the Thunderbird.

In the trunk he flipped through the heavy pages of the key binder to find the pouch marked 215, and slipped it out, then slammed the lid. He palmed it and walked back to Truax's crash pad.

The key twisted easily, retracting the bolt. If there was an alarm, it would go off right away, and he'd have to abort. He took a breath, and pushed open the door, and stepped inside.

There was no sound, and no alarm panel here. Closing the door behind him, he pocketed the key and called out, "Gas company." Standing motionless for a moment, he listened, but the place was quiet.

This was a tiny room, just deep enough for a sofa and a side table. It was probably meant to be the foyer and to have no furniture at all. A set of carpeted stairs led upward, and directly opposite the door to the street was another door with a deadbolt in it.

The thumb turn was on this side, and it wasn't bolted, Slater found when he tried the handle, and pulled it open. It was a garage bay for a single car, currently devoid of a vehicle. He flicked on the lights and looked around. It was spare except for the electric car charger mounted on the wall, its thick black cord coiled on a hook. On a shelf nearby was an array of cleaning products, sponges, and rolls of paper towel. Parked next to that was an upright vacuum cleaner, and on the floor in the corner was a bulky camping cooler.

Killing the lights, Slater pulled the door closed, but then paused. Something snagged in his mind. Why would Truax have camping stuff here? This was a week-night place. His house and his cis-het nuclear family were in another town. That's where he'd start his camping trips from.

Turning, he stepped back into the garage, and crouched to inspect the cooler. A blue plastic box, it had a tight-fitting white lid. All the components were thick and heavily insulated to keep the beer cold for days on end. He gingerly pried open the lid with his fingers. No ice, no beer—instead there was a stack of familiar cylinders wrapped in waxy brown paper.

More freaking dynamite. What was this guy up to? Slater wasn't going to touch them, even with his gloved hands, but he didn't need to. From the neat arrangement he could see there were a dozen sticks. He pulled out his phone and snapped a photo.

Once he'd resealed the lid on the cooler, he went back into the apartment and up the stairs. There was more space up here, but it was small, one bedroom at the back and a main room with a kitchenette. It wasn't personalized in any way, with generic art prints on the walls, bland linens on the bed. The only book in the place was on the coffee table, a picture book about 1950s cars.

Slater pulled open all the cupboards. There were a few basic pots and pans and dishes. In the bedroom he dropped to his knees to look under the bed, but there was nothing there, not even dust bunnies. He dug through the clothes in the bureau drawers. It was all bland straight-guy stuff. A couple of suits hung in the closet, with dress shoes and a pair of sneakers on the floor underneath. Against the wall behind the shoes was a small black zippered bag. Lifting it out, Slater zipped it open.

Greenbacks—a jumble of bundles of cash. They were all new racks, still with the mustard-yellow currency strap on them. He picked one up and fanned through the bills, the crisp paper buzzing against his latex-clad thumb. It was real, as far as he could tell. Sequentially numbered mint-fresh C-notes.

There were six racks in all, he found, rummaging in the bag. That made sixty grand. It wasn't from drug runners or arms dealers or some other illicit source—this was new money from a bank. But no way was this for a legit purpose. Sixty grand was the exact dollar amount of the kickback the Magnesia goon had promised the politicians in that video. This was a bribe, and Truax was the delivery boy.

Slater arranged the racks on the carpet next to the bag and took a photo of them, then put them back in and zipped it closed. He'd seen enough. Downstairs he relocked the front door with his ghost key, and walked out to the street, and peeled off the gloves.

TWENTY-FIVE

T HE SUN WAS LOW in the northwest, the light turning golden as Slater drove back to his own neighborhood. On the street out front he saw Pike's SUV, and once he'd pulled into the garage, he hustled up the stairs.

He found Pike out on the deck, reclining in a lounger, a mostly empty bottle of Corona on the deck beside him. He was still dressed for work, with his ratty old cowboy hat covering his face. As Slater stepped outside, he stirred, and pulled the hat off, and squinted at him.

Pushing his knees apart, Slater sat facing him on the lounger, and leaned in, ravishing him, mouthing his neck, breathing in the heady scent of his skin. Eventually he pulled back.

"Hello to you too," Pike said.

"You're so fucking beautiful. I can't stand it. You drive me crazy." Slater grasped his forearms and squeezed them. He raised his voice. "Crazy."

Pike chuckled, his eyes bright. "Suck it up."

"You look tired."

"I was up early," Pike said. "It was a lot of driving. I'm hungry, but it's too late for lunch, too early for dinner."

"I'm in the middle of something, but I kind of need to eat too. There's stuff to make burritos."

"Sold."

Rising, Slater snatched up his hat from the deck and put it on his own head. Pike followed him inside.

"You look totally fuckable in that hat."

"It was the first thing I ever noticed about you," Slater said. "At that gas station in Voirrey's Corner. From the neck down it was all business-casual, but up top it was the wild West."

In the kitchen, Pike started pulling stuff out of the icebox.

"You're not going to want to eat again?" Slater said, and tossed the hat on the dining table.

"Maybe later we can do that thing French people do in the summer. Eat super late. That hotcha place downtown with the floor show has vegan grub for you. I bet it's open late on Saturday night."

"Greenleaf. Let me check."

On his phone, Slater checked the kitchen hours, then looked through the roster for the floor show. There was no sign of the vocalist Woody Newkirk. It would be awkward to run into that guy with Pike on his arm. He tucked the phone away.

"Let's do it. There's a big band on after the floor show."

Once they'd thrown together a couple of burritos and microwaved them, they sat at the dining table to eat.

"So how's your case going?" Pike said, his mouth half full of food.

No way was he going to tell him about Truax and finding another stash of dynamite. That had already caused enough trouble between them.

"More bullshit and drudgery," Slater said. "How was Fresno?"

"Hot. It seems worse than the desert for some reason. Hopkins calls it Nickel-nickel-nine."

"Why?"

"It's from the area code."

"That's a terrible nickname." Slater frowned. "It's

longer than the actual name of the place. What is wrong with that guy?"

Pike chuckled and gestured with his half-eaten burrito. "We also went to Merced. It's a little farther up the road. Hopkins calls it Mer-dead."

"It sounds like he has his finger on the pulse of the Central Valley."

"He's been working up there for a while."

After they'd eaten, Slater rose. "Do you mind cleaning up?"

"It's putting two plates in the dishwasher. I think I can handle it."

He leaned in to kiss him good-bye, lingering in it for a moment, then went down to the garage and opened his gear cabinet.

In a little plastic zip-top bag he found one of Svetlana's electric-socket cameras. A flat plate with three prongs on the back, the face was white with the three slots painted on it in black to mimic the socket it was pressed into. Svetlana's thinking was that you wouldn't notice it unless you tried to plug something into it, and even then it would easily be mistaken for a childproofing device, as the camera lens was a lone minuscule pit hidden in the black paint. Plugged into an electric socket, it didn't need a battery, so it was thin, and broadcast its video stream over the cell network.

Truax knew a lot, but he didn't know that Slater had tipped Finley to flee. He wasn't sure if Truax knew what building or what unit Finley was staying in, but if he planted this surreptitious camera in the condo, he'd soon know if Truax or one of his thugs broke in to the place.

Slater waited for the garage door to roll up, then backed into the street. The deep blue of twilight was fading, and the streetlamps were on. He drove to Pico Union, with the navigation sending him on surface streets instead of the freeway. It must be jammed. Saturday night was busy everywhere, and when he turned onto Finley's street, there was nowhere to park.

Cruising down the block, he spotted the dark-blue Volvo at the curb. At least Finley had listened to him and not taken it. He circled the block, trolling for a street space. These dense old neighborhoods were frustrating at night. Eventually he found a spot a few blocks away, on the boulevard, at a meter space.

As he climbed out, he tucked the little camera into his shirt pocket. It was completely dark out now. He assumed a brisk pace as he strode the few blocks back toward Finley's hideout.

When he turned onto the block with the condo, he saw two guys standing in the street, about halfway up to the next corner. They were near the Volvo. Could these be Truax's guys? But as he got closer, he saw that one of them had a hand jack. He disappeared from view as he dropped to the asphalt. A moment later the back end of one of the vehicles at the curb rose a few inches. That was the Volvo. They were going to steal the catalytic converter.

The other guy stood close to the vehicle, holding something heavy—an electric saw. His head swiveled toward Slater, and he locked eyes with him. That was ballsy. They weren't even trying to be stealthy about it.

It wasn't his battle, but that was Finley's ride. If they weren't armed, Slater might be able to scare them off.

When he was a few paces closer, he shouted, "Hey."

The guy holding the saw shifted it to his left hand and reached for the small of his back. Slater quickly crouched behind an SUV parked at the curb, waiting for the gunshot. He took a couple of breaths. No sound came—maybe the guy was waiting for him to reappear.

He could hear their voices, speaking in Spanish. He

couldn't parse any of it except the word *pendejo*. That was about him. Then came the sound of steel scraping on asphalt. The jack. Were they pulling it out, abandoning the attempt?

For a moment he debated rising to take a look, but that upped the risk of him getting capped. In the middle of that thought came a sudden flash of light that lit up everything around. For an instant it was broad daylight, with a loud *boom* that punched into his ears and pulled the air out of his lungs.

Slater grabbed the bumper of the SUV to keep his balance. What the hell just happened? It felt like somebody had thrown a grenade. His heart pounded with a rush of adrenaline. Stuff was falling on the sidewalk and on the cars, he realized. Chunks of metal and plastic struck the asphalt.

The blast had been so loud it had messed up his hearing. Something landed beside him on the concrete sidewalk with a *clank*. It was a license plate, bent into a parabolic curve.

He kept his hands on the SUV and rose enough to see over the vehicle. Up the block where the Volvo had been was an orange ball of flames. It wasn't even a car anymore. He stepped past the vehicle to look for the catalytic converter thieves. They were in the street, almost at the end of the block, illuminated by the flicker of the flames. One of them was on his feet, staggering, like he'd been injured. The other guy was flat out. Slater started toward them, and watched as the ambulatory one rolled the other guy onto his side, then pulled him up to his knees. With help the other guy made it to his feet. They must have been running away when the blast hit—if they'd been under the car, or even next to it, they'd be toast.

They didn't need his help, Slater decided, and paused

in the street, and worked his jaw to try to recover his hearing. He stepped closer to the fire, already growing smaller as it burned itself out. The steel frame of the Volvo's safety cage and the engine block were visible amid the flames, but everything else was either burning or gone.

There was debris all over the street, he saw, looking around. Some of the chunks were still smoldering. People were coming into the street now, out of the apartments up and down the block, standing to gawk at the scene. Nobody moved too close to the fire.

It struck him then that he needed to get out of here. Turning away from the wreckage of the Volvo, Slater walked toward the end of the block, passing several people who stood eyeing the scene, eyes wide, mouths agape.

Stepping between the parked cars, he moved onto the sidewalk. On top of a fence fronting a little yard he spotted a leaf, and picked it up as he passed. It was green and fresh, newly shorn from its tree by the percussive force of the Volvo blowing up. A bauhinia. He'd noticed them on this block the other day. In the spring these were all gravy, with a riot of glamorous blossoms, but things got messy at this time of year as they dropped their janky seed pods all over the street.

Gazing at the gentle curving shape of the leaf as he walked, he twirled its short stem. He was dazed, he suddenly realized. In shock from his proximity to the blast. He dropped the leaf and eyed a guy approaching him on the sidewalk.

"What happened?" the guy said, his tone intent.

Slater could hear him, but the sound was muffled.

"I don't know." His own voice felt weird and loud.

He turned the corner and looked ahead. The boulevard was at the end of the next block. Soon the

Thunderbird came into view. The sirens were audible now, and getting louder. Had it taken them a long time to come, or was his perception of time messed up too?

Climbing into his car, he started the engine and quickly pulled into the street. He needed to put distance between him and the scene. There was no telling how much of the neighborhood the cops or the fire department would tape off and lock down.

Ahead on the boulevard he could see flickering blue and red lights approaching, then a prowl car blew past, siren blaring. Next came a lumbering ladder truck, laying on its horn even though no one was impeding its path.

Glancing at his phone, Slater checked Svetlana's tracking app. Finley was still in Koreatown. He dialed his number.

"We need to talk," Slater said when he answered. "I'm going to pick you up."

"What's going on?"

"I'll be there in a couple minutes."

"Why don't you just come up?" Finley said. "I'm alone here."

"What's the door code?"

"It's easy to remember. It's the year the UFO era began."

Slater thought about it, pushing through the dazed muddle in his brain. "1947?"

"That's it." Finley laughed. "Do you want Margo's address?"

He already knew where it was, but Finley didn't need to know that. "Sure."

Finley rattled it off, and he ended the call.

This was another dense neighborhood, and he had to park a block away, on the boulevard, and walk to the building. Once he was upstairs, he rapped on the door.

When Finley pulled it open, he was wearing a gray

T-shirt and tight black stretchy shorts that emphasized his bulky junk. It was hard to tell whether they were workout shorts or underpants.

"You look great," Slater said.

"You don't." His brow furrowed. "Come in."

It was a studio apartment, he saw, stepping inside. The bed was in the corner, and there was a kitchen counter. On the desk under the window he spotted Finley's copy of *Saucers over the Southwest.* Of course he'd bring that with him. That's where his extortion material was hidden.

The room was wallpapered in blue and green paisley, and a swag lamp hung over the little dining table. Next to the sofa a clear Lucite bubble chair dangled from the ceiling.

"Groovy pad," Slater said, taking it in.

"Margo's into the 1970s."

"Where is Margo?"

"Shanghai. For work." His eyes narrowed. "You look a little rattled."

"Does Margo have any sauce?"

"Help yourself," Finley said, and pointed him to the liquor cupboard.

There weren't a lot of options, just vodka and tequila and a cloying liqueur, but behind those in the shadows he spotted the prize—a bottle of Glenmorangie. It was dark for scotch, he saw as he pulled it out, and the label said it was eighteen years old. This was decent stuff. The bottle had a red bow taped on it, and it hadn't been opened. Did Margo even know what she had here? Why wasn't she drinking this? Cracking the seal, he poured three fingers into a tumbler.

"You opened a new bottle?" Finley said. He folded his arms. "There was stuff open already."

"Not the good stuff."

"Well, I'll have to explain that to Margo."

"Tell her a rat got into it." He gestured with the tumbler. "You want a taste?"

"No," he said flatly. "Your hand is trembling. What's going on?"

He dropped into the armchair adjacent to the sofa, across from the bubble chair, and slurped at the scotch, closing his eyes for a moment to savor it. He rarely got such good booze. Finley perched on the sofa and leaned toward him.

Eyeing him, Slater took another sip. "I can't believe Margo left this alone and neglected. Good booze needs to be appreciated. Tell her she needs to smoke 'em if she's got 'em."

Finley gestured impatiently. "Did something happen with Truax?"

Slater took a breath. "I was going to check out the condo. To see if Truax had sent his goons for you. I was about fifty feet from Irwin's Volvo when it blew up."

He frowned. "What?"

"Two guys were messing with it. They had a jack and a saw. They were going to steal the catalytic converter. They must have set off Truax's explosives."

"Irwin's car blew up?"

"That's what I just said." He slurped at the scotch, and coughed a little at the fumes in his throat, and closed his eyes to savor the delicious burn.

"How do you know it was explosives?" Finley said. "Maybe the thieves accidentally punctured the gas tank with the jack."

"Gasoline burns fast. It doesn't explode. There's chunks of burning Volvo up and down the street. Debris all over the block. Gasoline fires don't do that. Explosives do that."

"You're sure it was Truax?"

"I didn't see him plant it on the Volvo, but I saw him

buy dynamite from a mining supply company. Now I know what it was for."

"It was meant for me." Finley looked pale now, he saw, and he was breathing hard.

"Why else would your car blow up?"

"What happened to the thieves with the jack?"

"I think they were trying to fade. They got flattened but I saw them on their feet after. If they'd been closer to the blast, they'd be pink mist."

He looked away. "I might have gotten myself in over my head."

"Is there any way Truax could know about this place, about Margo?" Slater said. "Is she connected to Magnesia? Do you have mutual friends at work?"

His brow furrowed, and he didn't speak for a moment. "I don't think so."

There were beads of sweat on Finley's brow, he saw, and the color had completely drained from his face.

"I could have died tonight, Slater. I think I'm going to throw up."

"Christ. You're going into shock." He set his glass on the coffee table and pushed himself out of the chair. He extended a hand. "Get up."

Finley took his hand and rose, and Slater pulled him over to the easy chair.

"What are you doing?"

"Sit in my lap," Slater said.

He didn't protest, and followed him down onto the chair, and draped an arm around Slater's neck. Finley was shivering now, and Slater rubbed his back, and his arms, and his thighs.

"You're safe here," he said softly. "No one's coming for you tonight."

Finley leaned into him, resting his head on his shoulder.

"Take slow, deep breaths," Slater said. "Through your nose."

He could feel him doing it, could hear his breathing gradually slow as he held him firmly in his arms. Eventually the shivering subsided.

"Better?" Slater said.

"My head hurts, but I don't feel like I'm going to pass out anymore." He kissed his neck.

"You should crash." Slater prodded him to rise and steered him to the bed.

"You've got a stiffy," Finley said, looking him over as he sat down.

Slater adjusted the crotch of his jeans. "It's involuntary. Because you're so beautiful. And those shorts aren't concealing anything."

He chuckled. "You want to ride this pony?"

"I do. A lot. But I'm not going to. Take off your shirt."

Finley pulled it over his head, then got under the covers.

"Can you stay?"

Slater dropped to one knee at the bedside and caressed his cheek. "No. Try to get some sleep."

"What am I going to do?"

"That's not a question for tonight. You can worry about it tomorrow."

Rising, he let himself out, and went down to the street. The night air felt good on the walk back to the Thunderbird. He needed to make some decisions. Why had he had that scotch? But maybe it didn't matter. Even with a muddled head he knew what he had to do.

On the drive to his house, he phoned Andy, glad that he answered.

"It's after dark, son," Andy said. "Well past my ... work hours."

"I know. It's urgent."

"You sound a little shook."

"Are you near your computer?"

"I'm doing other stuff," Andy said.

"With that gunsel Kyle?"

"Better known as my ... husband. What do you need?"

"That video. I need it to go to every local journalist you can think of."

"Tonight?"

"That's why I called."

"Oh, man." Andy huffed. "It'll have to be sent ... anonymously. Setting that up is a ... bit of work."

"I'll pay you golden time. Whatever you need."

"I didn't keep a copy of it. You'll have to share the file with me."

"I'll do that now," Slater said. "Send it to the *Bugle*, the TV stations, all those gossipy local websites."

"You're a pain in the ass sometimes, Ibáñez."

"I know," he said, and ended the call.

TWENTY-SIX

When Slater got to his house, he found Pike upstairs in the bedroom. He was getting dressed up, already in dark pants, pulling on a sharp blue shirt.

"We're going out." Slater ran a hand through his hair, taking in the scene. He'd completely forgotten about that.

Stepping over to him, Pike embraced him, and kissed his neck. "You look a little rattled."

"It's work-related."

"If you need to decompress, we can stay in."

"It'll be good to go out. Eat a meal in the middle of the freaking night. We'll feel like Frenchmen."

Slater changed out of his jeans into a pair of black dress pants. He hated the way they felt, like he was wearing nothing, but Greenleaf was high-tone, and he didn't want to look like the help. He pulled on a tan linen shirt that Doris had bought him, then stood next to Pike in front of the floor mirror.

Slater met his gaze in the glass. "You look so fuckable right now."

"Keep your eyes on the prize." He squeezed him around the waist. "A Frenchman's dinner."

As they trooped down the stairs, Slater said, "Can we take your rig?"

They climbed into Pike's SUV and headed downtown. Two floors above a street-level restaurant, Greenleaf dated back nearly a century, in a big room clad in lots of rich dark wood, with a bit of the redwood forest motif carried over from the dining room downstairs. The bar stretched the length of the side wall and was crowded with patrons.

"I love that people dress up," Pike said, as they stood at the front desk, waiting for the host.

"They have to. This is where the hep cats come to groove."

Up front was the bandstand, with a low stage, in a roomy alcove painted powder blue. Half a dozen musicians, dressed in black and white, were seated with their instruments—a bass guitar, a keyboard on a stand, plus a trombone and a sax and a trumpet. The front of the drummer's big bass was emblazoned with GREENLEAF and the bar's logo. They were playing a fast-paced tune he didn't recognize, and on the parquet dance floor fronting the bandstand, three couples were gyrating to the music.

The host led them farther back to the tables, each with a little fake battery-powered candle. They sat facing the band and ordered some food.

"The dancers are really good at it," Pike said, gesturing toward them with his chin. "Are they real, or are they part of the show?"

Their drinks arrived, two margaritas, and Slater leaned back as the server set them down. He tapped his glass on Pike's. "Who knows? They're all dressed differently, so if I had to guess, I'd say they were customers like you and me."

The band ran through the end of the song they were playing, and people around the room clapped. As the musicians rose and filed off the stage, the woman with the trumpet paused at the mike stand. "We'll be back a little later. Right now we return to the floor show. Please welcome the lovely Mary Jane Bamber."

A rail-thin woman, maybe still a teenager, stepped onto the stage. Her hair was butched short, and she was wearing a pink minidress. After a perfunctory bow from the neck, she stood sideways, reaching her arms over her head, then bent her knees, leaning back until her palms connected with the floor.

"A contortionist?" Pike said.

"Maybe it's yoga. I've seen poses like that."

Not content just to hold the pose, the woman started to move her feet, her black shoes clacking loudly on the stage. She was tap dancing.

"That's not yoga," Pike said.

The server set down their plates and then stepped away.

"I'm not going to be able to eat with her doing that," Slater said. "She's making me nauseous."

Pike laughed. "How long can she possibly keep that up?"

He was right, and soon the woman stood erect, red-faced and beaming, and took a deep bow. As she walked off, a guy in a tweed jacket stepped out, followed by three little white dogs.

"Jack Russels," Pike said. "Those are smart dogs."

Slater didn't reply, as he was working on his food. It felt good to eat, like the activity itself was pulling him back down to the ground.

Upbeat recorded music came through the sound system, and one of the dogs jumped into the guy's arms. He extended his arm, and the dog walked out to his elbow, carefully maintaining its balance. The next dog jumped, and walked out on his other arm, and then the third jumped onto his shoulder. People around the room clapped at each successive feat.

"Those are good dogs," Pike said.

Slater had to laugh, almost gagging on a mouthful of food. It seemed so absurd, the yoga tap-dancing, the performing dogs, Pike's inane reaction to them. Maybe he was still punch-drunk from that explosion.

The man in tweed held up a bright-red hoop now, and the dogs jumped through it in sequence, not hesitating as he twirled around with it, leaping at just the right moment. People clapped, and the guy took a bow, then stepped up to the mike. "Up next is the lovely Roquelle."

A woman in a long midnight-blue dress came out, her jewelry sparkling in the spotlights against her dark skin. Her hair was swept back. Without any music, she launched into a song:

> A tinkling piano in the next apartment
> Those stumbling words that told you what my
>   heart meant
> A fairground's painted swings
> These foolish things remind me of you.

Done with his food, Slater slurped at his margarita and folded his arms, only half listening to Roquelle's troubles. Even though those thieves had walked away from the Volvo, they still might be injured. He was extremely lucky he'd been able to walk away too.

"You're a million miles away," Pike said.

Everyone was clapping for the torch singer, he realized. "It's work stuff." He leaned closer to Pike. "So if a car blows up on the streets of LA, do they call in the feds?"

His eyes narrowed. "Is this about your dynamite guy?"

"I heard on the radio earlier that a car blew up over by K-town. I'm just curious who was handling it."

"It depends on why it exploded. Probably it's local PD."

Roquelle launched into another song, and they sat

back and took it in.

"Is it odd she has no accompaniment?" Pike said.

"A little, I guess. But she has the pipes to pull it off."

After Roquelle, the band came back to play. The music was fast, and people drifted over from the bar to dance. The second song was slower, and Pike shifted his chair back.

"Come on—let's dance."

"I'm no good at it," Slater said. "And you're really good at it. It makes me look like a chump."

"Just let me lead. As objectionable as that sounds."

Slater rose and followed him onto the parquet. Pike took hold of his hand and planted his other palm firmly on his back.

"You're the only man on the planet I'd do this for," Slater said.

Pike told him how to move his feet, demonstrating with his own, and eventually Slater picked up the rhythm. Once they were into it, and had a groove, Pike steered him around the floor.

When the song ended, Slater pulled him closer and nuzzled his neck. "I get it now. This is extremely hot."

"Plus nobody can stay cranky when they're dancing. It always feels good." The next song started, and Pike shuffled his feet. "One more."

Eventually they left, and rode back to the house in contented silence. Pike went to get undressed, and Slater trudged up to the kitchen, and poured his ration of bourbon into a tumbler. He'd had a drink at Greenleaf, but that didn't count.

Stepping onto the patio, he gazed out at the towers of the Financial District beyond the hillside. The evening finally felt cool, and he sipped at the heady golden elixir. The low rumble of the city filled his ears. It never stopped. Some of the noise might be residual from

Arapahoe Street, he realized, or even that torch singer's high notes. Either way it was about this place, the weight of it, the constant grinding roar.

Pike stepped out onto the deck behind him, and he turned to look. He was naked except for a pair of high-cut red briefs.

"The fire-engine skivvies," Slater said. "They're back."

"I got a new pair." He jutted his chin, and waggled something in his hand. It was a little plastic tube of lube. "There was talk earlier this week of some rock-hard action."

"I'll fuck you right here, if that's what you want," Slater said.

"Put down your applejack."

Slater set it on the table and stepped closer, running his hands over Pike's warm back, nuzzling his neck.

"I should ditch the dress pants," he murmured.

"Leave your clothes on. It's hot."

Slater met his mouth, and slid his fingers into the red underpants, and pushed them down.

"Over here," Pike said, and stepped out of his skivvies, and stood at the low wall surrounding the deck. Facing the dark city, he braced his hands on it.

Slater stepped behind him, reaching around to run his hands over his belly and his pecs.

"You drive me fucking crazy," he said, and unzipped the fly of his flimsy pants, and pulled out his cock, already hard.

Once he'd lubed up, he pressed into Pike, who stifled a groan, and working together, they gradually got into it. Slater wrapped his arms around his torso as he thrust into him, breathing hard, both of them drenched in sweat.

"You're so fucking beautiful," Slater said as he got close.

Finally he pressed in hard as he climaxed. With Slater still inside him, Pike guided his hand to his cock. As Slater stroked him, Pike arched his back, leaning on him, and grunted through his teeth as he came.

They stood together for a moment, Slater's chin on his shoulder, Pike leaning on the wall, Slater holding him close. Eventually Pike turned to him and mouthed his neck.

"How did I get here?" Slater said, still panting, and ran a hand into Pike's sweaty hair.

"I'm thinking you climbed the stairs, like I did."

"I mean, how did my life get so fucking good?"

Pike chuckled and grasped the sides of his belt, tugging on it, pulling him closer. "I was wondering the same thing."

TWENTY-SEVEN

I N THE MORNING SLATER's head hurt. It wasn't a hang-over, he decided. More likely from being caught in a damn explosion. Daylight filled the room, and Pike was up already.

Grabbing his phone, he checked the newspaper. Andy had done it. The story about the video was right up top: "County Supervisors in Racist Rant." Below it was a still photo from the video of the meeting. Scrolling down, he saw the subtitle: "Motor Pool Acquisitions Called into Question." Doris was right—the name-calling eclipsed the actually illegal part, the contract fixing and the kick-backs.

In his hand his phone buzzed with a text from Doris:

Cue the tsuris. Was that you?

His instinct was to swipe it away, but she'd helped him on this job. He sent her a reply:

Sunlight sterilizes things. Maybe some of those trash bags will be forced out of office.

He checked the front page again and scrolled down. The second story was headlined "Two Injured in Car Explosion: Botched Catalytic Converter Theft." The ar-ticle didn't contain much detail, but it was interesting that the cops hadn't called it a bombing. At least not yet.

Setting his phone aside, Slater looked at the hazy sky outside the sheers. In the sober light of morning, he knew what he had to do.

Forcing himself out of bed, he got dressed, a clean pair of jeans and a short-sleeved shirt, and went upstairs. Pike was out on the deck, sitting at the patio table with a mug and a half-eaten bagel on a plate. Once he'd poured himself a cup of java from the pot, he went outside, and leaned in to embrace Pike.

"You didn't sleep very well," Pike said. "You seemed agitated. Do you think it was the dancing, or the upright sex thing?"

"Last night was a blast," he said, and took the adjacent chair, and set his mug on the table. "It's just my case. It's getting intense."

"You finally tracked down your target?"

"I did, and he's a handful."

"I'm going to go over and swap out one of Doris's wall sconces today. You want to come with?"

Slater frowned. "It's your day off. You don't have to work for her. She already likes you, if that's your angle. Tell her to hire a damn handyman."

"It's not an angle." He chuckled. "I genuinely want to help her out."

"It makes me look bad. Like I'm neglecting her."

"Or," Pike said, raising his eyebrows, "it makes us both look good. Like we're a team that gets stuff done. Plus it gives me a chance to get to know her better."

"OK," he said evenly. "Just watch your back. She's tricky."

Pike rose, and dropped to one knee in front of his chair, and grasped his thighs. A wry smirk on his face, he looked into his eyes. "She's scheming to derail your life?"

"Since day one."

Leaning in, he mouthed Slater's jaw, and squeezed his arms, and they spent a minute with their mouths tight together. Once Pike left, he sat back and turned his face to the morning sun, willing the joe to kickstart his brain. It felt good to warm up.

Eventually he sat up and phoned Conrad.

"I'm busy, Slater," he said when he picked up. "What do you need?"

"I've got something for you. Is there any chance you're working the car bombing in Pico Union?"

"I'm not on it, but I heard about it. We haven't actually said that it was a bombing. That implies that you know something about it."

"I know who did it," Slater said. "A guy named Truax. He works at a company called Magnesia Motors. I had you look into him last week. Are you writing this down?"

Conrad lowered his voice. "Christ, Slater—how are you involved in this?"

"I'll text you Truax's details."

"I remember the name. He's the car tamperer."

"Truax hired me to find the guy who was driving the Volvo. The registered owner is a croaker named Irwin Ganz, but he wasn't the target of the bomb. That's the guy who borrowed the car. Irwin's brother-in-law. He also worked at Magnesia. His name is Finley López."

"You had me look him up too," Conrad said. "No record, Chinatown, lots of parking tickets."

"Good memory."

"How do you know Truax booby-trapped the car?"

"I was shagging him," Slater said, "and I saw him buy dynamite at a business called Cali Rock and Mineral in Wilmington. The guy had a hard-on for Finley. If he didn't rig the Volvo himself, he paid someone to do it." Slater took a breath. He could feel the adrenaline surging just from talking about it. "It's him."

"If this is valid, it's going to save a whole bunch of people a whole lot of time."

"It's good dope," Slater said. "Get yourself on the case. If you bring this info, they'll have to put you on it, right? Get yourself a nice pat on the back."

"I don't think I'll be able to keep your name out of it. With all this detail I can't really spin it as an anonymous tip."

"I figured. I'll come in and make a statement. Just not today."

Once he'd ended the call, Slater texted him Truax's phone number, and the address of the townhouse, and Finley's new phone number. Rising, he went inside and set his mug in the dishwasher. His phone buzzed in his pants, and when he pulled it out to check, he saw that it was Finley.

"I don't know how you did it," Finley said, "but I know it was you."

"You're welcome. It sounds like you're over your shock from last night."

"You ripped me off," he shouted.

"I saved your ass," Slater said. "I saved you from yourself. Now Truax doesn't have any reason to come for you again."

"I was trying to cash in on that video."

"And Truax was trying to grease you."

"I could have handled that."

"No, I handled that," Slater said, raising his voice. "When I told you not to drive the Volvo."

"How did you get the video?" Finley demanded.

"Listen, have you had lunch? I'll pick you up."

"You don't get to be all glib. You're an asshole," he shouted.

"I know that," Slater said. "I'll be there in twenty."

Hustling down to the garage, Slater backed the Thunderbird into the street and drove to Margo's. As he pulled up out front he texted Finley, who appeared a minute later, scowling at him as he climbed in the passenger side.

"Thief," Finley said intently.

Slater sighed and pulled into the street. "I know you want to be pissed at someone. It doesn't need to be me."

"Where are we going?"

"Have you ever been to Wet Bar?"

"A bar? It's barely past lunchtime."

"It's more like a pub. There's good vegan food."

Slater turned onto Western and drove a few blocks, nosing into a street space near the pub. Inside it was busy, with all the booths occupied, and loud conversation filling the air. They sat on stools at the bar.

The bartender, a guy in his twenties with a little mustache and his black hair pulled back into a knot, stepped over and raised his eyebrows.

"Bring me the plant burger," Slater said.

Finley was looking over the menu card. "Eggs over easy and oatmeal."

"Drinks?" the guy said.

Finley shook his head. "Not before five."

"It's Sunday," Slater said. "Cocktail hour starts at breakfast." He snapped his fingers. "I know—an Irish car bomb. He'll have one too."

The bartender's eyes narrowed. "What's that, exactly?"

"A pint of dark beer with a shot of Irish whisky dumped in it. Don't use Guinness, though. They make it with fish guts. Use a red ale from the tap, and whatever whisky you have in the well. It doesn't even have to be Irish."

"Easy enough," he said, and stepped away.

Finley looked at him sidelong. "Gross."

"Fish guts? Extremely gross."

"A cocktail called a car bomb."

"I thought it was funny," Slater said, and waved a hand. "Somebody tried to kill me."

"But you didn't die. You're sitting right here in one piece. Isn't that cause for celebrating?"

Finley looked away and folded his arms.

"Right now I'm in the middle of this narrative complex," Slater said. "I think it's messed up my judgment in a way. You know that feeling when it's really, really intense? We're just getting through that part. Although I still can't keep my paws off the guy. He even bought these red skivvies that I like. They're the color of a fire truck."

"Fascinating," he said flatly.

"Even though it's distracting, and it feels like I've been caught in a whirlwind, it didn't make me stupid." He jutted his chin at Finley. "What were you planning to do with the video?"

"I thought you knew the whole story."

He paused as the waiter set down their drinks, two pint glasses filled with dark liquid, a thin yellowy head on top.

"I figured out enough of it." Slater lifted his glass, and tapped the other one with it, even though Finley hadn't touched it, then took a slurp. "You put the squeeze play on Magnesia. You tried to extort them for that footage."

"I'm not extorting anybody. I just thought I could make some extra cash. I wasn't actually going to publish it."

"You're lucky I published it. I did you a favor. The next time Truax came after you, he might not have missed. No amount of gravy is worth your life."

"I talked to one of the VPs at Magnesia," Finley said. "One of the guys in the video. I sent him a few seconds of the meeting footage. I thought he'd negotiate payment. But he shut me down and sent Truax after me.

I got scared. That's the real reason I cleared out of my apartment. But I still thought I could get them to pay up remotely. I knew they'd never find me."

"Well, I found you," Slater said. "You're just lucky I figured out what Truax was planning for you. How long do you think you'd have been able to squeeze them? Were you ever going to go home again and live your own life?"

"I admit that it's possible I hadn't really thought that far ahead." He waved a hand. "How did you get the video? It's right where I left it. I checked."

"The only book that followed you from your apartment in Chinatown all the way to Margo's place was *Saucers over the Southwest*. I knew it had to be important. My mistake was thinking the content was the reason you took it. That led me to Eustace Burke and Olivia Howard and the Great Mojave Summoning."

"You met them?" Finley grinned. "Olivia is such a great person. A pioneer in the field."

"She's a grifter who charges people to talk to her."

"The woman's got to make a living. You went to see Eustace?"

"Talking to him was free," Slater said, "but he laid his mack down pretty hard."

"Oh, yeah, I saw that too. He's what my abuela would call a *sucio*."

"Did you do him?"

"We made out a little." Finley reached for the beer glass and took a sip.

"Tasty, right?"

"I disagree." He grimaced and set it back on the bar, then met Slater's gaze. "Do you think Truax might come after me again?"

"He has no reason to now. The video is out there."

"Maybe for revenge?"

"Truax isn't going to be worried about you. He'll have bigger problems."

"He wasn't in the video. It won't affect him."

"That car bomb almost killed those catalytic converter thieves. I can't let that go."

His eyebrows shot up. "You're going to turn him in? Great idea. The man is a menace."

"The thing is, the bombing has no logical motive without your blackmail scheme." Slater grabbed his beer glass. "That's going to be part of it too. It's all going to come out."

"Fuck, man." Finley scoffed. "First you shut down my side hustle, then you're going to send me to jail? I thought we had a connection."

"Your side hustle got Irwin's Volvo blown into molten smithereens. You won't go to jail if you cooperate with the prosecutors."

"Why would I do that?"

"You can be a witness or a defendant. It's your choice. If you don't cooperate, they'll go after you, and you'll wind up in the hoosegow. But if you help them bench Truax, you won't get charged with anything."

"Both of those choices suck hard. Maybe I'll just take off. That's worked pretty well so far."

"It took me a week to track you down, and I'm just one guy with limited resources. The cops literally have thousands of people to do the same thing. No matter how long it takes, the clock doesn't run out, and they won't give up."

"So I'll go to Brazil."

"Look at me," Slater said, and waited for him to meet his gaze. "No one is beyond redemption. Get yourself a lawyer, and cooperate with the prosecutors. You can pull yourself out of this and walk away with zero jail time. Doing a bunch of interviews and sitting on the witness stand is better than living as a fugitive for the rest of your life. Plus you'll get to help send Truax over."

Finley looked away. "I wish I'd never met you."

"You're lucky you did, you damn ingrate." He sipped from his glass, savoring the heady sweetness of the whisky and the yeasty beer. "Otherwise you'd be dead right now."

TWENTY-EIGHT

AFTER THEY'D EATEN, SLATER dropped Finley at Margo's apartment and drove to Silver Lake, cruising onto the hillside street with the row of townhouses. There was no guarantee that Truax was here. If he wasn't, he'd have to drive out to Thousand Oaks or wherever the idiot's house was where he abused his wife. But this place was a lot closer, and worth a shot.

Walking up on the front door, he pressed the bell. A minute later Truax pulled it open, dressed in a lustrous green track suit with white stripes on the arms and legs.

Truax frowned at him. "What are you doing here?"

"You owe me money."

"How did you find me?"

"You don't get to question me," Slater said.

He scoffed and slammed the door. Slater heard the bolt snap into place. Digging the ghost key out of his pants, he twisted it in the lock and stepped inside. Striding through the odd little foyer with the sofa, he trotted up the stairs. Truax stood in the middle of the main room, and turned when he heard him mounting the stairs, his eyes wide.

"What the fuck are you up to?"

"Like I said, baby, you owe me money. I found Finley and led you right to him. Assignment completed."

Truax pursed his lips and gestured helplessly. The guy wasn't intimidated by him, not even a little, Slater saw. That was typical of a lowlife.

"I actually got the information I needed through another means," Truax said. "I no longer require your services. What I paid you up front is all you're going to get."

"Not good enough."

Slater stepped toward him and threw a right hook. Truax hadn't been expecting that, and his reaction was a little slow. The blow landed solidly on his jaw. He quickly punched back, and Slater fended it off, but Truax grabbed him, grappling with him for a moment, boxing his ears, until Slater managed to pull away. As he did, Truax landed a solid gut punch.

Slater crumpled forward around the searing pain in his abdomen and sank to his knees. The guy knew how to brawl. Why hadn't he assumed that he would? At this angle he'd already missed his shot at a dick punch. The one move he had now was the knee. He punched hard at the side of Truax's leg. You had to hit it just right, and he quickly knew he'd succeeded when Truax howled and hopped and pounded a fist on the back of Slater's neck.

Gasping for air, Slater forced himself upright, swinging with an uppercut and then a left hook to the head. Both blows landed, and Truax looked dazed for a moment, and stumbled backward. He couldn't get his balance on his messed-up knee, and he flailed his arms as he stumbled, a blur of fluttering shiny-green rayon. When they'd been grappling they'd got turned around, and the staircase was behind Truax now. He took another uncontrolled step and lurched back toward it.

"Whoa," Slater said, as he realized what was happening, and lunged to grab for his arm.

But he was too late—Truax fell backward down the stairs. He landed on his ass and then tumbled down on his back. Slater stepped over to watch his descent. It didn't look like he hit his head, at least not too hard. When he reached the bottom, he lay motionless.

"Idiot," he muttered, and trotted down after him, stepping over his legs on the bottom few stairs.

Sprawled flat out, Truax wasn't moving, and a trickle of bright-red blood crept from his nose. Slater pressed two fingers to his neck. He had a pulse. Grasping his jaw, he rotated it, and lifted his head, assessing the resistance. His neck wasn't broken either. He'd just knocked himself out.

Slater rolled Truax onto his side on the carpet, propping him in the crash position, and went over to the door into the garage. The fuggly red plastic car was in here now. From the array of cleaning supplies he grabbed a sheet of paper towel and used it to open the camping cooler so that he wouldn't leave his prints. It was still full of dynamite.

That actually made sense—he'd found this stash yesterday, but Truax had planted the tracker on his car on Thursday, so he'd likely rigged the Volvo that night or maybe Friday. It had to be Friday night, he realized— Finley had driven to Palos Verdes that day and hadn't blown up. But what was Truax planning to do with all this? He closed the lid of the cooler again and went back into the house.

Truax hadn't moved. He trotted up the stairs and into the bedroom, where he pulled the little black bag out of the closet and zipped it open, grasping the tab with the sheet of paper towel. The money was still here.

Two racks seemed fair, he decided, and took them out. Rising, he stuffed them into a hip pocket. Thinking about it, though, it had cost him a small fortune to go to Giant Rock, and he'd paid plenty to Andy, and to Etta. Plus Truax was just going to give this to crooked politicians. He grabbed another couple of racks. Forty grand for this job wasn't unreasonable. Almost getting blown up and then fending off a murder justified the surcharge.

Max was going to be pissed that the cash was accumulating in the safe again faster than they could move it out. Once he'd zipped the bag closed, he put it back in the closet and then stood erect, but he froze at the sound of movement downstairs. He listened for Truax coming up, but instead heard a familiar voice—Conrad.

"Show me your hands," Conrad snapped.

He remembered that tone, Conrad projecting his authority. Even now it put lead in the pencil. What was he doing here, and why hadn't he heard him knock?

It struck him then that he'd left the front door ajar when he'd let himself in. That would give any cop a clear indication that something was amiss. Of course they'd walk right in.

Loosening his belt, Slater tucked the racks under it, in the small of his back. All four bundles were too bulky. Pulling one out, he stuffed it down the front of his pants, compressing his junk. It was a lot of volume, but he had nowhere else to put it. He could put up with the tuck for a little while. He adjusted his shirt over the racks in the back of his belt. It hung low enough to cover them, he decided.

Once he'd tightened his belt, he walked to the landing and raised his voice. "I'm coming down the stairs. I'm not armed." As he descended and stepped into the little front room, he kept his palms visible at his sides.

The front door was hanging open, and Conrad stood there, in his tan summer suit, his shirt open at the collar. Next to him was a woman in a gray suit, her hair tightly bundled back, a badge on her hip. Conrad's weapon was holstered, but the woman had hers trained on Slater.

Slater scowled at her. "Put your gun away. I said I'm not armed."

Truax was sitting on the sofa now, and looked up at him, murder in his eyes. There was a rosy blotch on his cheek—that was going to bruise. He'd smeared his nosebleed onto his face, the blood now dried in a nauseating shade of puce.

Conrad frowned. "Are you wearing a wedding ring?"

"It's just a ring. A symbol. There's no paperwork with it."

"What have you done to Pike? That poor man."

"He's wearing one too."

The other detective glanced at Conrad, and gestured to Slater with her weapon. "You know this lowlife?"

"I'm his ex," Slater said. "The fuck are you?"

"Watch your mouth," Conrad said, and jutted his chin at him. "This is Chávez."

Chávez holstered her weapon. "I guess that explains why the brass put you on this. You're sleeping with the perp."

"I'm not the perp, toots," Slater said, raising his voice. "I gave you the perp."

"And I'm not sleeping with him, not anymore," Conrad said. "What happened here?"

Truax waved a hand at Slater. "This psycho attacked me in my own home."

"It's the other way around," Slater said. "We were talking, and he attacked me. I pushed him away in self-defense. He lost his footing and fell down the stairs."

Conrad's eyes narrowed. "Have you got a woody right now?"

"Of course I do. From seeing your pretty face." He spoke louder. "Stop looking at my crotch. What are you doing here, anyway? I thought it would take you a week to slog through all the details."

"When you dynamite a Volvo on a public street," Conrad said, "things tend to move faster. We came to interview Truax."

A uniformed cop stepped in the open front door and stopped. Thick, with his hair buzzed short, he was wearing a ballistic vest under his uniform.

"Detectives," he said, in a lilting Caribbean dialect, and glanced around the room. "Do you need a hand?"

"Clear the upstairs, officer," Chávez said, briefly eyeing him.

Slater stepped aside to make room as the guy drew his weapon and headed up the staircase.

"There's nobody up there," Slater said, but the guy ignored him. He eyed Conrad. "If you just came to do an interview, why are more of you showing up?"

"I called for backup when we found him crawling around on his hands and knees and bleeding," Conrad said.

Slater nodded. "Since you're already here, you should look in the camping cooler in the garage." He gestured to the garage door. "I'm pretty sure I saw explosives in there."

"Are you kidding me?" Conrad demanded, his brow furrowing.

"Serious as a heart attack, brother."

"You trust this guy?" Chávez said.

"Not for a hot second," Conrad said, "but I'll take his word on this. It can't hurt to look."

Chávez pulled a pair of blue latex gloves from her hip pocket and started to wriggle into them, then stepped toward the garage door.

"You don't have my permission to go in there," Truax said, raising his voice.

Chávez ignored him, and stepped into the garage, closing the door behind her.

"We don't need your permission," Conrad said. "We entered the premises because the door was wide open and an injured person was in plain view. One of the occupants reported the potential contraband unsolicited."

Truax half rose from the sofa, speaking louder. "That's an unlawful search."

The uniform came down the stairs, his weapon holstered now, and stepped over to Truax. "Settle down."

Looking pained, Truax sank back onto the sofa, and massaged his forehead with his palm.

Eyeing Conrad, the uniform said, "There's no one up there."

"Good work," Conrad said, then looked to Slater. "Chávez has been trained in explosives. We call her bomb squad–adjacent."

"Stop talking to him like he's on your side," Truax said, waving at Slater. "He busted in here and assaulted me. You need to arrest him."

"Bullshit," Slater said. "The door wasn't forced. You can check. This yutz opened it for me, and left it ajar for the breeze, and offered me a Fresca. When I asked him to pay me for the work I'd done for him, he just freaked out and started throwing punches."

"Fuck you," Truax snapped.

"Why is it that the guys who try to mix it up always turn out to have a glass jaw?" Slater demanded. He jabbed a finger at Truax. "You tried to grease Finley, and you're going over for it."

The garage door flew open, and Chávez stepped in, breathing hard, her eyes bright.

"I'm seeing dynamite," she said, speaking rapidly. "There's enough to level half the block."

"Do we need to get the bomb squad?" Conrad said.

"It's factory-made. There's no blasting caps. A cooler isn't the best place to store it, but it's secure."

Conrad put his hands on his hips and eyed Truax. "Any comment?"

"I don't know how that got there," he said, and shrugged. "This is a company apartment. Many other people have access."

"His prints will be all over it," Slater said.

Conrad scowled at him. "Thank you for your input. I actually know how to do my job." He eyed Chávez and gestured to Truax. "You found the stuff. You should hook him up."

"On your feet," Chávez said, stepping over to Truax.

The uniform moved in next to her, and Truax slowly stood up.

Eyeing Slater, his lip curled in disgust. "Why couldn't you just stop when I told you to stop and chill the fuck out?"

"I wouldn't be here if you'd paid me what you owe me," Slater said. "And I'll chill out when they drag your lifeless carcass out of the gas chamber."

The uniform frowned at him. "They don't do that anymore."

"It's still on the books, though." Slater eyed Truax. "We might get lucky."

Chávez took hold of Truax's arm, and guided him to turn around, and snapped the cuffs on him. The uniform stepped in and took him by the bicep, steering him out the front door.

"You have the right to remain silent," the cop began, and Chávez followed them outside.

Conrad took a deep breath, and rolled his neck. Slater could see the tension melting away.

"I really hope you find a connection between him and the Volvo debris," Slater said. "Otherwise it's just holding the dynamite without a permit. Isn't that like a parking ticket? He won't even be in overnight."

"We'll get him." Conrad glanced toward the door and lowered his voice. "There's other reasons we prioritized this interview. When I looked into Truax this morning, I found license-plate reader data that shows his car was on that block Friday night. That puts him at the scene. It'll be rock-solid when we subpoena Magnesia for the records on his electric vehicle. Those stupid things don't even have a spare tire but they record video of everything, including who's driving."

"That seems invasive. But I get why the cops would love it."

"We also got doorbell camera footage across the street from where the Volvo was parked. It's a little low-res, but it shows a guy get on his back to work under the Volvo. He's wearing a flu mask, so you can't really see his face. But he's also wearing a green track suit. A lot like what Truax is wearing today."

"It sounds like you got him." Slater raised his eyebrows. "I'm a little startled you're actually that competent. I thought you'd be balls-deep in Sullivan on Sunday afternoon."

"Sweet Sullivan." Conrad chuckled. "Why are guys like that always such a handful?"

"The phrase 'demon twink' comes to mind. The question is, why are you into him?"

"You don't need to worry about me. You, however, are going to have to come across. Your relationship to this knucklehead, how you knew the dynamite was in the garage. You've got some explaining to do."

"I'll spell it all out," Slater said. "Give me a day or two to regroup."

"To get your story straight and rehearse it, you mean."

"It's not a story. Just the cold hard facts, elegant in their inherent lack of distortion." He drew loops in the air with his finger. "The golden strands of objective immutable truth that stitch the world together."

Conrad scoffed. "Why did you come over here, knowing what he did? He could have iced you."

"He had no reason to. Truax didn't know I knew about the Volvo." Slater shrugged. "And he owed me money."

———◆———

www.ingramcontent.com/pod-product-compliance
Lightning Source LLC
Chambersburg PA
CBHW011851300726
48970CB00009B/2748